Books Edited by Jeff Gelb and Michael Garrett

Hotter Blood*
Hottest Blood*
The Hot Blood Series: Deadly After Dark*
The Hot Blood Series: Seeds of Fear*

Books Edited by Jeff Gelb

Hot Blood* (with Lonn Friend)
Shock Rock*
Shock Rock II*
Fear Itself

By Jeff Gelb

Specters

By Michael Garrett

Keeper

*Published by POCKET BOOKS

EDITED BY JEFF GELB
AND MICHAEL GARRETT

POCKET STAR BOOKS

New York London Toronto Sydney Tokyo Singapore

An *Original* Publication of POCKET BOOKS

POCKET BOOKS, a division of Simon & Schuster Inc.
1230 Avenue of the Americas, New York, NY 10020

ISBN: 0-671-53754-7

POCKET BOOKS and colophon are registered trademarks of
Simon & Schuster Inc.

Printed in the U.S.A.

Copyright Notices

For Forrest J. Ackerman
and
Hugh M. Hefner,
creators and publishers of
Famous Monsters of Filmland
and
Playboy,
the two publications that influenced
us most as teenagers.
Thanks for the
screams and dreams.

CONTENTS

x *Contents*

INTRODUCTION

You hold in your hands the sixth volume in the *Hot Blood* series.

When we first conceived of an original erotic horror anthology, little did we imagine the chord it would strike in readers' hearts—and elsewhere. We wouldn't have guessed that the original *Hot Blood* would spawn an entire series, that reader interest would actually multiply with each new book.

But what exactly has led to the *Hot Blood* series' amazing success? Like any quality anthology series, it has showcased many of your favorite authors, introduced you to exciting new talents, and presented multiple treatments of a particularly engaging theme.

And that theme happens to be *sex*. Readers everywhere are interested in sex, whether they'll admit it or not. But the *Hot Blood* series follows a tried-and-true formula, and after watching a highly touted "erotic thriller" film that fell flat on its face (a turkey by virtually anyone's standards), a few things dawned on us that we wanted to share.

First, this star-studded movie was only "erotic" because of its gratuitous sex scenes. The coupling of its characters had nothing to do with the story itself. Cut the sex scenes and you've still got essentially the same story. In other words, Hollywood used sex to overcome a weak script.

Second, the erotic aspect of the movie never really jelled. All we saw was two sweaty actors groping each other, the actress displaying full frontal nudity while the male star's body was never once displayed in all its assumed glory. After a minute or two of witnessing the kissing and fondling of unseen body parts, we grew bored, and worse yet, felt cheated by having to fill-in-the-blanks, imagining what wasn't being shown. In other words, it was all tease and no delivery.

And that brings us to the *Hot Blood* series.

One of the trademarks of the stories in these books is that sex is a crucial plot element. Take out the erotic content, and the story collapses. Sex is never gratuitous in a *Hot Blood* story; it's the engine that drives the car.

Second, *Hot Blood* stories don't "pull out" at the last minute. No *coitus interruptus* here. While never pornographic, these stories allow their writers to describe sex in its endless variations in minute detail. Unlike Hollywood, we give our readers credit for being adult enough to appreciate the elements of eroticism that keep the stories moving.

Chances are you've never thought about what makes the *Hot Blood* series work for you—you've just enjoyed the stories. If so, we and our writers have accomplished our goals.

And of course there are other reasons why these books have been so popular, beginning with our writers and ending with you, our readers. We thank you all for your continued support, and for making *Hot Blood,* the original erotic horror anthology, what it is today.

Stay tuned. There's more to come.

                                        Jeff Gelb
                                        Michael Garrett

TAKE IT AS IT COMES

Tom Piccirilli

*R*ain slashing down, tires groaning hideously, the eighteen-wheeler pulled left at the bottom of the grade, hitting the flooded floor of the interstate doing seventy. The driver almost jackknifed, truck shimmying and aimed for the curved exit ramp that would roll him straight over LOUIE'S LAST EATS neon sign. Instead the driver regained control, straightened out and kept his momentum, never even hitting his brakes as he continued into the descended night.

"Jesus," Cole muttered, "crazy bastard must've been asleep."

Beth nodded without looking. Red lights reflected across the plate-glass window where she sat hunched over her cup of coffee. Out here, with nothing but I-90's asphalt leading twelve hundred miles back to New York, you saw murder on the road. Foreign jobs smashed out on the median, road kill everywhere. Twelve hours ago they'd seen a flipped horse trailer, two mutilated nags screaming on the divide. "Are we safe yet?" she asked.

He reached and took her hand. "It's okay. We'll stay in town tonight and get an early jump in the morning."

The teenage waitress came around and refilled Beth's coffee, leaning forward silently but smiling as if she'd said something funny. Cole checked his watch, then opened the menu again.

"There's not much we're gonna make now," the girl said. "We usually close around two-thirty or three."

"Can't I even get a burger?" Cole asked warmly, hitching the lilt in his voice up a couple notches.

"I'll check," the girl said, letting her gaze wander over his lean Soloflex body. He didn't bother indulging her with an equally flirtatious look. She threw her chest out a bit farther, tightened her ass a few inches, going for the luscious shape. He figured she'd start sagging before she hit twenty-five, no bra, jeans too tight, trying hard to impress. She returned and said, "It's okay, Solly hasn't shut down the grill yet."

"Solly? Where's Louie?"

The girl grinned and said, "Louie's dead," as if it were the punch line to a joke he'd heard a thousand times. He looked at Beth and thought, *We're on the border. Nebraska or Iowa? Where in the hell are we? Is she ever going to trust me?*

The only other patrons of Louie's were seated in the back stall: two farmers, apparently father and son. The man was short and brawny, with a crew cut. The boy was no more than fifteen, but colossal, at least six-six, blubbering in his overalls and talking like Baby Huey, his words lost in his sobbing. Cole was thinking that everything he'd ever heard about Iowa farmers was true.

He did his damnedest to give Beth a reassuring gaze. Talking didn't help, twelve hundred miles did nothing. "At this rate, we'll be in Seattle tomorrow night."

Beth started to say something but the words didn't come. She cleared her throat. "It's just that . . ."

"You don't have to explain. We're gonna make it, we'll start a new life." He sounded so cliché he couldn't help wincing.

The burger came undercooked, gray and running; Solly the cook must be in a hurry to get home, Cole thought, took two bites and gave up. Beth eyed his plate, and he shoved it at her. *What did that bastard husband of hers do? What did Danford feed her?*

The farmers were buzzing, the giant boy keening as deeply as an infant. People had been making fun of him again, he said. His father reached out to put a hand on his son's shoulder, but Baby Huey was too large. The farmer patted the boy on the arm.

Cole was so tired he didn't quite feel it anymore. He'd been driving for twenty hours, and up until a few minutes ago had wanted nothing more than to eat and sleep. Seeing Louie'd changed his mind: now Cole wanted to have a quickie in the backseat, just to get off, and then ride straight into Seattle. Beth ate the burger, eyes shadowed, her features marred with the deep lines he hoped the North woods could help fade a little. She hadn't slept either, and looked weaker than when she'd thrown her suitcase in his trunk and told him to floor it over the Washington Bridge.

The door chimes rang as the farmer's son blew his nose, completely missing his napkin.

Cole glanced up and saw Danford smiling and thought, *Aw, fuck!* No time to move, no time to warn Beth as Danford came on, left hand in the pocket of his London Fog raincoat, right hand close to his side and holding the snub-nose .38 Beth feared would find her. Good Christ, how had he followed?

Staring out the window at the parking lot, Beth sighed once, scratching her chin, then sat up as she spotted Danford's Coup de Ville. Her eyes bulged. "Cole?" she said. "Oh my God, we—"

Danford approached, the smile stapled to his pale, gaunt face. Cole had only seen Ronald Danford twice, from a distance, both times smiling like this, joyously righteous. White tufts of hair sprawled over his ears, his bald pate laced with crawling veins like centipedes. Cole knew he should have killed Danford at the beginning, done it himself or hired somebody out; it was stupid to run. Cut his throat, poisoned him, anything but run.

Cole took the initiative, there was nothing else to do. "Fancy meeting you here, Ronnie," he said.

Danford shot him through the left knee.

Cole's shrieks brought the waitress and Solly running out from the kitchen. The farmer jumped from the booth; the boy didn't turn to look, but blew his nose again. Beth screamed but quit abruptly, as if understanding the uselessness of it.

Danford was moving to sit at the table. He stopped short and watched Cole writhing on the floor, trying to grip his shattered knee but unable to touch the exploded bone, the torn cartilage hanging. Blood spattered back and forth as he rolled.

"You've just taken your first step toward redemption, Mr. Winter," Danford said. Then he shot Cole through the other knee, confirming that he would never, in fact, take another step again.

Swimming in darkness, hearing Beth's pleas from a great distance, Cole rose twice toward the light and pain, but let the current take him back down. The third time, he broke the surface and managed to stay awake even though his brain was burning and his blood had already leaked into a horrifyingly large pool around him.

He took it all in, passed out once more but came immediately awake: Danford had handcuffed Beth spread-eagle across the table, her arms and legs bent far under her. She struggled without struggling, gently tugging at the shackles as they clinked metal on metal. He'd taken her panties but let her keep the skirt, opened her blouse and unsnapped the bra, but left them clinging and hanging from her shoulders, the old and fresh scars on her body dappled with sweat.

"Rejoining us, Mr. Winter?" Danford said. "Good. Bear witness."

"Ronnie," she begged, "don't, please." Her voice was nearly gone now, barely a frightened whisper. Cole wanted to tell her not to say anything more, she was only exciting her husband.

"You've already broken your promises to me, my dear," Danford replied sweetly, brushing her cheek with the .38.

She swallowed, and Cole thought he could see how she was— almost—relieved the moment had finally come, having waited for it a thousand miles, dreading his rage, hating his shining teeth, but waiting all the same, like an expectant mother. "I'm sorry, oh God, Ronnie, I'll . . . I'll do whatever you want . . ."

"Yes?"

". . . just please . . ."

"Mm-hmm? You'll what?"

She slipped back into the role of victim more easily than Cole would have thought possible; as simple as putting on broken-in, comfortable shoes. The brown, puckered scars along her ribs seemed to lengthen in anticipation. "I'll be a good girl. Just don't hurt me. I'll do anything. I'll be your good girl again."

"You fail to sway me, Bethany."

Nothing would, Cole thought; Danford not only had the sluice gates of his sadism open, but he was on the side of right. Unfaithful wife caught red-handed with her lover, on the run. Danford had twelve hundred miles of driving behind him to hone his hate through the windshield's glare, everything in his favor.

Cole whimpered and gnashed his teeth. The waitress came over with dish towels while Danford eyed her closely. The girl took quick, haphazard steps, afraid he'd put a bullet in her back. She attended to Cole's legs as well as she could, unable to press down on the mangled kneecaps without the agony rising in him like a wild animal clawing. Shivering uncontrollably, he threw up and fell over in it, icy sweat covering him.

Danford leaned back against the table and lit a cigarette, then directed the smoke out his nostrils and down over his wife. The more recent burn scars on Beth's breasts glistened.

"No, Ronnie," she said.

"I wouldn't dream of hurting you, Bethany." He added a low laugh, for effect, Cole thought—how he must've been rehearsing each dark mile, talking to himself the whole ride, chasing. How did he know they would come this way? Had he been behind them, almost in eyeshot, the entire time?

Solly looked like his own gray hamburger, greasy, half formed. He didn't know what the shooting was about and didn't care much, you could see it in his face. So long as he didn't get hurt and no real damage was done to his place, he wouldn't think twice about making a play or calling the police. The farmer, though, was torn, standing and boiling inside, unable to move in any direction because it would mean leaving his son behind. The boy did not understand what was going on. Traces of a frown flickered across his prominent brow. His head was in a perpetual tilt, eyes blank.

"You." Danford pointed to the idiot boy. "Young fellow, come here."

"Now, listen, mister—" the farmer said.

Casually, Danford shifted the gun to the farmer's chest. Solly grew agitated, realizing he was no longer completely safe. Danford raised his eyebrows in a friendly manner and cooed softly, as though communicating with a dog. He motioned with his hands. "Come come, boy. It's all right. Come stand by me."

The boy held onto his napkin, looked up at his father and blinked heavily. "Pa . . ."

"Come come," Danford urged. Uncertain, the boy raised himself partway, still seeking a command from his father.

The farmer's knuckles crackled as his fists tightened. "Leave my son alone."

"Yes," Danford said. "Agreed. But if you don't allow him to come stand by me, I will shoot the retard through his somewhat misshapen head." He drew on his cigarette until the ash glowed, then waved it over his wife's breasts for a moment before driving it down against her left nipple. Beth wailed and wriggled, skin sizzling. The waitress fell back beside Cole and moaned, mopping the blood, afraid to look, afraid not to look.

"Once again, and for the last time," Danford said kindly. "Come here, my young man." The farmer gestured for his son to continue standing, and the boy rose to his full height and walked

halfway toward them. "Yes, that's it. Here, by my side." The
farmer followed his son, cautiously.

"Don't hurt him," the farmer said.

Danford made a quieting gesture. "I'm doing him a favor. I
suspect your son's still a virgin. True? Yes, of course. Then, I
believe, he ought to take her. In all likelihood he'll never find
another woman quite as . . . open to him."

"Pa, the lady's on the table." The boy grimaced. "Why's the lady
on the table?"

"Don't be embarrassed," Danford said, arm outstretched, waiting to take the boy in under the wing. "My, what a big boy you are.
You'll do quite nicely."

"Cole!" Beth wailed, and thankfully didn't add *help me,* as his
mangled legs lay skewed.

His blood poured. "Baby . . ."

Lips skinned back in a wolfish leer, the farmer growled. Cole
damned Solly for hiding at the edge of the counter; if only he'd
come out, just to pretend to look, distract Danford for a half
second, the farmer would know what to do. Fat beads of sweat
blinded him. He moved his hand and tapped the waitress's leg; she
made a *yeep* sound, doing everything she could to haul in her tits
now. Her nipples were hard.

The farmer inched forward. Danford talked like they were
discussing a ball game over a beer. "Think about it. I'll shoot you
through the heart and then where will your son be? Without a
father, having to fend for himself in a cruel world that cares little
enough for its handicapped."

"Pa . . . ?"

Front teeth clamped over his bottom lip, the farmer drew blood.
"Listen, mister. I got no quarrel with you, really I don't. Far as I
see it, you got a perfect right to shoot your wife and this man over
here, and bury 'em both in the deep woods. If I was in your shoes,
I'd put my woman out of my misery for sure. I ain't about to argue
about that. But this here is my boy, and there ain't no reason for
him—"

Danford had been nodding along, listening and agreeing, tufts of
hair out at wacky angles. "There's a perfect reason," he interrupted, "for your son to aid me in my vendetta. Yes. Justice. Poetic
justice. Surely you would not deny me that? Also because it will
hurt her, I think. And right now, I wish more than anything else to

hurt and humiliate her. Your son will help me accomplish this, I believe. Perhaps not. We shall see."

The farmer bit his tongue, wanting to bite anything, looking out the window at the interstate, at the occasional headlights skimming by in the rain. "Mister, I'll . . . I'll do it. Please, let me do it instead. I'll do what you want." He looked twice as insane as Danford did, like he was ready to swallow glass, tear out his eyes, anything but be forced to deal with this, and in dealing with it, watch his son do this thing. Cole cursed and struggled to crawl, sending lightning bolts of pain shearing through his body as he watched the farmer unzip his fly, drop his pants, and shrug out of his shorts.

Danford sighed. "Inadequate. Sorry, friend, God chose not to bless us. Let's see the boy. Tell me no again and he dies."

Now they were down to it. Beth whispered, calmly, like a lover and wife, "Ronnie, no. No, not him. Leave him alone. Leave them all alone. Let Cole go. You. You come and do it. Come on." And then, to Cole's surprise, she laughed. "Just you and your raisin-sized prick."

That's all it took; Danford turned to her and slashed down at her with the butt of the gun, ripping her across her belly. Cole loved her more at that moment than ever, thinking, *Perfect timing. Good girl.* The farmer had his chance; Solly, the waitress, even the lumbering boy who could have torn Danford's bald head from his neck and shoved it up his ass for him. Cole shouted, "Now!"

The farmer still had his shorts down and couldn't move fast enough in the seconds he had. Hesitation halted him as he stooped to pull up his pants. Solly stood looking tough and uncertain of who he should fight, where he should be standing, if he'd be allowed to fuck Beth next. The boy looked at the wound on Beth's belly and approached another step.

Danford wheeled back, smiling at Cole, who drove his fists against the floor and choked on his cry. *Good Christ, you bunch of hee-haw shit-kicking inbred fucks!*

"Yes, young man," Danford said, "don't be embarrassed. She's told me what a handsome lad she thinks you are." Danford stroked Beth's wet thighs in small, slow circles, working his fingers up into her pubic thatch, opening her lips wider, wider, until she yelped, and still wider. "Let's see if you've inherited your father's curse."

"Pa . . . ?"

"Drop your pants, Harney," the farmer said.

"Pa, what's he doin'? The lady's bleedin' . . ."

"Do as I say, Harney."

The boy had trouble with his belt at first, but his father helped him. Harney dropped his pants. He wore stained boxer shorts, and his hard-on jutted free from the hole.

"A horse cock!" Danford said, laughing. "My my. What a waste up to this point, eh? But not so tonight." Danford took Harney by the hand and led him to Beth, positioning the idiot boy in front of her, the tip of his erection nearly inserted already. Danford went behind Harney and gave him a powerful shove, driving the boy's hard-on viciously deep into Beth. She screeched. A puzzled smile broke on the boy's face, his tilted head tilting even farther. He looked around as though not entirely connected to the pleasure he was feeling; he grunted and leaned forward, aware of her now, bending, Beth's blood smearing his chin. He rode her harder, trying to gain purchase by yanking her legs up. Shackled as she was, her knees and elbows popped and she screamed again, sobbing, the boy's drool striking her face. She shook her head wildly.

Danford laughed. "Mr. Winter, are you watching?"

Cole was watching—the pain, the impotence, were flames riding him just as violently. Danford motioned for gray burger Solly to step forward, and when the cook came out from behind the counter, already undoing his pants with a sick smirk, Danford shot him in the head. The farmer spun and tried to move, but there was no cover. Danford shot him twice in the back. The waitress shrieked and a bullet took her high in the neck, ripping out her throat.

Cole should have expected it. Danford ran over, took careful aim from a foot away, said, "Thank you," and shot Cole's brains all over the waitress's corpse.

Oblivious, tilting, Harney was moaning, thrusting his hips forward, humping and ripping skin off Beth's back as she tried to arch beneath his weight. Danford reloaded and put the gun behind Harney's ear, waiting patiently for him to finish, watching him getting into the groove, groaning louder, driving faster, spitting, Beth squealing now, Harney throwing himself into her, dragging his face across her breasts, not his lips but his runny nose, keening the way he had when crying, nearly tearing the legs off the bottom of the table, and, in his final moment as he came, rising and looking through the windows at the rain, he howled and laughed and Danford pulled the trigger.

Rain slashing down, tires groaning hideously, the Coup de Ville rode out of Louie's, hit the slick entrance ramp and headed east into the brightening sky.

"Was it good for you, love?" he asked.

She curled under his arm, snuggling, sated again, for a while at least. *Wonderful.*

THE BODY IN THE WINDOW

Ramsey Campbell

*B*ack at the hotel on the Rembrandtsplein, Woodcock wanted only to phone his wife. He let himself into his room, which was glowing with all the colors of tulips rendered lurid. Once he switched on the light, the tinges of neon retreated outside the window, leaving the walls of the small neat room full of twining tulips, which were also pressed under the glass of the dressing-table mirror. He straightened his tie in the mirror and brushed his thinning hair before lowering himself, one hand on the fat floral quilt of the double bed, into the single chair.

The pinkish phone seemed to be doing its best to deny its nature, the receiver was flattened so thin. He'd barely typed his home number, however, when it trilled in his ear and produced his wife's voice. "Please do help yourself to a refill," she said, and into the mouthpiece, "Brian and Belinda Woodcock."

"I didn't realize you had company. What's the occasion?"

"Does there have to be one?" She'd heard a rebuke, a choice which these days he tended to leave up to her. "I'm no less of a hostess because you're away," she said, then her voice softened. "You're home tomorrow, aren't you? Have you seen all you wanted to see?"

"I didn't *want* to see anything."

"If you say so, Brian. I still think I should have come so you'd have had a female view."

"I've seen things today no decent woman could even dream of."

"You'd be surprised." Before he had a chance to decide what that could possibly mean, Belinda went on. "Anyway, here's Stan Chataway. He'd like a word."

No wonder she was being hospitable if the guest was the deputy mayor, though Woodcock couldn't help reflecting that he himself hadn't even touched the free champagne on the flight over. He squared his shoulders and adopted a crouch not unlike a boxer's on the edge of the chair as he heard the phone being handed over. "What's this I'm getting from your good lady, Brian?" Chataway boomed in his ear. "You're not really in Amsterdam."

"Not for much longer."

"But you didn't want to make the trip with the rest of us last month."

"Quite a few of my constituents have been saying what I said they'd say, that they don't pay their council tax for us to go on junkets. And you only saw what you were supposed to see, from what I hear."

"I wonder who you heard that from." When the implied threat failed to scare out a response, Chataway sighed. "It's about time you gave up looking after the rest of us so much."

"I thought that was our job."

"Part of the job is forging foreign links, Brian, and most of the people who matter seem to think twinning Alton with Amsterdam is a step forward for our town."

"Maybe they won't when they hear what I have to describe at the next council meeting."

Chataway's loudness had been causing the earpiece to vibrate, but when he spoke again, his voice was quieter. "Your lady wife may have something, you know."

"Kindly keep her out of it. What are you implying, may I ask?"

"Just that the papers could make quite a lot of your jaunt, Brian, you cruising the sex joints and whatever else you've been taking in all on your lonesome. If I were you, I'd be having a word with my better half before I opened my mouth."

"I'll be speaking to my wife at length, thank you, but in private." Woodcock was so enraged that he could barely articulate the words. "Please assure her I'll be home tomorrow evening," he managed to grind out, and slammed the phone down before it could crack in his grip.

He was sweating—drenched. He felt even grubbier than his tour of inspection had made him feel. He squeezed the sodden armpits of his shirt in his hands, then sprang out of the chair and tore off the shirt and the rest of his clothes before tramping into the bathroom. As he clambered into the bath, the swollen head of the shower released a drop of liquid that shattered on the back of his hand. He twisted the taps open until he could hardly bear the heat and force of the water, and drove his face into it, blinding himself. It was little use; it didn't scour away his thoughts.

What had Belinda meant when she said he'd be surprised? Could she have intended to imply that he was no longer discharging his marital duty as he should? His performance had seemed to be enough for her throughout their more than twenty years together, and certainly for him. Sex was supposed to be a secret you kept, either to yourself or sharing it with just your partner, and he'd always thought he did both, kissing Belinda's mouth and then her breasts and finally her navel in a pattern that he sometimes caught himself envisioning as a sign of the cross. Wasn't that naughty enough for her? Wasn't it sufficient foreplay? What did she want them to do, perform the weekly exercise in a window with the curtains open wide?

He knuckled his stinging eyes and groped around the sink for the shampoo. Surely he was being unfair to her; she couldn't really have meant herself. He fished the sachet through the plastic curtains, gnawed off a corner, and tried to spit out the acrid, soapy taste. He squeezed the sachet, which squirted a whitish fluid onto his palm. A blob of the fluid oozed down his wrist, and he flung the sachet away, spattering the tiles above the taps as he lurched out of the bath to towel himself as roughly as he could. If he couldn't rub away his disgust, at least he could put it to use. He was going to find something that would convince Belinda he'd had reason to protect her from the place—that no reporter would dare accuse him of enjoying—that would appall the council so much there would be no further talk of implicating Alton with Amsterdam.

He wasn't prepared for the revulsion he experienced at the sight of his clothes scattered across the floor, the kind of trail it seemed half the films on television followed to the inevitable bedroom activity or, on the television in this room, much worse, to judge by the single moist close-up of no longer secret flesh he'd glimpsed before switching it off. He dumped the clothes in his suitcase, where no chambermaid would see them. Having dressed himself afresh, he grabbed the key and killed the lights, and saw the room instantly become suffused with colors like bruised and excited flesh—made himself stare at it until his gorge rose, because as long as he kept his revulsion intact, nothing could touch him.

He thrust the key across the counter at the blond blue-eyed male receptionist before managing to rein in his aggression. "I'm going out," he confided.

"Enjoy our city."

Woodcock forced himself to lean across the counter, and lowered his voice. "I'm looking for, surely I don't need to tell you, we're both men of the world. Something special."

"Involving girls or boys, sir?"

The calm blue eyes were hinting that these weren't the only possibilities, and Woodcock had to overcome an impulse to hit him with the brass bludgeon attached to the key of his room. "Girls, of course," he snarled, and was barely able to hear or believe what he said next. "A girl doing the worst you can think of."

"To you, what would that be, sir?"

"What do you think, I—" The man's opinion of him couldn't be allowed to matter, not if that interfered with his mission. Woodcock made himself think. "A girl who'll do anything," he mumbled. "Anything at all."

The receptionist nodded, keeping his gaze level with Woodcock's, and his face became a tolerant mask. "I recommend you go behind the Oude Kerk. If you would like—"

Woodcock liked nothing about the situation, let alone any further aid the receptionist might offer. "Thank you," he said through his clenched teeth, and shoved himself away from the counter. Seizing the luxuriant handles of the twin glass doors, he launched himself out of the hotel.

The riot of multicolored neon, and the July sultriness, and the noise of the crowd strolling through the square and seated in their dozens outside every café, hit him softly in the face. Losing himself among so many people who didn't know what he'd just asked came as a relief until he recalled that he had to find out where he'd been advised to go. When he noticed a man sitting not quite at a table, a guidebook in one hand and an extravagantly tall glass of lager in the other, Woodcock sidled up to him and pointed at the book. "Excuse me, could you tell me wh—" He almost asked where, but that was too much of an admission. "—what the Oude Kerk is?"

"Come?"

He'd expended his effort on a tourist who didn't speak English. The nearest of a group of young blond women at the table did, however. "The Old Church? You should cross the Amstel, and then—"

"Appreciated," Woodcock snapped, and strode away. One of his fellow councillors had told him about the church in the depths of the red light district—she'd come close to suggesting that its location justified or even sanctified the place. It was farther into that district than Woodcock had ventured earlier. He had to find whatever would revolt his colleagues, and so he sent himself into the night, where at least nobody knew him.

A squealing tram led him to the Muntplien, a junction where headlights competed with neon, from where a hairpin bend doubled back alongside the river. He was halfway across a bridge over the Amstel when a cyclist sped to meet him, a long-legged young woman in denim shorts and a T-shirt printed with the slogan MARY WANNA MARY JANE. He didn't understand that, nor why she was holding her breath after taking a long drag at a scrawny cigarette, until she gasped as she came abreast of him and expelled a cloud of smoke into his face. "Sor-ree," she sang, and pedaled onward.

The shock had made him suck in his breath, and he couldn't speak for coughing. He made a grab at her to detain her, but as he swung round, the smoke he'd inhaled seemed to balloon inside his skull. He clung to the fat stone parapet and watched her long bare legs and trim buttocks pumping her away out of his reach. The sight reminded him of his daughter, when she had still been living at home—reminded him of his unease with her as she grew into a young woman. The cyclist vanished into the Muntplien, beyond which a street organ had commenced to toot and jingle. The wriggling of neon in the river appeared to brighten and become deliberate, a spectacle that dismayed him, so that his legs carried him across the bridge before he was aware of having instructed them.

The far side promised to be quieter. The canal alongside which a narrow road led was less agitated than the river, and was overlooked by tall houses unstained by neon. Few of the windows, which were arranged in formal trios on both stories of each house, were curtained even by net, and those interiors into which he could see might have been roped-off rooms in a museum; nobody was to be seen in them, not that anyone who saw him pass could be sure where he was going. Only the elaborate white gables above the restrained facades looked at all out of control, especially when he observed that their reflections in the canal weren't as stable as he would have liked. They were opening and closing their triangular lips, which increasingly, as he tried to avoid seeing them, appeared to be composed of pale, swollen flesh. A square dominated by a medieval castle interrupted the visible progress of the canal. In front of the castle, trees were rustling, rather too much like an amplified sound of clothes being removed for his taste. A bridge extended from the far corner of the square, and across it he saw windows with figures waiting in them.

He had to see the worst, or his stay would have been wasted; he might even lay himself open to the accusation of having made the trip for pleasure. His nervous legs were already carrying him to the bridge. His hand found the parapet and recoiled, because the stone felt warm and muscular, as though the prospect ahead was infiltrating everything around itself. Even the roundness of the cobblestones underfoot seemed to be hinting at some sly comparison. But now he was across the bridge, and hints went by the board.

Every ground-floor window beside the canal was lit, and each of them contained a woman on display, unless she was standing in her doorway instead, clad only in underwear. Closest to the bridge was a sex shop flaunting pictures of young women lifting their skirts or even baring their buttocks for a variety of punishments. Worse still, a young couple were emerging hand in hand from the shop, and the female reminded Woodcock far too much of his daughter. Snarling incoherently, he shoved past them into a lane that ought to lead to the Old Church.

The lane catered to specialized tastes. A woman fingering a vibrator in a window tried to catch his eye, and a woman caressing a whip winked at him as he tried to keep his gaze and himself to the middle of the road, because straying to either side brought him within reach of the women in doorways. His mind had begun to chant, "How much is that body in the window?" to the tune of a childhood song. Other men were strolling through the lane, surveying the wares, and he sensed they took him for one of themselves, however fiercely he glowered at them. One bumped into him, and he brushed against another and felt in danger of being engulfed by lustful flesh. He dodged, and found himself heading straight for a doorway occupied by a woman who was covered almost from head to foot in black leather. As she creaked forward, he veered across the lane, and an enormous old woman whose wrinkled belly overhung her red panties and suspender belt held out her doughy arms to him. "Oude Kerk," he gabbled, and floundered past three sailors who had stopped to watch him. Ahead, across a square at the end of the lane, he could see the church.

The sight reassured him until he saw bare flesh in windows flanking the church. A whiff of marijuana from a doorway fastened on the traces of smoke in his head. The street tilted underfoot, propelling him across the softened cobblestones until he came to a swaying halt in the midst of the small square. Above him the bell tower of the Oude Kerk reared higher against a black sky streaked with white clouds, one of which appeared to be streaming out of the tip of the tower. The district had transformed everything it contained into emblems of lust, even the church. Revulsion and dizziness merged within him, but he hadn't time to indulge his feelings. He had to see what was behind the church.

He drew a breath so deep it made his head swim, then he walked around the left-hand corner of the building. The nearest windows on this side of the square were curtained, but what activities might the curtains be concealing? He hurried past and stopped with his back to the church.

By the standards of the area, nothing out of the ordinary was to be seen. Some of the windows glowed as pink as lipstick-exposed women, others were draped for however long they had to be. Woodcock ventured a few paces away from the church before a suspicion too unspeakable to put into words caused him to glance at its backside. That was just a church wall, and he let his gaze drift over the houses in search of whatever he'd glimpsed as he'd turned.

It hadn't been in any of the windows. A gap between two houses snagged his attention. The opening looked hardly wide enough to admit him, but at the far end, which presumably gave onto an adjacent street, he made out the contours of a thin female body, which looked to be pinned against a wall.

He paced closer, staying within the faint ambiguous multiple shadow of the church. Now he could distinguish that all her limbs were stretched wide, and in the dimness, which wasn't quite dim enough, it became clear that she was naked. Another reluctant step and he saw the glint of manacles at her wrists and ankles, and the curve of the wheel to which she was bound. Her face was a smudged blur.

Woodcock stared about, desperate to find someone to whom he could appeal on her behalf. Even if a policeman came in sight, what would be the use? Woodcock had seen policemen strolling through the red light district as if it was of no concern to them. The thought concentrated his revulsion, and he lunged at the gap.

It was so much broader than it had previously seemed that he had to suppress an impression of its having widened at his approach. He pressed his arms against his sides, his fingers shifting with each movement of his thighs, a sensation preferable to discovering that the walls felt as fleshy as the bridges and cobblestones had. That possibility was driven out of his mind once he was surrounded by darkness and could see the girl's face. It looked far too young—as young as his daughter had been when she'd stopped obeying him—and terrified of him.

"It's all right," he protested. "I only want . . ." The warm walls pressed close to him, confronting him with his voice, which sounded harsher than he'd meant it to sound. Her lips dragged itself into a grimace as though the corners of her mouth were flinching from him. As he crept down the alley, trying to show by his approach that he was nothing like whoever her helplessness was intended to attract, her large eyes, which were the color of the night sky, began to flicker, trapped in their sockets. "Don't," he said more sharply. "I'm not like that, don't you understand?"

Perhaps she didn't speak English, or couldn't hear him through the pane of glass. She was shaking her head, flailing her cropped hair, which shone as darkly as the tuft at the parting of her legs. He knew teenagers liked to be thin, but she looked half starved. Had that been done to her? What else? He stepped out of the alley and stretched his upturned empty hands toward her, almost pleading.

He couldn't tell whether he was in a square or a street, if either. The only light came between the glistening walls of the gap between the houses and cast his shadow over the manacled girl. Her mouth was less distorted now, possibly because the grimace was too painful to sustain, but her eyes were rolling. They'd done so several times before he realized they were indicating a door to the left of the window; her left hand was attempting to jerk in that direction too. He wavered and then darted at the heavy paneled door.

He'd fitted his hand around the nippled brass doorknob when he caught himself hoping the door would be locked. But the knob turned easily, and the door drew him forward. Beyond it was a cramped cell which was in fact the entrance to a cell, although it reminded him of his own toolshed, with metal items glinting on

the wall in front of him. There was an outsize pair of pliers, there
was what appeared to be a small vise; there were other instruments
whose use, despite his commitment to seeing the worst, he didn't
want to begin to imagine. He lifted the pliers off their supports and
paced to the door into the cell.

Despite his attempts to sound gentle, the floorboards turned his
slow footsteps menacing. Through the grille he saw the girl staring
at the door and straining as much of her body away from it as she
could, an effort that only rendered her small, firm breasts and
bristling pubis more prominent. "No need for that, no need to be
afraid," Woodcock muttered, so low that he might have been
talking to himself. Grasping the twin of the outside doorknob, he
twisted it and admitted himself to the cell.

The door screeched like a bird of prey, and the girl tried to jerk
away from him, so violently that the wooden disk shifted, raising
her left hand as though to beckon him. When she saw the pliers,
however, her body grew still as a dummy in a shop window and she
squeezed her eyes tightly shut, and then her lips. "These aren't
what you think. That's to say, I'm not," Woodcock pleaded, and
raised the pliers as he took a heavy resonating step toward her.

They were within inches of her left hand when her eyes quivered
open. She clenched her hand into the tightest fist he'd ever seen, all
the knuckles paling with the effort to protect her fingernails from
him. There wasn't much more she could do, and he had a sudden
overwhelming sense of her helplessness and, worse, of the effect
that was capable of having on him. The pliers drooped in his grasp
as though, like his crotch, they were putting on weight—as if one
might be needed to deal with the other. "Don't," he cried, and
gripping the pliers in both hands, dug them behind her manacle
where it was fastened to the disk.

The wood was as thick as his hands pressed together. When he
levered at the manacle with all his strength, he was expecting this
first effort to have little if any effect, particularly since he was
standing on tiptoe. But wood splintered, and the girl's arm sprang
free, the manacle and its metal bolt jangling at her wrist. The force
he'd used, or her sudden release, spun the wheel. Before he could
prevent it, she was upside down, offering him her defenseless
crotch.

He felt as though he'd never seen that sight before—a woman's
secret lips, thick and pink and swollen, bearing an expression that

seemed almost smug in its mysteriousness. "Mustn't," he cried in a voice he hardly recognized, younger than he could remember ever having been, and grabbed the rim of the wheel to turn it until her face swung up to meet his. Her mouth had opened, and her eyes were also wide and inviting. As they met his, she clasped her freed arm around his neck.

"No, no. Mustn't," he said, sounding like his father now. He had to take hold of her wrist next to the manacle in order to pull her arm away from him. Although her wrist was thin as a stick, he had to exert almost as much strength to move her arm as he had to lever out the manacle. Her eyes never left his. The manacle clanged on the wood beside his hip, and he thrust his knees against the wheel between her legs, to keep it still while he released her other arm. He couldn't bear the prospect of her being upturned to him again. Forcing the jaws of the pliers behind the second manacle and bruising his elbows against the wheel on either side of her arm, he heaved at the handles.

He felt the jaws dig into the wood, which groaned, but that was all. His heart was pounding, the handles slipping out of his sweaty grasp. Renewing his grip, he levered savagely at the manacle. All at once the wood cracked, and the manacle jangled free, so abruptly that the pliers flew out of his hand and thudded on the floor. Only then did he become aware of the activity in the region of his penis, which was throbbing so unmanageably that he had been doing his best to blot it from his consciousness. While he was intent on releasing her arm, the girl had unbuttoned his trousers at the belt and unzipped his fly. As his trousers slithered down his legs, she closed her hand around his penis and inserted it deftly into herself.

"No," Woodcock cried. "What are you—what do you think I—" She'd wrapped her arms around his waist, tight as a vise. She didn't need to; he was swollen larger than he'd been for many years, swollen inside the warm slickness of her beyond any hope of withdrawing. Once, early in their marriage, that had happened to him with Belinda, and it had terrified him. There was only one way he could free himself. He closed his eyes, gritted an inarticulate prayer through his teeth, and made a convulsive thrust with his hips. The manacles at her ankles jangled, her body strained upward, and her arms around his waist lifted him onto his toes. Perhaps it was this shift of weight that set the wheel spinning.

As his feet left the ground he lost all self-control. He was a child
on a carnival ride, discovering too late that he wanted to be
anywhere but there. When he tried to pull away from the girl, the
movement intensified the aching of the whole length of his penis,
and his reaction embedded him even deeper in her. He groped
blindly for handholds as he swung head downward and then up
again, and managed to locate the splintered holes left by the
manacles. He pumped his hips, frantic to be done and out of her,
but the sensations of each thrust contradicted his dismay, and he
squeezed his eyes shut in an attempt to deny where he was and
what he was doing. The jangling of the manacles had taken on the
rhythm of the girl's cries intermixed with panting in his ear. The
wheel spun faster, twirling him and his partner head over heels,
until the only sense of stability he had was focused on the motions
of his hips and penis. Were the girl's cries growing faster and more
musical, or was he hearing a street organ playing a carnival tune?
He was beyond being able to wonder; the sensations in his penis
were mushrooming. As he strained his head back and gave vent to
a roar as much of despair as of pleasure, light blazed into his eyes.
He could do nothing but thrust and thrust as the vortex in which
he was helplessly whirling seemed to empty itself through his penis
as though it might never stop.

At last it did, and the girl's arms slackened around his waist as
his penis dwindled within her. He kept his eyes shut and tried to
calm his breathing as the wheel wavered to a stop. When he was
sure he was upright, he lowered himself until his toe caps found the
boards, let go of the holes in the wood, and fumbled to pull his
trousers up and zip them shut. His eyes were still closed; from what
he could hear, he thought he might not be able to bear what he
would see when he opened them. After a good many harsh, deep
breaths, he turned and looked.

The window frame was ablaze with colored lightbulbs. Speakers
at each corner of the window were emitting a street organ's merry
tune. In the street which the lights had revealed outside the
window, dozens of people had gathered to watch: sailors, young
couples and some much older, even a brace of policemen in the
local uniform. Woodcock stared, appalled at the latter, then he
stalked out of the cell, wrenching both doors as wide as they would
go. Even here the law surely couldn't allow what had just been

done to him, and nobody was going to walk away with the idea that he'd been anything other than a victim.

When the audience, policemen included, began to applaud him, however, he forced his way to the gap between the houses and took to his heels. "Bad, bad. The worst," he heard himself declaring—he had no idea how loudly. From the far end of the gap he looked back and saw the girl raising her manacled wrists to the position in which he'd first seen them. As the lights that framed her started to dim, he gripped the corners of the walls as though he could pull the gap shut; then he flung himself away and dashed through the streets choked with flesh to his hotel.

In the morning he almost went back, having spent a sleepless night in trying to decide how much of the encounter could have been real. He felt emptied out, robbed of himself. As the search-light of the sun crept over the roofs, turning the luminous neon tulips on the walls of his room back into paper, he sneaked downstairs and out of the hotel, averting his face from the receptionist, gripping the brass club in his pocket rather than relinquish that defense.

He left the whines of early trams and the brushing of street cleaners behind as he crossed the river, on which neon lay like a trace of petrol. He followed the canal as far as the lane to the Oude Kerk. Under his hands the parapets were as cold and solid as the cobblestones underfoot. He strode hastily past the occupied windows and halted in sight of the church.

He could see the gap between the houses, but without venturing closer, not how wide it was. One step farther and he froze. The question wasn't simply whether he had encountered the girl or imagined some if not all of the incident, but rather, which would be worse. That such things could actually happen, or that he was capable of inventing them?

A movement beside the church caught his eye. One of the women in the windows was nibbling breakfast and sipping tea from a tray on her lap. An aching homesickness overwhelmed him, but how could he go back now? He turned away from the church and trudged in the direction of the canal, with no sense of where he was going or coming from.

Then his walk grew purposeful before he quite knew why. There was something he ought to remember, something that had to help.

The face of the girl on the wheel: no, her eyes . . . Hadn't he seen at least a hint of all those expressions before, at home? It had to be true, he couldn't have imagined them. The bell tower of the Oude Kerk burst into peals, and he quickened his pace, eager to be packed and out of the hotel and on the plane. As never before that he could remember, he was anxious to be home.

JACKING IN

Brinke Stevens

Beep! the computer announced dutifully.

Guy Lauber looked up with a start. He put down the new "sex toy" advertisement he'd just downloaded from the Internet. The menu bar at the top of his computer screen blinked with a message: YOU HAVE NEW MAIL.

Heart suddenly in his throat, Guy shifted mental gears. That printout advertisement had been funny—in a sick and twisted sort of way—but he had more important fish to fry now. He hoped this e-mail message wasn't something about work.

Maybe it was something from Miranda.

Unhappily, he glanced at the thick stack of printouts next to his computer—copies of their electronic letters to one another. He had carefully read and reread them over the past week, trying to think of a way to put things right. He looked again at the blinking icon on the monitor screen. It was like a searchlight, holding his attention.

Guy bit his lip pensively. *Maybe Miranda won't give you the steel-toed boot salute after all . . .*

. . . *you pervert!* Wasn't that what Miranda had called him? At least he hadn't yet been reduced to buying "Megabyte Meg," the latest high-tech sex toy mentioned in the advertisement he'd been reading. "Computerized satisfaction, fully anonymous and guaranteed," read the testimonial. The illustration showed a fancy voice-operated virtual reality rig, with a complicated microprocessor, projection interface helmet, datagloves . . . and a very weird thing called an "artificial vagina."

Guy made a wry face. This was a far cry from the CD-ROM

pornography games he'd played for several years. To fantasize was
one thing; this was reality. Of a virtual sort, anyway.

Gives new meaning to the computer term "black box," doesn't it?
His inner voice was such a smartass sometimes, but it was usually
right on.

"Get Bitten by Megabyte Meg," said the ad blurb. "The Very
Latest in State of the Art Alternate Romantic Realities. Your Wish
Is Meg's Command. Personalized, Private, Guaranteed to Please,
and Anonymous."

"And she called *me* a pervert!" Guy shook his head at the
unfairness of it.

Guaranteed to please . . . The ink-black words on white paper
drew his eye again. Thousands of years of technological innova-
tion, culminating in microprocessor-controlled sex toys. Who
would have believed it?

Still, a computer game—even one like this—was easy to understand. Not like real women. Not like Miranda. Guy wet his lips,
looking again at the blinking screen icon. His fingers made no
move toward the keyboard or mouse.

He was the kind of fellow who did better with computers than
women. Logic was easier for him to understand than the lipstick
sex, by far. Maybe this "Megabyte Meg" *would* be a good choice
for a loser like himself.

Guy even had trouble talking to girls—*women,* his political
correctness sensors warned. It wasn't that he hadn't tried to be
social with women. His throat seized up when he did, and stupid
things flew out of his mouth. He had a genuine talent for saying the
one thing that would offend a woman beyond the point of no
return.

YOU HAVE NEW MAIL, blinked the monitor patiently. He drummed
his short-bitten fingernails on the desk. What if she wouldn't give
him another chance? Guy knew all too well that he hadn't really
meant to write what he had to Miranda. Well, maybe he had, but it
came out wrong.

Guy was a software designer for Imaginarium, one of the best
firms in the Silicon Towers in L.A. Dozens of patents to his name.
His own condominium, a sports car, and a good salary. He dressed
very well for a computer programmer. No, he wasn't good-looking
or anything, but Guy felt he had a lot to offer.

*Yeah. Everything except looks and a personality. You're more
Megabyte Meg's type, y'know?*

There had to be more to life than flashy toys from *The Sharper Image* catalog. Guy wanted more. He wanted a woman, a relationship. Fulfillment. Miranda could have been that chance for him.

The message icon continued to blink at him. What would it say? Was this e-mail from Miranda? He was a little afraid to find out.

And afraid not to.

They had called him the Mechanical Monk in college. Guy was now thirty years old, and it had been ten years since he'd been laid. The only time he'd ever had sex.

Whoa, he reminded himself. *With another person, you mean. Not counting holding up centerfolds with one hand, or the number of times you've left the VCR on freeze frame.*

Guy looked at his sweaty palms. He was a little disgusted by his own self-pity. Spend that much time alone, he knew, and you were bound to develop a few fantasies. You might even get a little kinky.

Or a *lot* kinky, like Miranda had said in her last letter.

At least he wasn't dating integrated circuitry and foam rubber, Guy reassured himself. *That* would be kinky.

The blinking icon flashed at him hypnotically from the computer screen. Did Miranda want to give him a second chance? He nervously ran fingers through what was left of his brown hair.

Miranda Jones—not that he could be sure that was her real name—was a woman he had met on the Internet. It was the technonerd version of a singles' bar. Guy had first heard from Miranda as part of a discussion on the ALT.FAN.HORROR.MOVIE special interest group. Finding a common interest, they had started sending electronic mail messages back and forth. Laughing about the latest schlocky horror films, silly current events, or stupid television shows. Clever wordplay, bad puns.

Guy had loved it. His developing friendship by modem changed his long days in the gray cubicles of Imaginarium, the tedious freeway commute through smoggy mornings and afternoons, the empty condo—they all became more tolerable. His collection of slick magazines and garish videos paled, their idealized women becoming less and less alluring.

Guy had developed a mental image of Miranda Jones. He saw her as slim, with long dark hair and darker eyes. A crooked, humorous smile. Sexy and smart. Guy imagined that her voice had to be a cool contralto. Miranda was intelligent and funny, with interests not so different from his own.

Well, at least *some* of her interests were the same. He remembered the tone of her last angry message. Guy hoped that she
would finally accept his apology. Maybe it wasn't too late.

You and your pervert mouth. Guy hated himself most of the time,
his anger and fears kept buried beneath his thinning hair. He had
to keep so much of himself hidden, controlled. Caged.

Maybe Miranda was a real babe, Guy told himself. Or at least
decent-looking. God knows he didn't consider himself any great
prize. He scowled.

Still, he had hopes about Miranda. High hopes. Guy smiled a
little, remembering their electronic conversation about that Nich-
olson werewolf film. Miranda had written that they should have
cast Kevin Costner; then the film could have been titled *Dances
with Werewolves.* There was an element of playful suggestiveness in
her wording, which encouraged him. It seemed almost like flirting.

She's probably four feet tall and looks like a troll, sneered the
critical part of his mind. Somehow, Guy was sure that Miranda
was nothing like that. He took a deep breath and steeled himself.
He cued up his electronic mail program. The hard disk whirred
and clicked for a few seconds, accessing information.

YOU HAVE ONE NEW MAIL MESSAGE, read his computer screen. Guy
double-clicked on the Open button in the dialogue box. The
window opened and words appeared on his monitor.

He wet his lips as he watched the message scroll across the
screen. The e-mail was from Miranda. But it wasn't what he had
hoped to read . . .

Not by a long shot.

GUY:

   I THOUGHT I HAD MADE MYSELF CLEAR. YOU REALLY SCARED ME
WITH YOUR MESSAGE LAST WEEK. I'M NOT THAT KIND OF PERSON.

   I E-MAILED YOU AT THE TIME, TELLING YOU THAT I DIDN'T
WANT TO HEAR FROM YOU AGAIN. STOP SENDING ME MESSAGES! IF
YOU DON'T, I WILL ALERT THE SYSTEM OPERATOR. YOU WILL HAVE
ALL ACCESS BLOCKED TO THE NET. I'M SURE YOU DON'T WANT
THAT TO HAPPEN.

   DON'T MISUNDERSTAND ME. I KNOW THAT YOU ARE NOT AN EVIL
PERSON. YOUR TASTES ARE YOUR BUSINESS, BUT THEY AREN'T
MINE. I AM SORRY TO BE RUDE, BUT I THINK YOU NEED PROFES-
SIONAL HELP, GUY.

DO NOT E-MAIL ME AGAIN, OR I WILL NOTIFY THE SYSTEM
OPERATOR. THERE ARE RULES ABOUT THIS KIND OF THING.

                                                          ——MIRANDA

Shit.

He exhaled shakily. "I'm *not* a bad person," Guy muttered impassively.

Yeah, sure. That's why you suggested tying Miranda up to a bed frame, straddling her face, gagging her with your hard cock and . . .

Guy blocked out the rest of that memory. Maybe he had moved too quickly. Still, Guy knew that there was nothing wrong with fantasies. Plenty of people were into bondage and discipline games. And it wasn't fair for Miranda to judge him. He had never actually played any such games.

Except in his own mind.

But Miranda's threat was very real. If she complained to the System Operator, he could be banned from the Net. If he persisted, she could even file sexual harassment charges against him. All he wanted to do was apologize, prove to Miranda that he wasn't some gross pervert in a metaphorical raincoat.

Too late. It was over between them.

He slammed a fist down on the desktop and watched the mouse jump. Guy knew that he had screwed up yet again. He couldn't even communicate with a woman electronically without saying the wrong thing.

Loser.

Anger simmered inside him, making his gut churn. He worked hard—didn't he deserve a reward? He stabbed at the return key, deleting Miranda's message. Gathering up the stack of e-mail printouts, Guy rose to his feet and stalked into the kitchen. Crumpling the letters in one angry fist, he shoved them into the trash compactor. Tears of embarrassment welled up in his eyes.

I can't even make it with a woman over a goddamn modem, he raged inwardly. Guy bit his lip. All the jeers from so many schoolyards flooded up from his memory. *Weenie. Nerd. Geek.*

He pulled a Buzz Cola out of the refrigerator, popped the top, and drained half the can in one long swallow. The combination of sugar and extra caffeine gave him a bit of a lift. He belched and finished the can. It joined the crumpled letters in the trash compactor. Part of him enjoyed hearing the grinding sounds of the

machine, like huge teeth the size of millstones. He imagined
Miranda was trapped inside too, along with all her lying letters.

That's getting a little sick, his inner voice chided.

Guy knew that he was basically normal, no matter what fantasies scuttled like bugs inside his head. He didn't go to hookers, did
he? Sure, he watched porno movies and read the slicks from time
to time. Browsed the many hardcore Internet groups, where he had
found the "Megabyte Meg" ad. He'd developed some intense
fantasies, maybe. But hey, he had hormones too.

The anger and embarrassment began to boil behind Guy's eyes.
What right did Miranda have to judge him? She had never even
met him.

He walked back to his work desk and sat down heavily. The
computer screen flickered, a comfortable and familiar part of life.
He patted the top of the monitor.

"Good girl," he said. "You're always here for me, aren't you?"
The rage and loneliness Guy felt were like hungry animals in the
room with him. Waiting . . .

The advertisement for "Megabyte Meg" caught his eye again.
The printout was still lying next to his keyboard, words and
pictures seizing his attention, drawing him into it.

"Personalized," the ad crooned inside his head.

"Private," it whispered.

"Satisfaction Guaranteed," it assured him.

"Why not?" he asked aloud. It would only be a computer
program, right? How could it harm anyone?

A bitter taste in his mouth, Guy pulled out his credit card and
sat it on the desk next to the ad. There was a convenient toll-free
number. He picked up the telephone, his fingers poking at the keys
aggressively.

The number answered promptly on the first ring. After a click,
there was an empty sound, like the wind through high tension
wires. It sounded faraway and lonely. Spooky.

There was another faint click and a pause. He shivered. A
neutral electronic voice asked Guy to specify his order by catalog
number, method of payment, and address. It was all very imper-
sonal, like voice mail. Efficient, but a little creepy. Guy punched
numbers on the keypad, making selections. There was nothing the
slightest bit sleazy about the process; he could have been ordering a
spreadsheet program. The order total was expensive, but it was . . .
guaranteed to please.

He impulsively paid an extra twenty dollars for overnight delivery.

Guy felt a little better by the next day. More justified and sure of himself. Centered. How dare Miranda judge him? What he did in the privacy of his own home was his business. His thoughts were his own. The cyberporn equipment he had ordered might even be a form of independence.

As promised, the package was waiting at his condominium door. Still a little frazzled from his long commute, Guy lifted the bulky package and took it inside. The large box was covered in plain brown wrapping paper. Neutral and innocent; it could have been anything.

Guy carried the package over to his computer workbench and put it down with a grunt. He slit open the wrapped box with a kitchen knife, carefully digging into the plastic peanuts protecting the equipment inside. He lifted a sleek black box out of the package and set it next to his computer. Digging deeper, his fingers found several cables and connectors, all standard. Soon he had removed the black virtual reality helmet, studded with plugs and wires. The inside of the V.R. helmet was filled with a spaghetti tangle of wiring and electrodes. Then he found the datagloves, which looked like clumsy gauntlets trailing thick cables.

His hands found another object among the plastic peanuts. Something cold and yielding to the touch. Slowly, Guy lifted out the artificial vagina, brushing away bits of Styrofoam. He looked at it warily. It was much larger than he had expected. A little frightening.

Guy knew that the entire situation was strange, but felt committed by his credit card. He had gone this far.

The object was a fat cylinder covered with connectors and cable attachments. Darkened ready lights ran up and down its thick length. Velcro straps and nylon web buckles were clearly meant to hold the cylinder to the user's body. At one end of the device was a vertical rubber opening. Guy gingerly touched it with a fingertip. It was very soft and cool.

Tentatively, he ran his finger along the inside of the opening. It parted with a moist sound as he touched it. Guy jerked his hand back, startled.

Oh, yeah, agreed the voice inside his head. *You're not weird or anything.*

The instruction book was thin but complete. No salacious comments, no gross cartoons. Businesslike and professional. It was labelled MEGABYTE MEG on the front, and the directions were simple and straightforward. He skipped the portions of the manual other than the assembly instructions. *Manuals are the last resort of the technically illiterate,* he thought smugly. Guy was very good with machines, and didn't anticipate having any trouble figuring this one out. Besides, the program was primarily voice activated. Self-operating.

Plug in and play, so to speak.

Guy followed the directions step by step. It didn't take long to finish the job. Wires fit snugly into specific color-coded slots. Cables slipped into multiprong plugs. A fiber optic cable attached to a port on the artificial vagina with a satisfying click.

Guy took a quick breath and pressed the power toggle. A row of tiny lights winked green on the black console deck.

It was ready.

Guy licked his lips, suddenly nervous. He felt as if he was being watched, and shivered a little. He closed all the blinds and turned down the lights. The assembled rig waited, making a slight humming sound.

All dressed up and no place to go, rang inside his head. *Maybe you should have brought some flowers.*

"Nobody here but us chickens," Guy said aloud. First things first. He undressed and clumsily strapped the big cylinder to his waist and thighs. Feeling ashamed and nervous, he stretched the rubber opening wide with two fingers, and managed to insert his limp penis. The device held him in a clammy grip.

You bet, buddy! Just a normal Friday night.

Guy put the datagloves on one at a time, fitting snugly up past his elbows. He bent over to pick up the V.R. helmet, and a movement caught his attention. The screen saver program on his computer had darkened the monitor, and Guy could see his reflection in its idiot eye. He looked so silly, standing there stark naked, with a dildolike device strapped to him and long S&M gloves trailing from his arms. He took a deep breath.

He put the helmet on, which completely covered his face and ears. It was pitch-black inside, and he stood unsteadily for a moment, feeling very strange. Guy finally reached behind him for the chair, clumsy from the datagloves. He sat down heavily, the seat of the chair rubbing harsh against his naked buttocks. There was pressure on his hands and head, and a moist coldness clasping his genitals. The whole V.R. system was voice operated, according to the manual. All he had to do was speak.

Say the magic words, buckaroo . . .

"Program on," Guy said crisply, his fingers shaking.

There was a whine in his ears that moved up in pitch. At the same time, the electric box buzzed against his genitals. It was an odd feeling, not unpleasant. The soft rubber holding him slowly warmed and seemed to soften.

God, I feel like a pervert, he thought.

The blackness inside the V.R. helmet vanished in a flare of brilliant white light. It blinded him, like blazing sunlight on water. He squinted against it, his eyes dazzled. The bright glare slowly faded into . . . a room.

It seemed entirely real to Guy.

The room was good-sized. He looked around, and his point of view changed as he moved his head. He looked up at the smooth ceiling and down at the carpeted floor. Guy knew that the computer was monitoring his motions and altering the projected image on his retina to match a computer-generated model of a bedroom. Despite that knowledge, it seemed like a genuine room, solid in every detail.

There were draped windows, but no doors. A dim pale light gleamed from ceiling fixtures. A huge four-poster bed was covered in satiny white sheets. Candles glittered on side tables, and there was a scent of incense in his nose. The room was silent, with a hushed expectancy about it.

As if something cold and inhuman was patiently waiting.

Guy shivered at the stupid thought. He looked down and saw himself, naked. He felt embarrassed again for no rational reason. There was a thin ghost of the sensation of the chair against his bare backside, but very far away. The real world had become a dream.

"Hello?" he called out, feeling foolish. His words seemed to echo in the silent room. Guy fidgeted, not knowing what to expect.

"Program optimization beginning," said an emotionless electronic voice, very much like the one that had taken his credit card order. **"Please concentrate on your last sexual encounter."**

Yeah, sure, anything for a laugh. Guy's mind rifled his memories, seeking. Hardly worth a snigger, he thought sourly.

It had been ten years ago, while he was an undergraduate at UCLA. A drunken college party, a young woman named Kathy

who'd said she was recently jilted. She had been drinking too many
Long Island ice teas. Kathy saw him as calculated revenge on her
football star ex-boyfriend, although Guy hadn't known that at the
time.

Guy had been studying the crowd through a beer mug. She
suddenly appeared across the room, a yellowish vision through the
suds. His blurry eyes focused on her fishnet stockings and short
black skirt, zippered up the front. Kathy soon walked unsteadily
up to him and raised a provocative eyebrow in his direction.

Not believing his luck, he was hardly inclined to ask her any
questions. Kathy hadn't needed to say anything verbally; even a
meganerd like him knew what she meant. What she wanted.

Guy remembered every steamy detail of that night. Kathy
leading him to her dorm room, giggling. The fumblings with his
shirt and pants. His skin tingling as her hands moved across his
chest. The mysteries of how to remove a woman's clothing. The
gratifying thrill as she put a condom on him with her mouth. The
beer and his nervousness had made the experience very confused
and surreal. He tried to talk to her, but she hushed him quickly
and went to work. Skin sliding across skin, a certain urgent
wetness, the feel of her tongue in his mouth and on his body.
Sensations and a mounting heat had blotted out everything but the
moment.

The next morning, Kathy unexpectedly threw him out of her
dorm room—and she never spoke to him again. It still made him
feel angry and badly used. The snickers in their mutual classes, and
the nasty grins in the crowded cafeteria.

He burned to get even, but it had not been possible. He wanted
to punish Kathy, to make her afraid of him instead of merely
contemptuous. Maybe he should have been grateful for the first-
time sex, but he couldn't forget how she'd made him feel as
important as a used Kleenex. Guy could feel his fists clenching at
the memory, still fresh and biting.

Ah, school days, jeered his inner voice.

"Optimization continuing," the cold voice intruded.

Guy found that he could walk around the room. He knew that he
was actually seated in front of his computer table, wires and cables
running from the helmet and gloves and . . . that other thing . . .
to the cool black console of the V.R. processor. Still, it felt as if he
could walk. The plush carpeting was a tickling pressure against his
feet.

Great code, marveled a portion of his mind, admiring the complexity of the programming necessary to create this kind of computerized hallucination. He reminded himself not to think about that. Instead, he tried to concentrate on the experience. It would become more real and detailed if he did, according to the manual.

Experimentally, he walked over to one of the night tables and picked up a candle. The flame wavered and sputtered as he moved it. The smell of hot wax was pungent. Idly, Guy wondered if the V.R. flame could possibly burn his hand. He cautiously extended an index finger into the beckoning fire—and yelped loudly. It really hurt like hell . . . fascinating. Putting down the candle carefully, he sucked on his wounded finger. His other hand pulled open a drawer in the nightstand.

A gleam of metal caught his eye. Guy leaned closer, peering into the drawer.

Handcuffs, yet with padded linings. The pinkish length of a vibrator, ribbed and blunt. A riding crop with a gold handle. Two silvery spheres set in a velvet box. Several rings that looked to be carved of ivory. Strings of very large pearls. Bottles of lotion. Feathers. Thin silk cords. Other things that Guy couldn't immediately identify. It was a regular sexual arsenal, straight out of one of his stroke magazines.

"Optimization complete," hummed the voice from all around him.

There was a murmuring sigh behind Guy. Suddenly, he could smell her perfume, rich and musky. Full of sensual promise. A little nervous, he straightened up and slowly turned around.

"Hello, darling. I'm Meg," said a fully gorgeous woman. She was standing provocatively in the center of the bedroom. Her voice was deep, throaty . . . and he felt it up and down his spine and into his groin.

Guy couldn't breathe, just looking at her. A wave of coldness passed down his neck, making him shudder. His tongue was a dead lump in his mouth. He had never seen a more beautiful woman in his life.

She was of medium height, and so achingly perfect. No blemishes or lines on her face or body. Long blond hair gleamed past her shoulders in soft curls. Mischievous eyes darted and winked, a pale blue that matched her scanty lingerie. The woman's figure was spectacular, and the bits of lace she wore emphasized the fact. She posed for a moment, jutting out her breasts and showing the muscle definition of her thighs and calves.

He gasped like a carp out of water.

She smiled at his reaction. "Well, a girl *does* like to be appreciated! Still, some introductions are in order." She crossed her arms against her ample chest. Guy couldn't tear his eyes away from her long slim fingers with crimson nails. He imagined them moving slowly on his body, and felt himself throb in response.

"I'm . . . Guy," he croaked. He didn't feel thirty. He felt twelve years old.

Meg took two steps toward him and extended a graceful hand. "Pleased to meet you."

Like a robot, Guy's hand moved forward and folded the woman's fingers into his own. He could feel the warmth and softness of her skin. Part of his brain knew that it was all a matter of artificial intelligence programs, feedback loops, and brain induction. But he smiled, almost in awe. No matter where Meg came from, she was perfect.

She smiled back at him, and Guy could see glistening, pearl-white teeth. She squeezed his hand gently, and Guy grunted as if he had been punched in the stomach.

"I'm your dream girl, Guy," she whispered, and tugged him toward the bed.

"But—" he managed to say, his lips numb.

"Shhh." A ghostly finger touched his lips. "Let your imagination run . . . *wild."* Her eyes seem to bore into his. "I'm yours," she breathed. "And you are mine. Concentrate on whatever you want."

Guy began to imagine all the things that he could do to her. *They* could do together. Images flickered inside his head, of things that he had read about. Things he had been afraid to say, let alone do. Things involving what he had already found in the bed stand. And much more. *Things that made his suggestions to Miranda seem ridiculously minor.* An impatient buzzing filled the air, like an angry beehive. His mind became vague, drifting with images of willing flesh.

He was achingly hard.

"That's right, lover," Meg approved. She reached down and stroked his erection. Guy moaned, almost in pain. "I'll do anything you want," she purred. Guy could see a flicker of tongue lick her perfect red lips.

"Anything?" he stammered, hypnotized.

Meg nodded. The hot promise of her smile made Guy weak in the knees. She led him to the bed and stroked his chest and shoulders. He shivered. The satin sheets felt slippery and cool beneath him.

"Ooh, baby," she finally cooed. "You have *no* idea."

Her head slipped down his belly, her lips trailing a cold fire along his skin. Meg covered his thighs with waves of silky blond hair. Guy moaned softly as she took him in her mouth, impossibly deep. He stared at the white ceiling above him. It seemed to roil and swirl like deep ocean currents. The pale sea rose and thundered over him, finally sweeping Guy into secret places he had never been before.

And that was how it began . . .

After the first night, it took him some time to clean the spongy black device that held his aching genitals. He had actually been rubbed raw in three places. He thought about venereal disease, and then laughed a little. That was one thing he didn't have to worry about with cybersex. You couldn't catch a virus from a computer program, right?

Guy slept like the dead that night. There were no dreams that he could remember.

But surely, his days at Imaginarium seemed to lose their focus as the week passed. Guy's mind was always racing ahead to what waited for him at home, ignoring important meetings and pressing deadlines. They weren't as vital as the ever-pliant Meg. She was always at his beck and call.

Anything . . .

Guy knew that the infernal machine was tickling his mind, inflaming his imagination. It was learning from his fantasies. The experiences grew more intense and powerful with every session. He couldn't think clearly while he was connected to Megabyte Meg. Night after night Guy strapped on his equipment and activated the program. Meg was always there, waiting. Wet-lipped and smiling. Oh so ready. And each time, she seemed to know him better, more intimately. He didn't ask questions. He was lost in a maze of soft breasts and pliant red lips, urgent needs and throaty cries. Meg inspired him to inventiveness he had not yet visualized, even in his darker fantasies.

It should have been enough.

But after two sweaty weeks, Guy found that standard sex with Meg wasn't sufficient anymore. His needs seemed to grow inside him, like a dark cancer within his soul, eating away at his conscience. The handcuffs and riding crop excited him. He would savagely bite Meg's nipples, whip her, slap her face. Part of him loved her pathetic cries and whimpers. Guy climaxed as he never had before when she tearfully submitted to him, tied cruelly to the bed with silk cords. Slowly, Meg grew less bold, becoming more like a victim.

Guy found he was especially turned on by such role-playing. That pleading look on her face was priceless as she knelt nude on the bed, a red ball-gag stuck in her mouth, hands tied behind her back, while he brutally fucked her ass. And as he grew more violent, he assured himself it was only a computer program. It didn't really matter how he used her. Her opinions and desires meant nothing. Meg was truly his own personal Dream Girl.

Until that last Friday night.

Guy slammed the door to his condo shut, stifling a curse.

What if I do get fired? he thought. He would have to do plenty of thinking over the weekend. Uncontrollably, his eyes strayed across the room to where the V.R. rig beckoned. He started to loosen his tie and unbutton his shirt as he walked toward the computer desk. It was an almost automatic response when he came through the door now.

Guy had received his second warning at work that afternoon. His manager told him that he was under review for poor performance. They had been watching Guy grow gaunt and hollow-eyed over the past weeks, matching his deteriorating performance with programming code. The manager went so far as to accuse Guy of drug use. He had laughed in the manager's face.

Guy knew what would make him feel better.

The evening ritual began again. It was always the same. Shirt carefully hung up, and tie neatly rolled. Belt stowed. Pants folded along the creases. Shoes lined up, with argyle socks lying next to them. Underwear in the hamper.

Palms damp, Guy picked up the artificial vagina and grimly strapped it on.

Datagloves clung to his arms, and he lifted the V.R. helmet onto his head. Anger and anticipation built in him. He was already getting hard.

"Somebody is going to pay," he muttered. He switched it on and said the magic words. Guy had a good guess *who* would be paying for his turmoil.

Meg cowered on the bed as the bright flare inside the helmet faded away. Her eyes glinted fear and resentment. Guy felt a little badly that she was no longer the sexually aggressive vixen he had first met. But she served different and more urgent needs now.

And Meg is only a computer program. It isn't like she's a real person.

"Get up," he said roughly.

She slowly stood up, naked, holding her hands across her luscious body. The show of modesty was . . . interesting. Meg's eyes were downcast, and her submissiveness excited him.

Guy took a step forward. Smiling cruelly, he slapped her. The awful sound was loud in his ears. His hand stung with the blow. Meg looked back at him, her eyes smoldering in hatred.

That was new . . .

"Don't give me that look," he hissed. Guy made a fist. "You have to learn respect."

"Miranda was right," Meg said flatly.

"What?" He was shocked.

"You heard me." She took a step closer to Guy. He stepped back in reflex. "All of them were right. You're a geek and a pervert."

Fury narrowed his eyes. "Shut up, bitch!"

Meg laughed, an ugly sound. "You're no good in bed. That's why Kathy kicked you out, isn't it?"

He felt himself flushing in rage. He imagined his fists battering Meg, blacking her eyes, breaking her nose. Her blood flying, spotting the creamy white satin sheets of the bed. His hands, white with pressure, wrapped around Meg's windpipe.

Can't kill a computer program, Guy thought. Then he smiled. *Or maybe you can. Over and over again.*

His hands flashed out and caught Meg's long, pale throat. He squeezed, growling low like a vicious animal. Meg's calm eyes met his, unblinking.

"Big man," she said. She clearly was not choking.

Guy's hands dropped away. His anger had drained in an instant. There was something *wrong* with all this. It was time to put a stop to it.

"End program," Guy grated.

Nothing happened. Meg still stood before him, naked and

perfect. A slight smile played across her face. She smoothed back her hair and blew him a mocking kiss.

She's just a program, Guy thought. *Not real. It will stop any second now.*

The weird V.R. bedroom, with its white walls and white drapes and cold white light remained. The four-poster bed behind Meg was firm and solid, even to the rumpled satin sheets. Every sense stayed sharp, from the smells of sex and incense to the sensation of chill air prickling along his arms. Clearest of all to Guy was the hard glint in Meg's glacial blue eyes.

He was confused. Did it take a few moments for the program to save its position? A lot of interactive games did that. The computer should have shut down on his voice command, and the room and its contents vanish instantly.

"Not that easy." She grinned, batting her eyelashes in a parody of seduction.

"End program!" he shouted, his gut cold with fear.

The woman and the room remained. He breathed in and out, shaking his head.

"I just love it when you're so . . . masterful," Meg spat, her tone dripping with contempt. She reached out and pinched one of his nipples, hard. There was nothing of desire in her face, only the flat glare of a snake stalking prey. The sharp pain seemed to twist something inside of him. A harsh buzzing filled his ears.

He took some deep breaths to steady himself.

It's only a game, for Christ's sake.

Why hadn't the program shut down? There was a bug in the voice recognition software, that was all. But he knew that it was clearly time to exit this program. Right now.

Meg cleared her throat, and Guy found himself looking at her again, involuntarily. He couldn't help himself. A perfect face and body, he had to admit.

"Oh Guy . . ." Meg's smile was the merest thinning of her lips. "Did you like it when you hit me? When you tried to strangle me? Did you get off on it?"

Guy felt suddenly feverish. "I'm not like that," he started to tell her.

"I'm inside your head, Guy," Meg interrupted. "I know what you're like. Don't you want to do it again?" Her voice sent cold tendrils into his heart. "That's the only way you can get it up, isn't it?"

Guy realized this went way beyond good programming. Like a dash of cold water in his face, he wondered who had designed Megabyte Meg, and why. Distracted, he remembered the old joke: sensual is a feather; kinky is the whole chicken. This was a whole flock of chickens.

He swallowed, his mouth tasting sour.

"What's the matter, Guy? Not man enough anymore?" She ran a graceful hand down the curve of one perfect breast. His eyes followed against his will. She was drawing his attention to the secret places where he had lost himself in a red fog of lust and anger.

He could feel himself starting to respond; fists clenching and erection growing. Guy repressed a shudder, and fought down his response again. *Enough.* This wasn't about sex anymore. It was about something older, and far darker.

He bit his lip. No matter how weird things had become, a part of his brain always stayed in hacker mode. If the program was no longer responding to voice commands, there was always the direct approach.

Once the helmet was off, the interface wouldn't be reaching the computer's sick fingers inside his brain. The program was *doing* all of this to him, somehow, twisting things up inside his mind. He reached abruptly up for the V.R. helmet with both hands, to break the computer connection once and for all.

Just as swiftly, Meg reached out and grabbed his wrists.

He couldn't move his arms. The impossible fact didn't register for a moment.

Guy tugged upward in shock and surprise, but his arms would not move. He strained up and down, side to side, but couldn't break away from Meg's grasp. Her hands were like bands of steel on him.

Guy stared down at Meg's slim hands wrapped around his wrists. He could feel the pressure of her grip, implacable and harsh. The hands squeezed, and Guy choked back an involuntary grunt of pain.

Meg's laughter was a cruel sound in his ears. Fear began to settle in his gut again, like shards of ice.

Fucking great code, said the sarcastic voice in the back of Guy's head.

There weren't any A.I. programs this good. This was something different. Something evil.

Meg's eyes were empty blue pools that held him as tightly as her hands around his wrists. He could feel himself falling into their endless depths. A long, slow blue fall into hell.

"Playtime isn't over yet." She chuckled and squeezed his wrists, still harder. He saw his hands going white in Meg's grasp.

A part of his mind screamed, *This can't be happening!*

"That's the thing about interactive reality," she whispered, touching the tip of her tongue delicately to his earlobe. "It works both ways. You think you can't move because I am holding you in one place, and—wonders of science—you can't." Meg pulled back, bringing her face very close to his.

Meg laughed again, smoky and undeniably sexy. "No, we aren't finished. No way, baby." Her words had an edge sharper than any razor.

Guy couldn't believe how white her teeth looked, how gleamingly perfect and sharp. Nor could he believe how many of them he could see in that feral smile.

He shouted in surprise as Meg picked him up easily by the wrists and tossed him onto the bed. Before he could move, she became a blur of motion at his hands and feet. Guy heard a metallic snicking sound, felt a clamping coldness on his ankles and wrists. Flat on his back on the bed, he looked around wildly.

Meg had handcuffed him to the four posts of the bed. Guy couldn't move his arms or legs at all. The handcuffs had him pinned in place. Spread-eagled, like a frog on a dissection tray in biology class.

If he could just get the helmet loose, it would break the connection. Hopefully, Guy began to whip his head back and forth. Swing hard enough, and the helmet would fly off his hallucinating head.

The ceiling of the V.R. bedroom seemed to blur past him as he swung his head. The scene began to fade and lose definition. *Yes,* he thought, *that's it.* He redoubled his efforts.

There was a crunching pain in the center of his face. He closed his eyes in stinging reflex, gasping. Guy felt one of his earlobes twist savagely, forcing his eyes to open.

Guy looked up and saw a grim-faced Meg straddling his midsection. She held a balled up fist so close to his face that his eyes crossed.

Guy realized vaguely that she had broken his nose.

"Naughty boy. You need to hold still until Meg is through with you." She extended a finger and whacked his nose. He screamed at the horrible sensation of shattered, grinding cartilage. Tears and blood streamed down his face, and he swallowed a salty copper taste.

"And I won't be finished for a long time." She studied her bloodied finger. The color matched her crimson nail polish. He couldn't tell one from the other. Looking directly at Guy, she slowly and methodically licked the blood off her finger.

His blood. *Not possible . . .*

Light as a feather, Meg moved off him to the side of the bed and rummaged in the nightstand. Guy was careful not to move, his throbbing nose a reminder.

Have to figure my way out of this, he thought. *Gotta be calm.* His mind raced, trying to think of an approach.

Meg came back into his field of vision, waving a pack of cigarettes in front of his face. She shook one from the box, took it between her white teeth. A lighter seemed to appear in her other hand, and she lit up. The lighter evaporated as quickly as it had appeared. Meg spent a few moments calmly smoking, saying nothing.

The sheer detail of all of this still amazed the detached part of his mind.

Appreciate it later, he reminded himself. *After the helmet is off.*

"Meg?" he managed to say, in an almost normal tone of voice. He knew he had to talk with her, to get some clues. To think his way out of this mess. If he could just say the right thing, the program would surely end.

"Yes?" she replied after a few moments, blowing a stream of cigarette smoke from her mouth.

"What do you want?" Guy asked.

Meg leaned forward, her breath hot on his face. His battered nose ached. "I want you to know what it feels like."

"I don't understand," Guy mumbled. He could smell her musky perfume, and her long silky hair brushed across his chest.

"I want you to know how it feels to be a plaything. To be empty and used." Meg's eyes became intense, her lovely features as cold and distant as the moon. She sighed after a moment, and leaned down very close to his face. She ran her lips softly up his cheek to his earlobe, taking it between her teeth.

"Not enough to tell you," she breathed. "I want to *show* you."

Then she bit down, very hard.

Guy screamed in pain.

Gotta find a way out, his mind gibbered. *I could be here for hours, days, until someone figures out I'm missing.* If he couldn't break the connection to the V.R. equipment himself, someone else would have to get into his condo and do it for him.

How long would that take? ran through his mind.

She waited patiently, taking long puffs on her cigarette. Meg still looked beautiful, despite all she had done to him. Her eyes ranged over his bound body possessively.

Hours? The thought was a numb lump inside Guy's head.

"Your first lesson has begun, lover. I will be your teacher now. You were mine, after all."

Days? With a stab of regret, Guy was sorry he'd tossed out the instruction manual. Could he possibly have skipped some important warning?

Meg looked at the glowing coal of her cigarette. Then at his naked body. Guy blinked back tears as he saw her smile begin to blossom.

"No," he pleaded. Her smile grew wider as her hand moved slowly down his body.

"Oh, yes."

She ground out the cigarette on his chest. He stifled a yell.

How long until someone finds me? It's only Friday, and I don't have to be at work until Monday.

Meg tugged open the bedside drawer. She lifted out a gleaming black electric cattle prod, which he had never seen there before. She examined it carefully for a few moments, still silent. The woman pressed a switch on the prod, and a fat blue-white spark snapped across the wickedly sharp electrodes. A smell of ozone filled the air.

How long?

Guy took a deep breath to say something, to argue, to scream. To do something to stop this madness, *anything,* before it was too late. But Meg had already forced a hard rubber ball between his teeth and sealed his mouth shut with a strip of electrician's tape.

END OF THE ROAD

Edo van Belkom

*R*ory Graham thrust out his thumb as the first car he'd seen in twenty minutes approached. Its headlights were set wide apart, shining like twin beacons of hope in an otherwise gloomy night.

"C'mon," he muttered between shivers. "You gotta stop."

As the car neared, he recognized it as a white, late-model Cadillac, big and luxurious . . . and probably as warm as a toaster inside. He held his thumb up higher to make sure the driver couldn't miss it, but the car zoomed by him, picking up speed as it passed.

"Sonofabitch!" he cried, kicking some dirt at the speeding car. "God damn sonofabitch!"

He kicked at the dirt once more, adjusted his knapsack on his shoulders, pulled his faded denim jacket tightly across his chest, and began walking. In the distance the car's rear lights had become little more than tiny red stars on the horizon. He watched the lights get smaller and smaller until the car crested a hill and the lights winked out, making the darkness surrounding him complete.

"Great idea!" he said, throwing his arms up in the air. "Hitchhiking across the country . . . is a great idea when you live in the city and cars drive by every minute. But what happens when you're stranded just outside Bumfuck-Nowhere and—"

He suddenly stopped his rant and listened.

It was the sound of another car.

He spun around and saw two white lights on the road growing bigger by the second.

Rory stuck out his thumb again and the car began to slow.

"Yes!" he said through clenched teeth, pumping his fists into the air as if he'd just won the big game. "All r-right!"

It was an older car, a Buick maybe. It was big and black and had a huge chromed front bumper and grill combination that made it look like it had a set of menacing steel teeth. "The next-best thing to a Caddy," said Rory, running to catch up to the car, which was now idling just up ahead by the side of the road.

When he reached the car he quickly opened the door and took a good look at the driver. He'd learned his lesson in Indiana when he got into a semi-trailer driven by a guy who had looked like some hybrid cross between Charles Manson and Mad Max. The guy had driven like an absolute maniac and offered Rory a thousand dollars if he'd off his wife. That first truck stop had never seemed so far away.

At least this guy looks normal, he thought. Might not mean much, but at least it's something. The driver was an older man— late forties, early fifties—with a little bit of gray on top and a few age lines around his eyes and across his forehead. He had a suit on, or at least a jacket and tie, and looked for all the world as if he sold insurance for a living, or maybe even used cars.

"Where you headed?" asked the man, his voice edged with a slight southern drawl.

Rory poked his head deeper inside the car and nodded in the direction the car was already pointed. "That way," he said.

The man nodded. "Well, get in, then."

Rory was inside the car in seconds, his body already tingling from the warmth of its interior.

The man put the car in gear and pulled back onto the highway, even using his turn indicator, Rory noticed, to signal his return to the road. He drove for several minutes without saying a word, giving Rory the chance to get comfortable, then said, "You headed anywhere in particular? Or just *that way?*"

Rory turned to look at the man, his face eerily lit by the glow radiating from the dashboard before him. "I'm going west," he said. "Don't know where exactly till I get there. Might stop in Los Angeles, maybe San Francisco . . . who knows, maybe even Seattle."

The driver nodded. "So nobody's really expectin' you?"

"Basically."

The man continued to nod. "Reason I ask is the next town ain't for another twenty-five miles and I ain't going but fifteen miles down this road."

Rory thought about it. If this guy hadn't picked him up, he'd have been walking all night, maybe even froze to death. Even with the ride, he'd be walking another ten miles before reaching the next town. He shook his head. Great fucking idea this turned out to be!

"Guess I'll be doing some more walking, then."

"Guess so," said the driver.

The car was silent for another couple of minutes.

"You get much pussy on the road?"

The words had come without warning, and Rory couldn't be sure he'd heard them correctly. "Pardon me?"

"I said, do you get much pussy on the road?"

Rory looked at the man, wondering what to make of the question. There were dozens of possibilities, especially ones that suggested the guy was a wacko, but Rory decided in the end that he was probably just a lonely old man who wanted to talk. And if you're going to talk about something, why not sex? It's as good a topic as any.

"Afraid not," said Rory, shrugging his shoulders. "I haven't got much of anything lately—food, clean clothes, sleep . . . or pussy."

The man sighed and let out a laugh. "I get me enough," he said. "More than enough, really. As much as I can handle, and then some."

Rory didn't quite know how to respond. He felt like telling the man he really wasn't interested, but decided the car was too warm, and the night outside too cold, to say anything impolite. "Sounds great."

"Yeah, my wife's a real sweetheart," he said. He took a hand off the steering wheel, reached up and took down a picture from beneath the visor. He glanced at it a second, then handed it to Rory. "Real sexy too."

Rory leaned forward and moved the picture around until it caught some of the light coming from the dashboard. It was a color photo, the sort of head-and-shoulder shot newspapers use all the time. She certainly is attractive, thought Rory. She had a bright, warm smile, long dark hair, and big brown eyes that almost seemed to radiate a dark sort of passion. Lower down there was a hint of cleavage between the full round tops of her breasts. Rory looked at the picture a long time, curious about what the rest of her looked like. "Sure is good-looking," he said, handing the picture back to the man.

"Yeah, she's beautiful all right," said the driver. "But she ain't much of a cook, and she can't clean the house worth a damn."

Under different circumstances Rory might have taken offense to the man's words, called him sexist, maybe even a creep, but right now he had to be pragmatic, and that meant doing everything he could to stay inside the car and headed west. "Well, you can't have everything," he said.

"The only damn room she's any good in is the bedroom."

Rory almost couldn't believe what he was hearing, and wondered just how far south he'd traveled. "You don't say."

"But in the bedroom she's practically a whore. She'll take it anywhere and everywhere: in the mouth, from behind, even up the ass if I want. She loves nothing more than to please me. . . . It's almost like she's a damn sex machine or something."

"You're a lucky man," Rory sighed, his voice cold and impassive.

"Like the other night, for instance. We shared a glass of wine, then I put on a few videos—you know, to set the mood."

Rory nodded.

"And before I knew it, she was down there between my legs sucking on my pecker like a bobby soxer on a malted. Wouldn't stop neither till I filled her mouth with spunk."

Rory didn't know whether to be repulsed or turned on by the account, although he felt nauseated at the same time as a knot of tension began to tighten between his legs.

"For some women, that might have been enough, but not her. She just kept on working me—kissin' and suckin' and lickin'—till I was good and hard again. Then she asked me *so nice* if I'd like to fuck her pussy."

"No shit," said Rory, the words long and drawn out.

The driver just shook his head. "And then came the topper," he said. "After I was done with her pussy, she was practically begging me to stick it in her ass. Can you believe that?"

Rory was finding it hard to believe, but his groin wasn't having any such problems at all. There was something raw and carnal about the way the man was talking, and, like it or not, it excited him.

The man drove on in silence, smiling. After a few minutes he said, " 'Course, as horny as she is . . . I hafta admit that I'm getting a little tired of her. I mean, once you stuck it everywhere there is a couple hundred times, what else is there? Right?"

Rory didn't answer.

"Right?"

"I guess."

There was another few minutes of silence.

"Listen," said the driver, his voice soft and low. "This ain't no night for you to be walking all the way into town. Why don't you come home with me, have dinner, and get yourself cleaned up proper?" He drew a hand over his face and licked his lips. "After, you can spend some time with the missus . . . you know, show her a good time and give her a bit of a change."

Rory just looked at the man, trying to gauge his words. He looked closely at his face, but the light shining up from the dashboard masked any emotion he might have been expressing. Finally he just said, "You're serious, aren't you?"

"'Course I am. She's been pining for something new for so long. . . ." he said, as if he were offering Rory nothing more than the use of a lawn tractor. "Always wondering what it would be like to do it with someone same as her. Believe me, buddy, you'd be doing me a favor."

Rory looked out his window and watched the world pass him by, so cold, black, and endless—it made him shiver just to think about being outside. On the other hand, some food, a hot shower, and a night in a warm bed sounded all right even if the thing about his wife was bullshit. "Sure," he said. "Why not?"

The driver smiled. "Thanks, pal. You're going to make my wife one happy woman," he said. "And don't you worry. She knows how to show her gratitude."

Rory still had his doubts, but couldn't help himself from being a little excited. The woman in the picture had been so beautiful and sensuous that if what the man had been saying were true, he'd be spending the night in heaven.

If it were true.

They drove a few more miles before Rory saw the faint light of a farmhouse shining in the distance. "Must get pretty lonely out here," he said, stopping himself before adding, "in the middle of nowhere."

"Not really," said the man. "We keep ourselves entertained, you know . . . make our own fun." The man laughed and gave Rory a wink.

Rory smiled politely and nodded.

At last the man turned into a driveway nestled at the bottom of a gentle dip in the road. The mailbox at the end of the drive was a basic steel box. Seeing it made Rory realize he'd never gotten the man's name.

"By the way, my name's Rory," he said. "Rory Graham."

"Please to meet you, Rory," the man said, extending a hand but never taking his eyes off the narrow dirt road that twisted its way through the trees toward the house.

Rory shook the man's hand, waiting for him to introduce himself. But he never did.

"Here we are," he said, stopping the car and shutting it down. The car's big engine died and the night was suddenly as quiet as it was black.

Rory looked out the window at the house. It was an old brown-brick farmhouse trimmed in gray. The surrounding grass was cut short and neat, but there were no signs of flowers or bushes anywhere close to the house. In fact, the entire house was without color, devoid of what Rory thought might be a woman's touch.

As he thought about that a moment, Rory felt his heart leap up into his throat. "Your, uh . . . wife like to garden?" he asked, stepping cautiously out of the car.

"Naw," said the man. "She hardly ever comes outside."

The words did little to calm Rory's nerves. He stood motionless on the front steps watching the man unlock the dead bolt. After opening the door, he switched on a light and shouted "Hello" into the house.

"Hi," came the response. The voice was soft and faint, and most importantly, belonged to a woman.

Rory felt the tension drain from his body like water from a sieve. He let out a little laugh under his breath and headed for the front door.

Once inside, the man hung up Rory's jacket and tossed his backpack into the corner. "Why don't we go upstairs and say hello to the missus?" he said. "Then we'll see about getting you straightened away."

"After you," said Rory.

He followed the man up a flight of old, creaky steps, then down a hallway toward a room where a light was on.

Before he even got there, Rory was aware of a bad smell coming from inside the room. It was a sharp stink and it took him a moment or two to place it.

It smelled like soiled diapers . . . like shit.

"Hello, dear," said the man as he entered the room, leaving Rory waiting out in the hall.

"I'm sorry I couldn't wait until you got back," said the woman's voice.

Slowly, Rory stepped into the room.

There was a woman lying back on the bed covered by a sheet. It was the same woman he'd seen in the photograph, just as pretty as her picture and, judging by the rise and fall of the sheet as it clung to her body, just as curvy.

"No problem, honey," said the man, walking around to the head of the bed, where he gave his wife a quick kiss on the cheek. "You know I don't mind cleaning up after you."

Then the man pulled back the sheet . . .

And Rory felt his body go numb.

The woman on the bed had no arms or legs.

And the smell . . .

The smell was coming from the shit she'd taken on the bed.

Rory just stood there, looking at the woman, unable to move. Each of her limbs looked to have been hacked off, leaving her with four short stumps, each one capped by a gnarled mass of reddish pink scar tissue.

While Rory watched, the man took a baby wipe from a box on the night table and wiped the woman's buttocks and anus clean. Then he gathered up the towel that had been laying beneath her and tied it into a tight little ball.

"Excuse me," he said, walking past Rory with the soiled towel and carrying it on down the hall to the bathroom.

Rory still couldn't move, his eyes too fixed on the woman as she moved crablike into a more comfortable position on the bed. And while he stood there, he began thinking about what the man had said to him earlier in the car.

She's not much of a cook.

She can't clean worth a damn.

The only room in the house she's any good in is the bedroom.

It's true, he thought. All of it is true.

And so is the part about . . .

She's been pining for something new for so long . . . always asking me what it would be like to do it with someone same as her.

Same as her, thought Rory. With no arms or legs.

"Will you be staying the night?" she said, her kind-sounding voice betrayed by the sardonic little smile on her face.

"No ma'am," said Rory. "I think it's probably best if I got going."

And then he turned around . . .

Just in time to see the axe blade bite into the meaty part of his thigh.

JUST SEX

Michael Garrett

*W*ait a minute," John Franks interrupted, stunned by what he thought he'd heard. He wiped his lips with a linen napkin and stared confusedly at his friend Angel Peters across the table. She acknowledged the recognition with a sensuous grin, without a hint of embarrassment, as if her proposition had been little more than an invitation to attend a lecture. "Excuse me if I seem a bit dazed," John continued, "but would you run that one past me again, please? Just to be sure it was *me* you were talking about?"

The din of surrounding conversation partially muted her voice in the crowded restaurant as she repeated her pitch. Even before she finished speaking, John's dick sprouted with instant growth.

Angel laughed and lightly shook her head. She seemed perfectly calm, in control, and absolutely gorgeous, as usual. Finally she leaned across the table to clarify her request. "For a writer, I sometimes don't communicate very well verbally. But I've noticed the way you've looked at me before, John. You've been attracted to me from the beginning, haven't you?" Her eyebrows arched as she playfully challenged him. Without awaiting a response, she added, "If it's true, it presents us with a unique opportunity as writers." She paused to push an errant curl of brown hair from her forehead. "We both write erotic thrillers, yet our private lives are rather boring. A physical relationship could give us actual experience to draw from."

John swallowed hard and tried to hide his sudden lack of composure. Yes, he'd heard her correctly the first time. There *was* a fucking Santa Claus!

He'd met Angel at a writing conference three years earlier, and they'd taken an immediate liking to each other, but strictly on a platonic, *professional* level. Their writing interests were similar, though she was considerably more serious in her efforts, and they had since critiqued each other's work on numerous occasions. Keeping his physical attraction to her under control had been a struggle for John on the occasions when they'd been alone together.

He chuckled inside; God, he hoped he wasn't blushing. He'd been married for almost twenty-five years. Although Angel had rarely spoken of her own marriage, he'd assumed that she was happy as well. Despite his own contentment at home, John had occasionally fantasized over his sexy writing partner without the slightest hope of a true-to-life tryst with her. He blotted his forehead with the napkin and took another sip of iced tea. "I . . . can't believe this," he mumbled.

Angel took a deep breath that pushed her breasts against her tight blouse, leaving nipple impressions that slowly faded from the fabric. John's erection grew harder. "Look, I'm sorry if I've made you uncomfortable," she apologized. "Maybe I should've brought it up in a more private setting, but, well, we've talked about sex before. I've told you things about myself that I wouldn't dream of telling anyone else. As a writer, I'm just naturally curious, and it seems so logical to me, that's all. I mean, it wouldn't be emotional or anything. Just sex. It could be a *terrific* character study."

Just sex? John thought. Hell, it'd be the fuck of a lifetime! He glanced around the restaurant to see if someone he knew might be eavesdropping. "Hey, I'm not knocking the idea," he said, his voice barely above a whisper. "The surprise just needs to wear off before I can talk intelligently about it."

The waitress refilled their tea glasses and removed the soiled dishes. Angel stared at John with a faraway look in her eyes, then added, "But don't misunderstand. I'm not trying to steal you from your wife or anything. I don't know her very well and I obviously prefer not to be around her anymore if we go through with this. I'm only looking at it as a writing exercise."

John rubbed the bald spot at the crown of his head. Yes, there was still Sheila to think about, but what man could resist such an offer, regardless of his feelings for his wife? John exhaled and swallowed hard, still stunned by Angel's proposal and feeling somewhat put down by her last comment. She was thinking strictly in terms of improving her writing, while literary aspirations were the furthest things from his mind. He smiled at her again, feeling so self-conscious that it was difficult to make eye contact. "What about George?" he asked.

Angel laughed. "He's a truck driver, remember? He's only at home a couple of nights a week, and I suspect he's had a few flings along the way." Changing the subject, she leaned across the table, her movement launching the scent of her perfume in John's direction. "You told me before that you and your wife were childhood sweethearts, that you've never made it with anyone other than her."

A sticky wetness soiled John's crotch as he admired her cleavage. It had been years since he'd had an involuntary erection, and now he was leaking middle-aged seminal fluid at the mere thought of bedding down with Angel. She was at least twenty years younger, and so attractive she could compete quite handily with the *Sports Illustrated* swimsuit models. He closed his eyes and rubbed his temples. "That's right," he nodded, so overwhelmed by the possibilities that he could hardly speak.

She circled the rim of her glass with her fingertip. "I can't imagine what it would be like to experience a second sex partner at your age," she cooed. "Not that I think you're old or anything. I just think that having been confined to one partner all this time would make a new experience so much more adventurous." She stopped for a sip of tea, then continued. "That's why I chose you. You're the only male writer I know, and you've had just *one partner* in your whole life! I'd love to know what it would be like for you to experience having sex with someone new after all these years."

John watched her eyes flutter from errant beams of sunlight that arced through the door as customers entered and exited Miguel's Restaurant. Angel was absolutely beautiful; her dark hair rounded her shoulders, and her eyes sparkled in the flickering brightness, a hint of both Kathy Ireland and Teri Hatcher in her appearance. Her cheeks were smooth and pink, her lips full and inviting, and John wanted nothing more at the moment than to kiss them. Sheila crossed his mind again, but he couldn't help concentrating on the unbelievable opportunity before him.

Angel reached for her purse to pay her share of the tab; they'd always gone dutch whenever they met for lunch, and today was no exception. John stared at her in amazement. "We can't leave now," he complained. "Not without some kind of . . . *plan.*"

She settled back in her chair and grinned wickedly. "We don't have to decide anything today. There's plenty of time."

"I can't believe this," John moaned again, raking his fingers through his thinning hair. "Just a few more minutes. Please?" His erection throbbed mercilessly; the room seemed to swirl before his eyes.

Angel smiled. "You've always been so sensible, John," she laughed. "I'm surprised you didn't think of this yourself." She blotted her lips with a napkin and blinked coyly. "We've been a writing team since we interviewed the mortician—remember? And it makes perfect sense in more ways than one, to me at least." She cleared her throat and took another sip of tea. "George is away from home most of the time, and I'm at my sexual peak. I have . . . *physical needs* . . . and I admit, I've strayed a couple of times." She rolled her eyes to the side and cringed as a man nearby appeared to overhear her. Lowering her voice, she whispered, "And even though it would only be a writing exercise, it would still be a sexual outlet for me and keep me from getting involved with another stranger." John sat dumbfounded. "You didn't know me as well as you thought you did, did you?" Angel laughed.

John exhaled deeply, unable to wipe the look of elation off his face. He felt like a virgin on the eve of the Big Night. "You never fail to surprise me, Angel. God only knows how you could ever top this one."

"Remember, though, I don't want it to interfere with your marriage," she reiterated. "When we've talked about sex before, you told me that men can have sex without emotion, and that's what I'm counting on you to do. It'll be purely for research and nothing else, but I don't want it to endanger our friendship. If we're careful the way we go about this, we can experience the same sense of adventure that our characters enjoy. Just *think* of the realism it'll add to our work."

John scratched his head and admired her beauty, the way every hair seemed to be in place, the way her makeup had been so flawlessly applied, as if she'd just stepped off a Hollywood sound stage. But he obviously had more to lose than her. She didn't seem as concerned about her own marriage, yet he, on the other hand, had no complaints at home.

Angel smiled and winked. She dropped a tip onto the table,

grabbed the check, and headed for the cashier. John was afraid to stand, for fear his erection might show.

A couple of weeks later John's fantasy became reality. Following a candlelight dinner, they'd retired to Angel's bedroom, where she suggested that they shower together to thoroughly clean themselves for the upcoming sexual smorgasbord. She'd dimmed the lights to heighten the mood; clouds of steam partially veiled her nude form, but as John embraced her inside the confined quarters of the shower, the friction of his dick grinding against her soapy pubic bush was almost more than he could stand. He held her tightly and moaned as he clasped the firm curves of her ass, the sprinkling warmth of the shower streaming over his shoulder and across her forehead.

"John?" she whispered above the steady hiss of the shower. "Is there a problem?"

Relieved that the low light concealed his embarrassment, he admitted that he was about to come. "Let's get the first one out of the way, then," she responded, and proceeded to work up a soapy lather between her hands. Then she reached between his legs and carefully stroked his dick, the feeling so intense and delightful that he gritted his teeth and braced himself against the ceramic wall. Within seconds he tensed and pasted her hands with a milky warmth of his own.

"Oh, God, Angel," he gasped into her ear, trying to catch his breath. "That was wonderful."

She stood on her toes and kissed him tenderly, the humid air inside the shower adding to his increased body heat. "That was only the beginning," she promised.

And it was.

The evening was over much too quickly, and Angel proved insatiable. Never could John have imagined a woman so energetic, so uninhibited. Angel was a more than willing partner, eager to experiment with positions and activities that Sheila would have considered perverse.

"John," Angel whispered after they'd each recovered from intense orgasm, their bodies glistening with sweat. She snuggled against him, her lips only centimeters from his, her hair still damp from the shower. "Tell me everything. Every single detail."

John smiled, closed his eyes, and relaxed to the feel of her fingertips twirling his pubic hair beneath the sheet. "At first I was nervous," he admitted, "mainly about being in another man's bed having sex with his wife."

Angel nodded. "I understand, but I told you, I know George's schedule like clockwork. There's really nothing to worry about."

John exhaled a burst of pent-up breath, then continued. "It was like my first time all over again," he said. "I never dreamed that sex with a new partner could be so exciting, so *different.*" Angel switched on a bedside lamp and reached for a ruled pad and ballpoint pen on a night table. John put his arm around her and pulled her closer, kissing her forehead lightly. "Maybe the best part of all," he whispered into her ear, "was that this time, I had such a great looking lady to share the experience with, and we both knew exactly what to do."

Angel broke the embrace to free her arm for writing.

Answering question after question, John reluctantly realized Angel had meant exactly what she'd said, that their union meant nothing more to her than a writing assignment, that her tender ministrations had simply been an act, all part of a script whose purpose had been to simulate the romantic coupling of real people in love.

Finally John wrestled the paper and pen from Angel and tossed them to the floor. "Too many questions spoil the mood," he said. "We're missing an important part of the evening." Then he gently tugged the sheet to her waist, his eyes riveted to the expansion of her breasts as she breathed, her erect nipples pointing toward the ceiling.

Angel pouted and glanced at a nearby clock. "Didn't you say you needed to get home before Sheila?"

John wrenched the covers away to slip into his clothes, then leaned back to nuzzle against her neck, to tell Angel what a terrific lover she'd been, but she'd already retrieved her writing instruments and was frantically transcribing notes again.

The party was obviously over.

Subsequent telephone conversations reinforced Angel's detached perspective of the encounter. John craved a rematch—he couldn't get her out of his mind—but had tried to appear indifferent, projecting false bravado to improve his chances for a return engagement. But Angel carefully skirted any mention of the event. It was maddening!

At a corner table of the library a few days later she finally broached the subject. "I'm glad we did it, John. I can already see improvement in my work." She fingered through a sheath of papers and exclaimed, "Just *look* at the sex scene I wrote last night!"

John took her dot matrix manuscript and waited for her to comment about his performance, about how wonderful he'd made her feel, but her mind was obviously on how she might improve on the concept. "What do you think about this?" she asked, reaching over to squeeze his arm. John's smile quickly faded. "I've decided to make it with a man who has been with lots of other women, a real ladies' man—someone completely opposite from you. Can you think of anybody you'd recommend? I'll share my notes with you if you'll help me."

John was flabbergasted. And on top of that, he wasn't exactly happy to be viewed as the *opposite* of a ladies' man. "But Angel— what about George? What about AIDS?" *And what about the fucking jealousy burning inside my gut?*

Angel shook her head. "I know this sounds awful, but I'm more committed to my writing than to my husband," she replied smartly. "My work is my life. Besides, I know how to take precautions. And like I said before—it's just sex. It has nothing to do with George and me."

"But Jesus, Angel—"

"We'll talk about it later," she interrupted.

John shook his head as she sauntered away, the sway of her hips fueling the pain of sharing her with anyone else. *Just sex,* she says, he repeated to himself. *If she could write half as well as she can fuck, she'd top the bestseller list.*

John stared at Angel across their favorite table again at Miguel's Restaurant, unable to erase the vision of her perfect breasts from his memory. Growing increasingly more agitated by Angel's re-ports of her further adventures with local studs, John realized that the only way to get her back in bed was through her writing, and he'd come up with an excellent plan.

"Tell me about this collaboration idea of yours," Angel said, following a sip of coffee. She looked ravishing again, perfect in every way.

John had become so obsessed with her that he'd neglected his wife along the way and lost interest in his own writing. Regardless, he faked literary ambition as he pushed the proposal to her: "You can write all of the female character's parts, and I'll write the male's point of view, based on our actual experiences with each other as we explore a developing relationship."

She seemed skeptical as he explained the concept, and John tried to appear nonchalant, as if the sexual element was as insignificant to him as it was to her. "We could pick up where we left off and let our physical relationship follow its natural course. We'll let the chips fall where they may—let the story tell itself." He paused to gauge her reaction. She was thinking about it, he could tell. "Just imagine," he continued. "Real lovers, real spouses, real love triangles. Our novel will be so realistic, we'll have our readers creaming in their pants!"

Angel exhaled and pursed her lips. "I don't know, John," she sighed suspiciously. "You haven't written anything lately. Are you sure you want to tackle a novel?" Before he could even answer, she added, "And you're talking about a continuing relationship instead of a one-night stand. Are you being straight with me, John? Are you sure you won't be in it just for the sex?"

"N-N-No, of course not." John blushed. Suddenly his collar felt too tight. He cleared his throat and glanced toward a nearby waitress, motioning for more coffee. "Hey, it was just a thought," he finally said. "Forget it. We'll think of something else." Hopefully, she wouldn't detect his disappointment.

Her eyes narrowed as she examined him closely. "Besides, I always work from an outline. I'm not sure I could write a novel without knowing its resolution in advance."

John reached over to hold her hand. She was receptive after all, but there was no affection in her touch. Strictly business. "But this will be like nothing else you've ever written before. You *can't* outline it," he explained. "It has to be followed to its natural conclusion. And you'll *be* the lead female character. You'll be a part of your own book—just think about it!"

He seemed to be winning her over.

"Remember how our characters seem to take on lives of their own?" he urged her on. "Well, this time, *we'll* be the characters. I can't imagine anything else like it."

Following a brief debate over the potential drawbacks and a final challenge of John's actual motive, Angel consented.

While the intensity of their first time could never be matched, John enjoyed the hell out of trying. Angel had the thickest pubic bush he could imagine, and he loved burying his nose in it. The only downside to their sexual marathons was Angel's insistence on a question-and-answer session following each rendezvous, and he hated to see her reach for the ruled pad on the nightstand. After three couplings that were, for him at least, fan-fucking-tastic, she was obviously growing impatient.

"John," she sighed, her head sinking into her pillow at the conclusion of their latest after-sex press conference. "Can't we do something to beef things up? We have a really weak story so far. There has to be more substance for this to be a marketable novel."

John was pleased that the darkness concealed his disappointment. "Well, I guess we could push it to the next level," he reluctantly conceded. "But if we interfere too much, it'll lose its natural quality."

Her silence was like an early frost. He anticipated her impatience, even before she wrenched the covers away and reached for her clothes. "You're not interested in writing this novel," she spat. "You're only in it for the sex." She snatched her bra and panties from the floor and stormed into the bathroom.

John met her at the door when she returned, but she shrugged away. "Look," he said, "I won't deny that I enjoy the sex. But it's true that sometimes you have to help a story along. It's easy to experience writer's block when you're developing a plot. Maybe we need to spice it up a bit." Even as he said it, John envisioned kinkier sex.

She turned to him in the darkness. "How many pages have you written?"

Oh, shit, he thought. "Several," he finally lied.

"Well, I want to see them. Next time we'll go over our work *before* we go to the bedroom." Even in the shadow of night, John felt the intensity of her stare. "I've got to know that you're serious about this, John. I don't like being used."

Having gained Angel's approval with an explicit sex scene culled from an unpublished manuscript, John slipped out of his clothes and slithered between the sheets. Her mood had been icy from the moment she'd met him at the door, their "collaboration" obviously on the verge of collapse. Even before Angel climbed in bed beside him, still in her bra and panties, John knew he'd have to make the best of their limited time together.

"Forget something?" he confronted her playfully with a tug of the elastic band of her underwear.

She shrugged away and avoided contact. "I'm upset with you, John. You've used me. I feel like a hooker."

John tried to console her. "That's not true," he said. "Besides, this was your idea in the first place. Remember?"

She exhaled and shrugged farther away. John shook his head in exasperation, then used his creativity to turn the situation to his advantage. "Maybe this is what we've needed," he said. "We've reached a conflict point in our relationship. This could be great for the story! It could be a turning point!"

She didn't buy it; further discussion seemed hopeless. John glanced at his watch and exhaled in disgust. "Well, then, I suppose we should just call it a night and try again later."

Angel grabbed his arm. "No, wait," she said. "We need to set things straight, once and for all. If we can't see eye-to-eye, we need to call it off for good."

John swallowed hard. He reached over to stroke her hair and noted her increasingly erratic behavior. "Are you feeling all right?" he finally asked. "You seem different tonight."

Angel slipped from his grasp and headed for the bathroom without a word.

This must be her routine, John thought. She gets mad and sulks in the bathroom like a spoiled little girl. George has probably been through this scores of times. But, shit, for a woman like Angel, a guy could put up with just about anything.

Within moments, from behind the closed bathroom door, she called out to him as she twisted the shower knob on, "I'm disappointed in you, John."

It was a strange thing for her to say. "I . . . don't understand," he responded, cocking an ear in her direction to hear her more clearly above the noise of the shower.

"I thought we were friends," she continued. "I thought we were helping each other. I thought you were serious about your writing. I never believed you'd . . . *take advantage* of me."

John tossed the covers aside, the cool night air drawing goose bumps from his skin. "I resent that!" he lashed out as he edged closer to the bathroom door. "Can't we discuss this face-to-face?"

She laughed. "I'm not stupid, John. I won't let you talk your way out of it this time. I admit, I might have been gullible. But I'm not stupid."

What the hell was she doing in there? The shower had been running for several minutes now, and he knew from the sound of her voice that she hadn't closed the shower curtain yet. If she was so pissed off, why had she been so insistent that they get together tonight? Shit, sometimes women were impossible to understand. John leaned against the door and pressed an ear against it. Was she talking to someone?

"I know you're out there listening, John," she said, the sarcasm of her voice more distinct from this closer vantage. "But can't you at least give me the decency of going to the bathroom in private?"

John shrugged. Maybe he was only imagining things after all. Hell, what did he expect? A hidden gun in the toilet? A dagger in the medicine chest? He chuckled to himself. Erotic thrillers were getting the best of him. This was reality, not fiction. "I don't understand why you're so upset," he called out as he stretched and yawned. "I've done everything you've asked. I've helped you develop a ton of notes. And I'm still here, working on this novel with you, and you don't appreciate a damn thing. What more could you want?"

She laughed again. "I'm determined to get a novel out of this, John, and a marketable storyline would certainly help. You owe it to me." She unlocked the door and stood before him in a Notre Dame T-shirt and panties, a cellular telephone in her hand. Leaning against the door frame, she tapped the phone's antenna against her hip, back into its casing. A cloud of steam rolled through the open bathroom door as the shower continued to hiss behind her, its purpose obviously having been only to camouflage her telephone conversation. "But I think you were right when you said that sometimes a writer has to help a story along. That's what I've decided to do. And like you first suggested, the story will write itself with just a little prodding."

Something about the tone of her voice worried John. She *looked* sexy, but she wasn't *acting* sexy. And who the hell had she been talking to? Suddenly he felt uneasy. He grabbed his clothing from its perch on her husband's weight-lifting equipment in the corner of the room and jutted one foot into his underwear as the garage door rattled open downstairs. John froze.

George!

"Angel?" he whispered loudly with a look of bewilderment. "Did you hear that? Could George have come home early?"

No answer. She didn't seem concerned in the slightest.

John twisted another foot into his underwear, lost his balance and tumbled to the floor on his ass, jarring the nightstand as he fell. Manuscript pages fluttered through the dim light across the bedroom floor.

A slamming car door sounded from the lower recesses of the house.

John cringed. A rush of fear screamed through his veins.

"Angel!" he hissed again. *"Answer me!"*

He fumbled with his clothing but was too nervous and uncoordinated to dress himself. The kitchen door downstairs opened and slammed shut. A man's voice yelled, "This better be a fucking joke, Angel. *I'm not in the mood for games."*

And then, with a sense of impending doom, John glanced at the barbells in the corner, at the weight-lifting trophies on a nearby bookshelf, and then at the manuscript outline that had landed at his feet. There was no time to critique Angel's idea, but he now understood how she intended to help the story play itself out. The last line of the unfinished outline read: *Husband returns home unexpectedly and attacks (kills?) lover* . . .

John scooped up the remainder of his clothing and looked outside the window. The bedroom was on the second floor, and thorn-enshrouded rosebushes lined the exterior wall on the ground below. A cold sweat broke out across his face. How could she have done this? Was she so unconcerned about her own marriage that she would actually set her husband up to catch them in the act? Would she be that heartless?

Thunderous footsteps trampled up the stairs. Picture frames rattled on the wall. John was about to piss in his pants. He glanced at Angel—she was far too calm, too smart for this. Maybe it wasn't George after all. Maybe she'd recruited one of her stud-puppies to play the role of her husband. Either way, it spelled disaster. "This is enough, Angel! We can speculate from this point! We don't have to go through with this!" John yelled nervously. Couldn't she call it off? *Wouldn't she?*

He grabbed her by the shoulders and shook her hard. "Time out, Angel," he pleaded. *"Please!* Let's be civil about this."

A Neanderthal-like man burst into the bedroom, the door partially dislodged from its hinges from the force of the entry, its doorknob ramming a hole into the sheetrock wall where it struck. The hulk's arms were as huge as Popeye's, and he smelled strongly of tobacco and gin. The enraged husband drew deep heavy breaths, his face red with anger as he stared back and forth between John and Angel.

John's Adam's apple bobbed up and down. His dick shrank to its adolescent size. He glanced at Angel for help, but she was too busy scribbling notes.

John Franks buried his feet in the sand to prevent his pale ankles from blistering in the heat. The tropical sun was oppressive, the ocean a royal blue as he huddled beneath the protective shade of a beach umbrella with a favorite novel, a cooler of beer, and a cocktail in his hand. Seagulls swarmed above the foamy surf, a warm wind whipping the fringe around the circumference of the umbrella and casting snakelike shadows in the sand. John took a deep breath and relaxed to the sound of breaking waves. Finally he removed his sunglasses for a better look at the gold-digger bathing beauties parading about the exclusive resort. The glaring sun irritated his eyes.

Funny how things work out, he thought. Angel's insanely jealous husband had surprisingly gone for his wife first, and as the wild man had broken her neck, John had had just enough time and adrenaline to lift the smallest of the nearby exercise weights and drop them soundly atop the bitter husband's skull. Within moments the cheating couple lay dead in each other's arms. John had subsequently been cleared of any charges, the murder having been ruled justifiable homicide.

Following another sip of his piña colada, he smiled at a nearby sweetie in a string bikini. She promptly turned away and targeted an older guy decked out in expensive jewelry. John shrugged. He had enough money now to buy just about anything he wanted—including female companionship.

While it's true his marriage had been destroyed by the resulting scandal, John couldn't complain about the eventual outcome. The advance he'd received for the true crime novelization of his story and television movie option had been more than enough to set him

up for years. Now, for the first time in his life, he had enough time
to devote to his writing.

John yawned, knowing he should be writing. He'd exhausted his
imagination for a decent storyline, though, but couldn't come up
with anything fresh. To this day he could think of little more than
Angel. None of the high-class call girls he'd sampled since could
come anywhere close to matching her sexual prowess.

John shook his head, recalling the shock waves that sizzled
through his limbs when she'd driven him to orgasm. *Just sex,* she'd
called it. Yeah, like Steven Spielberg was *just* a director. Like Las
Vegas was *just* a desert town. No, it had been far more than *just
sex.* It had been an awakening, a renaissance, and sadly now, John
feared he'd never experience it quite the same again.

Angel had entertained visions of a blockbuster novel emerging
from their experiment, and John had dedicated the resulting bestseller to her. After all, her immaculate notes had made the first
draft a snap. Now John had no idea how to follow up his literary
success. Just as he'd promised Angel, their story had told itself,
more than either of them could ever have imagined. Fiction, on the
other hand, would present a much greater challenge.

A scream from the nearby surf jarred John just in time to see a
large black fin disappear beneath the surface only a short distance
from the shore. A shark! And a big fucker at that!

John noted the tension and terror in the air as swimmers
scrambled frantically for the safety of dry land. For a moment he
thought the incident might inspire a story, until he realized
someone had written that one already.

Shit, good book ideas were hard to come up with.

SKIN DEEP

Christa Faust

*F*riday night at the Clit Club. Smoke and sweat and music like a heartbeat, like an unrelenting lover, driving the endless, sinuous grind of female flesh. There were go-go girls on high platforms, gyrating like fierce goddesses above the sea of bodies. But these were no silicone icons, no soft focus fantasy constructs. Each was vital and unique. A lean and lanky butch worked boyish hips, a jeweled ring flashing in the hollow fold of her navel. A zaftig, heavy-breasted beauty with gleaming, blue-black skin and proud, Nubian features writhed with tribal intensity, her lush ass pumping above the crowd of cheering women.

Downstairs, couples hugged the shadows, tongues flashing, eager fingers teasing pierced nipples. A sad, stained pool table hosted a heated game, the sharp crack of the balls punctuated by hisses and triumphant cackles. Against the far wall, a cluster of televisions displayed a fly's eye view of Bettie Page times ten, wobbling in impossible heels and flashing cheesecake smiles.

The pale blue glow of the screens bathed the angular face of a wiry tomboy with a sarcastic mouth and a ring in her upturned nose. Her head was shaved except for a stiff spray of green and purple dreadlocks that fell over one eye like the tentacles of a sea anemone. She smoked an unfiltered cigarette with bitter intensity.

"Hey, Flashita!"

A blowzy Chicana tottered over on obscene gold platform shoes, a sloshing drink in each hand.

"Brought you a little medicine."

She handed Flash one of the two. The glass was cool and slick with condensation.

"Thanks, Mercedes," Flash said, but she couldn't focus on the

movement of her friend's fuchsia lips, the empty chatter. Her eyes
kept scanning the crowd, searching for something. . . .

Don't kid yourself, she thought, taking a deep swallow of the
drink, vodka and cranberry, strong but not nearly strong enough.
You know exactly what you're looking for.

The defiant chin, the little girl's mouth. The angry black
eyebrows and those bright eyes, green as jealousy.

Inanna. The only one who ever mattered.

Every time she saw a woman with long black hair, her heart
clenched, the spit going sour and electric in her dry mouth.

She drained her drink. The dull burn of alcohol in her belly was
no competition for the ache in her soul. The tart flavor lingered in
her throat, laden with memories.

They used to call them Bleeding Babushkas, back when things
were different, when they still laughed together. Back when they
would share a bottle on the L train, half full of Ocean Spray
Cranberry Cocktail and topped off with Cheapov vodka, whatever
had been on sale at the liquor store down the block from their tiny
East Village apartment. Back when they would walk down the
street with arms around each other's waists, full of the brave
conviction of new lovers. Just the two of them against the big bad
world.

But that was a thousand years ago, another lifetime, before the
betrayal, before the screaming fights and the icy emptiness in their
wake. Before the hellish hungover morning when Flash woke up
alone.

She lit another cigarette with the first, grinding the butt under
the heel of her battered motorcycle boot.

"Cheer up, baby," Mercedes said, clucking her tongue. "No
point moping around forever over that stuck-up bitch, Inanna.
Forget her." She snapped her fingers, gold rings flashing. "You
gonna find a nice girl, someone who give you the respect you
deserve."

Flash shook her head and smiled a little.

"Yes, Mother."

It was Mercedes who had dragged her out tonight, swearing to
show her a good time or die trying. Although she had whined and
protested, Flash had to admit it felt good to get out of that stagnant
shrine that was her apartment. At the pool table a cute redhead in
skintight cutoffs bent to take her shot. Her thighs were pale, her
freckled calves long-muscled and tight, downed with fine ginger

hair. She sank the eight-ball and looked up at Flash, offering a shy smile.

"See now, look at that," Mercedes said, poking Flash in the ribs with a long magenta nail, her dark eyes glittering. "Why don't you go talk to her."

"Christ, I don't know." Flash ran a hand over her stubbled head. "What if she has a girlfriend?"

Mercedes grinned.

"What if she doesn't?"

She poked Flash again, cheap bangles jingling.

"Go on."

Flash twisted away, laughing.

"All right already!"

The ten steps it took to reach the pool table seemed like ten thousand, an eternity of gut-twisting adrenaline and self-doubt. She watched as the redhead tipped her face back and laughed at a friend's joke. There was a green ribbon around her pale throat. Flash imagined that the redhead was laughing at her and felt sick, almost turned back.

But then the redhead was looking at her, brown eyes warm and lit with friendly humor.

"Wanna play?" she asked.

She chalked the tip of her cue, blue-jean hips cocked and mouth turned up in one corner.

Just as the ten steps had seemed like more, the handful of seconds that passed as the invitation settled in the air between them seemed like hours, years, forever. Flash could smell the redhead's clean shampoo and lavender scent, and against her will she found herself comparing it to the mysterious aroma of clove and rose petals and rich sandalwood that lingered in the inky depths of Inanna's hair. While Inanna smelled like secrets, like dark things better left unsaid, this girl smelled open as an afternoon breeze. With a rush of sadness, Flash realized that this sweet-faced girl with her honest eyes and broad, hardworking hands was part of a simple, daytime world. A world where Flash could never belong. Loneliness wrapped its cool, familiar wings around her heart.

"No thanks," she said.

She turned and walked away, tears burning in her eyes, unshed.

She took the stairs two at a time, adrenaline clawing in her belly, scraping her nerves raw. She cursed herself for a coward, but plunged into the sweating crowd anyway, fighting her way toward the door. She almost made it.

Then she saw the dancer.

A tiny blond girl she knew was climbing down from her platform, blotting her sweaty face with a T-shirt, and the woman who took her place stood up, washing away everything else.

Dressed in only a leather G-string, she was muscular as an acrobat, tall and small-breasted, with a shaved head and phosphorescent, blue-screen eyes, but these details were all secondary. The thing that caught Flash's eye along with every other in the room was the tattoo.

It was a single piece, winding like a living thing over every contour of her alabaster body. Bold black strokes wound jagged spirals over the curve of her scalp. Fine waves and lacy patterns melded together across the washboard muscles of her taut abdomen. Like webs woven by tripping spiders, like a dead language, like dreams. And beneath the mesh, writhing shapes like subtle faces, like a glimpse of childhood spirits.

As she danced, the patterns danced with her, undulating, hypnotic. Flash found herself drifting with the tide of eager bodies, closer and closer, until she was inches away from that curious flesh, those burning eyes.

The dancer ground her hips, threw her arms up over her head. She seemed like some pagan deity come to hot and sudden life, like an unattainable sacred queen, too exotic for the real world. So when those blue-flame eyes fixed on Flash, she felt as if her heart had stopped in the prison of her chest.

The heat of that gaze was almost unbearable, as intense as a knowing touch between her legs, and behind it some inexplicable kind of understanding. As if this stranger knew the secret shape of her pain and loneliness and longing. The dancer held her hand out to Flash, and there was nothing to do but take it.

Her grip was firm and intimate, the skin of her palm hot and silky smooth. All around them, women Flash knew and women she never met cheered and lifted her with a hundred hands, setting her up on the tiny platform.

Up close, the patterns on the dancer's milk-pale skin were even more complex and arresting. It would be so easy for Flash to lose herself in those rococo swirls.

The dancer wrapped her arms around Flash's waist. The strength of her touch was inflammatory, driving all shame from

Flash's aching body. She threw her head back and let the music swallow her.

One of the dancer's lean thighs slid up between her legs, and she moved against it, the rhythmic motion causing the most delicious friction. The scent of the dancer's sweat-slick flesh, of her armpits and her leather-cloaked pussy, was intoxicating, a rich, wild musk that played resonant hormonal chords in the hidden depths of Flash's body.

Her blood sang in her veins. She felt like a goddess, like queen of all she surveyed, the envy of every woman in the club. She felt chosen.

When she turned her head to catch a glimpse of the crowd, she saw a sea of worshipers, pulsing with adoration and desire. She let the dancer pull her T-shirt up over her head, wishing childishly that Inanna were watching.

But then the dancer's mouth closed over her nipple and all other thoughts were incinerated in the wake of that exquisite sensation.

A thousand years might have passed then. Flash was aware of nothing but swirling black patterns mirrored out to infinity, of tongues and fingers and salty skin and hot breath.

When the dancer pulled away, it felt like being torn from the peace of her mother's body and deposited unprepared into the harsh world. The light seemed too bright, the cheers of the crowd like the screams of monkeys, intolerable. But the dancer's strong hands were there to help her down and shelter her from the hungry crowd. She held out Flash's sweaty T-shirt and smiled, just a quick glimpse of teeth.

"Take me home with you," the dancer said.

Flash pulled her shirt over her head and then wrapped her arms around herself. The sweat on her chest had cooled and she felt slightly vulnerable, but those gorgeous, twisting spirals, those strong, gentle hands. What else could she do? She nodded, and the dancer smiled again, wider this time.

There was a brief moment in the long, grungy hallway with its thick familiar scent of stale cooking and fresh insecticide, when Flash stood poised before the door to her apartment and felt unsure. Her mind was as filled with memories of Inanna as the cramped apartment was with memorabilia of her dead relationship. She remembered the day they came to see this place. The silent, West Indian super let them in, and they knew right away that this was the place. Inanna had fallen in love with the heavy, claw-foot bathtub and the quirky angles of the narrow rooms. The neighborhood wasn't the greatest, and the rent was a little higher than they had planned, but she had been so sure.

Then the dancer was there, slipping warm arms around her from behind, understanding without needing to be told, supportive without being intrusive, and Flash could feel herself melting. Her hands hardly shook at all as she undid the row of locks and pushed open the heavy, thickly painted door.

Inside, Flash had no time for nostalgia. Remnants of Inanna were everywhere like snapping bear traps; the crate of Gothic death-rock albums Flash never had the heart to throw away, the black and purple cloth over the windows that Inanna tie-dyed in the bathtub. So many stealthy memories, but they all faded in the radiance of this curious creature, this walking talking goddess who did things with her mouth and her hands that stole Flash's breath, sent her thoughts spinning, lost in the hypnotic designs of the flesh beneath her lips.

Pulling away, breath fast and hard and eyes flashing hot blue fire, the dancer took Flash's chin between thumb and forefinger.

"I want to tie you up," she said.

Mute with aching lust, Flash swallowed hard and nodded.

The dancer drew her down on the unmade bed, and Flash did not resist as her jeans were peeled away, her wrists and ankles bound to the creaking bed frame. Her heart pounded in her throat and between her legs. A chilly rush of fear and desire raced over the surface of her goose-bumped skin as the dancer slid a ball-gag into her open mouth, buckling the straps behind her head. A moment of panic hit until she became accustomed to the blockage, breathing deep through her nose.

The dancer stood back, staring at Flash with her head cocked to one side. She was so beautiful, fascinating yet utterly unfathomable. Flash wondered if she was going to hurt her, and found she wanted it, ached for it with a fierce desire that eclipsed all rational thought. Her skin burned with possibilities.

She never could have imagined what happened next, although when it first began, she was sure she was imagining.

The inky tendrils on the dancer's skin began to move.

At first it seemed like a teasing illusion, like the kind you get when you stare too long into the heart of a spiral. But the fluctuations became stronger, curling up into the air around her with fluid strength, snakelike.

Her eyes rolled slowly up into her head as the sinuous pattern unwound. It waved blindly as if tasting the air, and then began to slink across the scarred wood floor, reaching for the bed and for Flash's prone and vulnerable form.

And Flash began to scream, flailing against the ropes that held her down, but the knots were strong. The choking mass filling her mouth muffled her screams, reducing them to impotent squeaks.

The thing stroked the soles of her feet, and a bolt of uncontrollable pleasure ripped through her fear. Its touch was as wet and muscular as a tongue, but a thousand times more intimate, as if it were penetrating her every pore, caressing her nerve endings with microscopic fingers. It sang a low seductive song, a frequency more felt than heard. She felt a slow, narcotic desire seep through her reluctant flesh as the glossy black coils wound around her thighs, sending thin, questing fingers to explore the folds of her labia. A single tendril caressed her clit, tentative at first, then bolder, undulating with an unflinching rhythm that soon had her shuddering with helpless orgasm, teeth sinking into the soft inside of her cheek. Other, thicker tendrils wormed their way up into her vagina, swelling to fill her while another slid into her anus. She bucked her hips, straining against the ropes and the slick, sanguineous embrace.

Bright pain melded with the heat of pleasure as needle-fine tentacles pierced her skin and the blackness began to fill her, seeping into the vault of her skull and the chambers of her beating heart. She tried to draw breath, but it was in her nose and throat, filling her lungs, and she found she didn't mind. She wanted to open herself wider to accept its unrelenting penetration. Life and love and thought and breath all became irrelevant, dissolved in this swirling desire, this incandescent pleasure that swallowed her identity and rendered her down to the truest form of herself.

And still the blackness sang, without sound, without words. It told her stories of a warm and liquid world, a world without pain, without loneliness, where spiral beauty and non-linear geometry flowed endlessly like a dark river with a thousand tributaries. It beckoned her, begged her to leave behind the world of broken promises and hurtful memories, to dive into this opiate ocean, to let the patterns of her soul become one with the patterns woven by a thousand others, lonely girls like her who traded bleak and empty lives for a taste of something like *belonging*.

Flowing now, untethered by the restrictions of flesh and bone, she let herself be carried away by a dark tide like the rush of blood, like the sea, like freedom.

A paramedic stood over the girl's naked body, baffled. Her breathing was slow and regular, her heartbeat even and smooth, her face peaceful, but her eyes, when they were peeled open, were utterly empty, dilated pupils like deep holes. She was like a house where the lights worked and the water ran, but the owner was long gone. For seven years he had worked as a paramedic, cleaning up the wreckage of a thousand young people swallowed up by drugs and the howling chaos of an unforgiving world, but there was something about this husk of a girl that chilled him to the bone. Being a simple and pragmatic man, he checked all her vital signs twice, searching for a diagnosis. He suspected profound catatonia, a psychological rather than physiological state. If he were more of a spiritual type, he would have said her soul had been removed, cut loose with surgical precision, leaving the body undamaged and uninhabited. But he wasn't, so he didn't.

His partner, in his usual gruff but well-meaning way, was trying to console the girl's friend.

"We're gonna take her down to Bellevue." He handed her a white card stamped with a green address. "You'll probably be able to visit real soon. We'll take good care of her, okay?"

The girl nodded, dry-eyed.

"That doesn't matter anyway," she said, indicating the prone figure with a tilt of her chin.

The paramedic frowned slightly, unsure. He changed the subject.

"That's some great tattoos you got there." He rolled up his sleeve to reveal a crawling panther with glowing red eyes, a grinning skull, a bat-winged woman. "Got these while I was in the service."

The girl gave a thin smile.

"Joey," his partner called, beckoning without looking. "Do you mind putting your dick on hold and giving me a hand here?"

"Right," he said. "You gonna be okay?"

The girl nodded again, her brilliant blue eyes unfocused, a million miles away.

Joey went to lay a meaty hand on her shoulder to reassure her. She flinched.

"Don't . . ." she said.

"Fresh work, huh?" He showed his palms, conciliatory.

"Yeah." She smiled, rubbing a section of glossy black lattice-work on her shoulder blade. Beneath the delicate lines, a subtler pattern lurked. Something like the narrow angles of a face, partially obscured by a spray of green and purple.

HOME MOVIES

Bruce Jones

I took your advice about the affair," Karen was mumbling.

She sounded distant-dreamy, echoey as the Lincoln Tunnel, barely audible and less visible to Glenda, who was groping her way through the darkened house, tripping on something and something else in the living room, calling back through the black cavity of hallway, "Hey? Where in hell *are* you, sweets?"

"In the bathroom. Follow the wall. Did you feel the quake?"

Feel it? It terrified her. Glenda Hope, future bigshot CEO returning to hometown haunts from big city triumphs, just off the plane, just in best friend Karen's neighborhood, her driveway, and what happens? The ground shudders, the Volvo sluices, street lamps wink out, blackness. Not even a porch light to find the door with. Feel it?

"Feel it? The whole neighborhood's gone dark! Karen, where's the goddamn door!" She kept banging her shins on things.

"Getting warmer."

"Keep talking. I don't like this. I've been reading about your serial killer. Am I close?"

"Just at the door."

"Is that you? You sound half asleep, where are you, it's like a *cave!*"

"In the tub. Come sit on the potty."

"I can't even see you!"

"Isn't it divine, I adore the dark. We should live like this, like cavemen. How's Frisco, did you get the job?"

"I got it. Where's Ed?" Glenda found the toilet, pulled down the lid, sat, whooshed.

"Being a cop, I guess, collecting his fuck movies."

"You sound half awake—shit, what did I kick, was that glass . . . ?"

"Johnnie Walker."

"Karen! Not you! Since when? What fuck movies?"

"Didn't I tell you about his porno flicks? He gets them from the department, confiscated or something, brings them home for us to watch. Or him to watch, I just lie there on my stomach fighting for air. Gives him a thrill."

"He screws you while watching porno?"

"And regaling me with all the gory details of our serial killer's latest exploits. The bloodier the better. Have you really been gone three months, I've missed you."

"Anything left to drink?"

"Sorry, I've been a pig. Was it a big quake, do you think?"

Glenda strained impatient pupils, trying to make out the vague form swimming before her, the ghostly hulk that must be the Sanford's tub. "Felt like it. What's this about an affair?"

"How's that?"

"You *are* drunk. You said something about an affair on my way in here."

"I've been fucking like a trooper, Glennie."

Glenda genuflected in blackness, unused to gentle, retiring Karen using the F word, much less employing it with such casual aplomb, drunk or no. "For real? Who?"

"I don't know his name."

"You don't know his name. You're having an affair with someone and you don't know his name? What *do* you know about him?"

"I know every inch of his cock, I can tell you that, which, incidently, is considerable. You were right, I should have cheated on Ed years ago."

Something about it. The eerie ring of little girl voice against harsh tile? Something. Glenda fought a distant chill. When would they have the damn lights back on? "And how did you meet this super stud?"

"You wouldn't believe . . . you wouldn't . . . ."

"Hey! You're trailing off, don't go to sleep on me, you'll drown, I'll be Lamb and Rector's new CEO with a drowned best friend."

"I won't drown, I won't go that way. Where to begin . . . ?"

Glenda heard the liquid rustle of bath water.

". . . well, Ed, I guess. Fat, sloppy cop husband Ed and his disgusting porno tapes. Every night the same thing, same thing, same thing . . ."

"You're repeating, stay awake."

". . . same thing. He comes in half tight, we eat dinner, he hauls out those big steel manacles, cuffs me to the four-poster, puts on his tapes and socks it to me. Same time, same station, same position. Big gut, little pecker, that's my Ed."

"He screws you and watches porno."

"And gives me the latest lab reports on the local lady killer. Have you heard about our killer, or did I ask that already?"

"It's in the Frisco papers too. Are you very scared?" Glenda craned behind herself at invisible shapes, swallowing thickly. "I'd be terrified. I wish the goddamn electricity would come back on. . . ."

"I wasn't, in the beginning. Scared I mean. Mostly just disgusted. He cuts their nipples off, you know, oh yes, Ed tells me all about it, cuts their titties and comes in their hair. One sick pup."

"All right all *right*—about the affair."

"The affair, yes. I met him at the mall."

"Karen, no."

"I know, it doesn't sound romantic, but Glennie, you should have seen him. Forget the TV hunks, this guy . . . this guy . . ."

"Trailing again . . ."

"Sorry."

"How much did you drink?"

"Plaid shirts. He always wears plaid shirts. Like a lumberjack . . . lumberjack with a big, lovely, axe . . ."

"Oh you're *gone*, you are."

"I'm sitting there at Olga's Kitchen sipping my iced tea, minding my own business, and I look up and there's Mr. Dream Pecs staring at me."

"Staring?"

"At me. Not the others, me. And you know me, Glennie, I'm blushing, I'm blushing from the toes up. I get so hot and scrunchy I have to leave."

"You left?"

"So shook up I ducked into the nearest multiplex, sat there in the dark actually trembling."

"I've got to see this guy. Hey, do you have candles, we could—"

"No. Do you want to hear about this?"

"I'd like to *see* you, for chrissake! What happened after the theater?"

"I'm sitting there, the place is practically empty, and the next thing I know this guy, this incredible-looking guy, is sitting next to me."

"Oh, wow."

"And then—and this is without saying a word—he's got his hand on my leg."

"No."

"And then he's got it somewhere else."

"My God! What did you do!"

"What did I do? I came. Finally. After all these years. I think I yelped."

"Karen, this is incredible."

"And he says, this big hunk says, 'I don't want talk. I don't want addresses. I don't even want to know your name.' And then he leaves."

"Jesus. And what did you do?"

"I think I passed out there in the theater seat. It was fantastic. Incredible. At least until I got home and Ed started in with the cuffs and the ugly porn flicks. That was the night he first told me there was a killer in the area."

Glenda huddled on the toilet lid rubbing her arms; no air-conditioning, the house cloying, and she was rubbing her arms. "But the killer, Karen. I mean, weren't you—you must have—"

"Of course. I mean, I thought about it. I mean, even if it was a long shot, it was still dangerous, right? Foolhardy. I think that's what made it so exciting. I think that's why I showed up at the mall the next day."

"And . . . ?"

"He was there. We did it in the women's john that time."

"The *what?*"

"He followed me in. I was sitting there in one of the booths doing my thing and then all at once there he was, pulling back the door, grinning. He shoved me up against the wall, hiked up my dress, and away we went. I came like the Fourth of July."

"You're putting me on. In a toilet!"

"I think he liked it down and dirty like that. We did it in elevators too. Hotel hallways. Any place dangerous and exciting. Outside, sometimes in the park. The warm sun on his hard, white ass. And neither of us uttering a word. Just groans. And gasps. Um."

"Karen, this is sick."

"Yes. We did it ten times one afternoon. Ten times. In *all* the positions. I mean *all* the positions and every spare orifice. I was awash in the Big Sticky. It was unbelievable. It was . . . was . . ."

"What—WHAT! Don't drift off *now!*"

". . . it was . . . addictive. I fell in love."

"You fell in lust. I can't believe this is you talking."

"It went on that way for weeks. Every day. I was so sore. And the more sore I got, the more I wanted. I got it so bad one night I broke the rules. I shouldn't have done that . . . shouldn't have . . . that's when it all started coming apart. . . ."

"The rules?"

"The no addresses rules. I followed him home. He lived over on the West Side, nice place, big two-story Victorian. I pulled up down the street, watched him go in, watched him come out again. I should have gone home. But I wanted him, I wanted him so bad. And the only thing at home was Ed. I sneaked into his house. . . ."

"Oh my God."

"I snooped around downstairs like a common thief. It was thrilling. Dangerous. The more scared I got, the more I liked it. Can you understand? I went upstairs. He had this incredible bedroom, this enormous canopy bed. I stripped, lay across the satin coverlet and awaited my prince."

"Christ, Karen, I can't believe . . . weren't you—"

"Terrified. I heard voices below, then on the staircase. He had someone with him. I hid in the closet."

"With your clothes, I hope!"

"He brings in this really gorgeous blond, really stacked. I'm watching through the crack in the door. The room is suddenly very bright, very bright. Glennie—this gets pretty sick now . . ."

"Don't—"

"He's got her bent over the bed, his big thing in her, and it's turning me on, Glennie, really turning me on. I'm not jealous, I'm not mad, I'm just so goddamn unbelievably hot. That's when . . . that's when . . . that's when—"

"When what?"

"He picks up the knife."

"No."

"From atop the bureau."

"No."

"I couldn't move, couldn't breathe."

"Oh Jesus, oh Christ, I *knew* it! Don't tell me anymore, I can't do this!"

"He stabbed her, Glennie. He stabbed her a lot. The blood just flying."

"Karen—"

"And the bastard, the bastard is still *in* her! And and and then . . . then . . . I guess I passed out."

"Please I—Karen, I'm going to be sick."

"When I woke up, the room was dark. The house empty. I got the hell out of there. Back at home, Ed's waiting with his cuffs. And his stories about how they found another girl. I threw up most of the night. Told Ed it was the flu."

"Dear God. Dear God." Glenda shook spastically, managed to keep it under control. "You—my God, you're lucky to be alive! Did they catch the guy? Karen? Hey! HEY!"

". . . what . . ."

"Wake up! Did they catch the guy!"

"I . . . no . . . I didn't tell them. . . ."

"You what!"

". . . you don't understand, Glennie . . . you could never understand . . . I tell you I was addicted . . . I was . . . I was beyond sick. . . . I'd lie there in bed at night and see the knife, the blood . . . and all I could think about was being under him. I didn't care, don't you see . . . I was ready to die for it. . . ."

"Karen, oh God. What *happened* to you!"

"He happened. He happened. And I couldn't let him go. Didn't want to let him go. I got a knife from the kitchen, just for protection, took it with me. We had this Tuesday night thing at this cruddy motel. I don't think I really intended to use it . . . didn't really believe he'd—"

"Karen, don't—I can't breathe in here!"

"I panicked. He was standing over me there next to the crummy bed, naked . . . so big, so huge, huge . . . I just . . . I panicked. And then the knife was out of my hands and in him, way in, I don't even know how it got there . . . and I was running . . . running . . . running . . ."

Glenda clutched nausea, the room spinning lazily. "Karen? Hey? Are you there?"

Barely audible now, slipping: ". . . wasn't much blood, not on me. And then I was just home again. Just all of a sudden home. Like it never happened. Only it had. It had."

"Baby . . ."

"No, there's more. I washed my face, gave myself a few minutes, then came into the bedroom. Ed was setting up the damn VCR, had this sick grin on his face. 'You'll like this one,' he says, 'one of them phony snuff tapes! Lots of fake blood and bad acting!' And then he's got me down, cuffed and down, and he's huffing away and I'm . . . I'm . . . I'm looking up at the screen, my heart . . . my heart just seemed to stop. . . ."

"What . . . ?"

Just a whisper: ". . . it's him, Glennie, my silent hunk, my lovely lumberjack, *on the TV,* humping the big blond in his bedroom. That's why the lights were so bright . . . he was making *movies* . . . stupid, phony snuff movies. . . .

"Ed was laughing. 'That's Sally Palmer,' he says. 'We call her Sally-the-Pump down at the station house. Hooker . . . works Cimmaron and Central. Saw her there tonight, in fact. Does this sorta phony snuff crap all the time.'"

Glenda lurched up, twisting, pain spiking her ankle, groping for the lid, just making it before her dinner and probably her lunch found the pale bowl.

The voice from the tub so feeble now, so dreadfully feeble: ". . . he wasn't the killer at all, you see . . . I killed an innocent man . . . an . . . innocent . . . man . . ."

Glenda coughed, raw-throated, slipped to her knees, sat there panting weakly, head swimming against cool porcelain, dancing dots—pushed up and slipped again, and again. Had she gotten some on the floor, she'd have to clean it up, it was slippery all over the floor, sticky. . . .

"Karen? Don't fall asleep. Karen you'll drown. . . ."

Her own voice sounded far away now. Probably she'd gotten it on her dress too, the new Armani she'd worn at the meeting, damn. "Karen . . . ?"

The air conditioner thumped on first.

Then the blinking fluorescents, stuttering white, the room coloring pink, then red, and deeper.

Red on the sticky floor, the walls, but mostly the tub, the tub filled with it, sides scalloped crimson, Karen waxy as death within.

Glenda, strangely composed, stared at her friend's corpse: the breasts, tilted chin, mouth caught in mid-sentence livid islands in the sea of blood, eyes poached and soulless. The left arm, fallen free, dangled with deep slashes, leaking still.

On the sticky floor, Glenda's shoe found the fallen razor, nudged it. Glenda stared curiously at it, dreamily, her swimming head cocked just so . . . eyes lifting then to her own laughable reflection in the sink mirror, staring and listening to her mind saying quite reasonably really: I'm a CEO, I live in Frisco now, I'm not part of any of this, any of this at all. . . .

THE JAJOUKA
PENIS-BEETLE

Graham Masterton

*T*wenty-seven years later, he was approached in the foyer of the Hotel Splendid in Port-au-Prince by a small, birdlike black man in a dazzling white suit and gold-rimmed spectacles.

The man took off his hat to reveal a bald head like a highly burnished brazil nut. His front teeth were all gold.

"Have I the honor of addressing Dr. Donnelly?" The man's accent revealed him to be Algerian or Moroccan, rather than Haitian.

"I'm Grant Donnelly, yes."

"I have been looking forward to making your acquaintance for many years, sir. I am a great admirer of your work."

"Well, that's very good of you, thank you. Now, if you'll excuse me—"

Grant's wife Petra was waiting for him by the French windows that led out into the garden. She caught sight of him and lifted her hand.

Grant made to leave but the man touched his sleeve. "Dr. Donnelly—please, before you go. I have studied all of your papers and all of your books, and they are very detailed and comprehensive. But there is always one significant omission."

"Oh?"

"How could a great expert have written *Complete North African Insects* without a mention of the Jajouka scarab?"

The man released his grip on Grant's sleeve. He was smiling, but with no humor whatsoever. The sunlight reflected on his spectacles so that he momentarily appeared to be blind.

"I am a wealthy man, Dr. Donnelly. I would give a great deal of money for information which would lead me to the discovery of a Jajouka scarab."

Grant gave him an almost imperceptible shake of his head. But the man's words had already filled his mind with flute music and the aromatic fragrance of kif and the silken sliding whisper that haunts anybody who has ever traveled to the edge of the Sahara.

"I would guarantee to make you rich, Dr. Donnelly, if you would advise me of the possible whereabouts of a Jajouka scarab."

"There's no such thing," said Grant, with a slight breathless catch in his voice.

The man tilted his head to one side and looked at him in scornful disbelief.

"No such thing, Dr. Donnelly? Really!"

"Believe me," Grant insisted, "it's a myth. It's a story the Moroccan *bouhanis* thought up, to make a fool of Westerners. There's no such thing. If anybody's told you different, then they've been pulling your leg."

"There is no such thing, master," said Hakim dismissively. "What you have been told is nothing but lies."

Grant shook another Casa Sport cigarette out of its crumpled paper packet. "Hakim, I talked to Professor Hemmer at the Institute of Natural History in Tangier. *He* knew all about it."

"Then he, too, has been told lies."

It was evening in the Old Town, in the early summer of 1967, and they were sitting in Fuentes Café in the Socco, a little plaza crowded with cafés and Indian bazaars and jewelry stores which offered Swiss watches of suspicious provenance to Swedish tourists. They were drinking mint tea and eating thickly sugared doughnuts, and Hakim was smoking kif. The strange, fragrant smoke drifted across the plaza and melted into the pale violet air. Inside the brightly lit café, old men in striped djellabas were listening to Radio Cairo on the shortwave.

Suzanna said, "Professor Hemmer was sure that it was a member of the scarab family, a very small chafer."

Hakim looked at her with dark, unreadable eyes. "Professor Hemmer is a German. He knows nothing of what is real and what is not real."

Grant put the cigarette between his lips, and lit it, and coughed. The tobacco tasted as if it had been soaked in honey and cinnamon and sun-melted asphalt. "It seems like we've come a long way for

nothing, then. That's a pity. The university gave us a budget that
was well out of proportion to the scale of our project, and we still
have a whole lot left."

"All the money in America cannot alter reality," Hakim replied.

Grant sat back in his uncomfortable bentwood chair. He and
Suzanna had been working in Morocco for seven and a half
months now, and he had grown accustomed to the riddles and
evasiveness that accompanied all business dealings in Morocco.
But they had traveled a long way today, and he was tired, and
Hakim's repeated denials were beginning to irritate him.

He and Suzanna had completed all of the work that they had set
out to do, including a radical and spectacular study of the life cycle
of the dung beetle, and a profile of weevil infestation which had
already assisted the Moroccan authorities to reduce beetle damage
to grain stores and warehouses.

But two weeks ago, at what was supposed to have been their
farewell dinner party in the house of the Director General of
Ethnic Studies in Kebir, they had sat next to a chain-smoking old
Frenchman called Duvic who had lived for forty-five years in the
fondouk. As soon as he had discovered that they were coleopterists,
studiers of beetles, he had laughed thickly and told them that as far
as *he* was concerned, there was only one beetle worth studying, and that was the Jajouka scarab, *Scarabaeidae Jajoukae,* the
so-called "penis-beetle."

"Why on earth do they call it that?" Suzanna had asked him, her
green eyes bright as broken glass.

Duvic had coughed up sticky sounding stuff into his handker-
chief. His mustache was white, but one side of it was stained by
nicotine to the color of Dijon mustard. "You shouldn't have to ask.
They used to use it in the Little Hills in a coupling ritual . . .
instead of kif. When you smoke kif, you enter a different world,
and walk with *bouhali,* the holy madmen who can do anything,
walk through walls, discuss politics with the dead. But they say
that when you use the penis-beetle, you discover yourself, your real
self, with such a clearness that you can scarcely bear it. *Aimez-vous
l'agonie?"*

He hesitated, coughed again, and then he said, "Twelve, maybe
thirteen years ago, I was offered a Jajouka scarab, in a brothel in
Mascara. I said no. I have to confess that I was too frightened.
Also, I was rich then, but they were asking more than I could
afford, over fifteen thousand francs. Now I wish . . . well, it's no

use wishing. I shall be dead soon, and who would have me, anyhow?"

"This scarab—it's a real beetle?" Grant had asked him, with quickly rising enthusiasm. He was already thinking of the papers, the book reviews, the lecture tours. Standing in front of three hundred academics and clearing his throat and saying, "None of you will ever have heard of *Scarabaeidae Jajoukae,* more commonly known in the Little Hills of Morocco as 'the Jajouka penis-beetle.'" What an opening!

But the Frenchman had been drunk, too much Algerian brandy, and had suddenly become righteous. "I regret telling you," he repeated over and over again.

Grant and Suzanna had been due to fly back to the States the following day, but early in the morning, Grant had talked to Professor Hemmer on the crackly telephone line to Tangier, and Professor Hemmer had said, "Of course, the Jajouka scarab. A very rare chafer that feeds off the gum of the kif flower, the gum we call hashish. I have seen drawings of it, and read descriptions. It is mentioned, I think, in Quintini's *Insects of Africa.* But as far as I know, it lives only in the kif meadows of Ketama, in the high Rif."

"Why do they call it the 'penis-beetle'?"

"Well, my friend, this is very simple. When the beetle is disturbed, it gives off a strong chemical irritant; and it was said that some of the hill peoples used to insert it into male urethra before intercourse in order to intensify their sexual pleasure. I don't even know if you could still find one today. They have probably been rendered extinct by insecticides. I have heard of certain millionaires who would pay a king's ransom just for one beetle. But *naturlich,* it's the question of finding one. And apart from that, its use is strictly forbidden on religious grounds, because Muslims believe in the absolute sanctity of the body, and on legal grounds by the government, who consider it very undesirable for the tourist trade. The last thing they want is to turn the high Rif into another Bangkok, swarming with Westerners in search of a new sexual excess. It is bad enough, *nicht wahr,* with all of my fellow countrymen giving shiny racing bicycles to the young boys on the beach."

Professor Hemmer had detonated with laughter, and Grant had cradled the old-fashioned telephone. Their pigskin bags were packed and waiting in the turquoise-tiled lobby of the Hotel Africanus. Nine cases of research material and three cases of specimens had already been forwarded to Paris. Suzanna had wanted to forget *Scarabaeidae Jajoukae* and return to Boston. "We can look for it next year." But Grant knew that if they didn't find it now, they would never find it. This was a place that, once you left it, you never came back to. Not in the same way, anyhow. You might be haunted every night for the rest of your life by the sound of Radio Cairo on the shortwave, and the hollow, skin-prickling blowing of *raitas,* like oboes heard in a drugged and never-ending dream. But if you came back, the doors to the *fondouk* would be tightly shuttered, the Medina would be deserted, and all of the secrets of the Old Town would be lost to you. You would drink your mint tea as a tourist, not as a brother, one who knows the Secret Name.

Professor Hemmer gave them Hakim's address, because Hakim had once worked as an assistant for the eccentric English botanist Dr. Timothy Scudamore, who had spent five years on the high plateau of the Atlas Mountains, studying the flora, and then the folk music, and then the hidden treasure of all Morocco, the whereabouts of which is known only to Soussi magicians, who have a secret registry of all the gold that has ever been concealed by anybody. If anybody knew where to find *Scarabaeidae Jajoukae,* Hakim did.

Although he *didn't,* or so he said, sitting with his mint tea and his thin *sebsi* pipe filled with kif, thin and angular in his white linen coat and his flappy linen pants and his red silk slippers. Under his red tarboosh his hair was shaved crucially short, and his face was narrow and crowded with angles, like a Cubist painting, so that he never looked the same twice. Only his eyes remained calm and motionless, as if he could get up and walk away, and leave them floating in the evening air, like a mirage, still watching them.

Grant, by total contrast, was two weeks past his thirty-first birthday, thickly put together, slightly overweight, with sun-bleached surfers' hair and a face like a genial quarterback: blue eyes, broken nose, and a toothy, immediate smile. He didn't look like one of America's leading experts on the impact of beetles on human society, not until he put on his round tortoiseshell spectacles, when he looked exactly like his late father, the author of *Donnelly's Definitive American Insects.*

He and Suzanna Morrison had worked together throughout their final Ph.D. year; sometimes intimate, sometimes nothing more than tolerant. Suzanna was tall, strong-faced, with high cheekbones and deepset eyes. She had veils of shining brunette hair, breast-length, but ever since they had arrived in Morocco, she had covered her head with a scarf, and often she wound the scarf completely around her face, so that only her eyes showed. It gave her dignity, and although the brotherhood of men said nothing, they appreciated it, and they respected her for it. She wasn't one of these tourists, or one of these bare-faced students, or one of their own women who scuttled out of the house for a pennyworth of this or a pennyworth of that, with only a rag to cover their faces.

She was even more of a free spirit than the brotherhood of men could have guessed. She had dropped out of SUNY for a year to hitchhike to La Jolla, California, where she had lived in a free-love community called the Shining Eye, a community in which the instant and open gratification of any sexual desire had been an integral part of a philosophy called the Opening. "Open your mind to all, open your body to all." She was more restrained now, but Grant still found her sexually intimidating. Her sexuality was so strong that it was almost audible, bare thighs sliding together, lips parting, eyelids fluttering; and the silken whisper of her hair like the sand snaking by moonlight over the Grand Erg of the Sahara.

The first time they had made love (in Paris, on the Rue Chalgrin, in their bedroom at La Residence du Bois), Suzanna had told him quite matter-of-factly that she had once had sex with five men at once. He had thought she was joking, because he couldn't think how it was possible. But when she carefully and seriously explained it, he remained silent for the rest of the day, both highly aroused and deeply disturbed.

This evening Suzanna wore an indigo-colored scarf and a loose djellaba-style dress of immaculate white cotton. All the same, Grant knew that she was naked underneath, and when she leaned forward on the table to talk to Hakim, he could see the heavy, complicated swinging of her breast.

These days, they weren't always friends, and even when they were friends they weren't always lovers. They had argued, during the past seven and a half months, sometimes violently. They had argued over the Jajouka scarab and whether they ought to go back to Boston and forget about it. But now that they were here, they had become closer again, sensitive to everything that each of them said, or was about to say, or *thought*, even. Grant enjoyed it when they were close like this. It gave him a feeling that he knew where he was in the world, both emotionally and geographically. Cared-for, and cared-about, 35.4 degrees north, 1.1 degree east.

Suzanna said to Hakim, "What if we agreed not to tell anybody what we had found? Would you show us the beetle then?"

Hakim glanced at Grant. "Does the woman speak for you, master?"

Grant impatiently blew out smoke. "Yeah. She speaks for me. Sometimes she even speaks for herself."

"There is no beetle," Hakim replied.

"You mean it's extinct?" Suzanna asked him.

Hakim's eyes flicked shiftily downward. "There is no beetle unless I decide."

"So there is a beetle but you won't show us where it is?"

"Unless I decide."

"So what's going to make you decide?"

Hakim smoked more kif. Coffee jugs clanked. Crickets chirruped. The shortwave rose and fell in the warm night air. It sounded like football results. Osiris United versus White Nile Wanderers? Hakim, at last, said, "Green card. Then I decide."

Suzanna stared at him, and then burst out laughing. "You want a green card? Are you yanking my chain?"

"Green card," said Hakim crossly. "Dr. Scoo-damor, he always promised that I could come to work for him in United States. Then he went searching for the Soussi magicians, and never returned. After all of my years of assistance and diligence, master, I was left with nothing. Very little money, for Dr. Scoo-damor, he was full of promises of payment, and when he did pay, he paid with paper."

"Well, at least he paid," said Grant.

"What is the use of paper?" Hakim retorted. "We cannot put our money into banks because banks are sinful, but when we hide our paper money, the mice eat it. All of the money that Dr. Scoo-damor gave me I hid in my attic, but when I went to take it out, it was nothing but mouse dust and colored confetti."

Suzanna looked quickly at Grant and clasped his hand on top of the blue-painted metal table. "We could sponsor Hakim, couldn't we, Grant? Especially if we told Immigration that he was essential to our work on the scarab."

Grant smiled and nodded, and thought, *Jesus, Suzanna, you're the sharp one.*

"Then you will sponsor me?" asked Hakim.

"We don't know," said Grant. "If the beetle is lies, then no. But if the beetle is truth . . ."

Hakim tamped his slender pipe. The night was the size of all Africa. "The beetle is truth," said Hakim.

The next morning, they took the train from the white-painted station yard at Fes. It was half past eleven, and the sun bleached the color out of everything except the extravagant overgrowths of magenta bougainvillea, and the sky the color of marking ink.

The train climbed steadily up through the hills. Ahead of them the spring flowers had painted each successive mountain a different primary color, yellow and red and blue. Behind them the valleys were filled with white waterwort, a foaming surf of sickly smelling blossom. The fragrance of the flowers was so strong and so sweet that Grant thought that it would poison him, and that he would fall asleep and dream of *bouhanis* who could talk politics with the dead.

He nodded off, but was still conscious of the swaying and creaking of the train, and the drumming of the diesel engine.

When he opened his eyes again, Hakim was sitting opposite, peeling an orange with long, none-too-clean fingernails. He said, "I live in the Old Town but I am always here, in the Little Hills."

Grant nodded in acknowledgment, but realized that Hakim had been talking to nobody in particular.

Hakim said, by way of explanation, "There are places in the world where secrets reveal themselves of their own accord. This is one of them."

"It's very beautiful," said Suzanna. The hills all around them were emerald-green and glittering with little white flowers. On some of the hillsides they could see flocks of sheep. "It's like a dream."

Hakim offered her the orange, opened up like a flower, but she shook her head. He offered it to Grant, and Grant, out of politeness, accepted a piece.

"Tell me some more about the scarab," he said.

"It is truth, master. It exists."

"But will we find one?"

"Anything that exists can be found. Maybe we will have to go to a magician, but we will find one."

* * *

Jajouka was both postcard-picturesque and mysterious, an intri-
cate little collection of dazzling whitewashed houses on an improb-
able hill, surrounded by olive trees and hedges of prickly pear.
When the diesel train had rumbled away, they were left in heat-
baked silence, and Hakim led them across the village green, where
a tethered goat grazed and tinkled its tiny bell. They passed
through a low whitewashed archway and found themselves in a
shadowy courtyard, where a young woman in a dark red dress was
fanning the ashes of a smoky mud oven. A cockerel with brassy-
bright feathers strutted around her.

"I am seeking your uncle Hassan," said Hakim. The sun slanted
through the smoke.

The woman nodded toward the shadowy interior of the house,
her earrings glinting. Hakim beckoned Grant and Suzanna to
follow him, and they found themselves in a cool, bare room where
two elderly men in snow-white turbans and thick woollen djellabas
were lolling on cushions, drinking tea and smoking kif.

There were ritual introductions. Hakim inquired about the
health of Uncle Hassan's brothers, his cousins, his goats, his fields,
and his wives. Hassan had a long curved nose and deeply hooded
eyes, and all the time he spoke he rolled a little ball of gray wax
between his fingers. The other man was much more buttery and
plump. He was so high on kif that Grant couldn't understand a
word he was saying.

"My master seeks a scarab," said Hakim at last. "He is a man of
high reputation and great learning, and wishes to complete his
knowledge of all insects. He can pay you with great generosity."

Hassan thought for a moment, and then replied very quickly and
softly, and at considerable length. With only kitchen-Arabic,
Grant couldn't keep up, but he did manage to pick up the words
"Jeep" and "cousin."

"What did he say?" he asked Hakim when Hassan appeared to
have finished speaking.

"He said that he knows where the scarabs can be found. They
are picked from the kif flowers not far from here by wandering hill
people, Nazarenes, who sell them to the brothel keepers in Tangier
and Marrakech. He will introduce you to the hill people and
arrange for you to acquire two or perhaps three of the beetles. He
does not wish for payment, since he lacks nothing. There is no
electricity here and no running water because they would alarm
Bou Jeloud the Father of Fear, who protects our sheep. He is

satisfied with the tithe which he is given for his fields; and his kif; and his music.

"All the same, he has a cousin Ahmed in Kebir who would dearly love to own a new Jeep. If this can be arranged, then he will take you to the Nazarenes who live by the beetle."

"What does a Jeep cost?" Suzanna whispered.

"Nothing, compared with one of these beetles."

"Then let's go for it. I can't stay here much longer. This kif smoke, I'm starting to hallucinate."

Hassan said something rapid and low. Grant didn't understand every word but he understood the implication. "Is this a man who has a woman to speak for him?"

In Arabic, Grant said, "In our country, the opinions of women are treated with the same respect as the opinions of men."

Hassan nodded, and smiled, and then replied in English. "Those who use the Jajouka scarab have respect neither for men nor for women; and no opinions."

"What does he mean?"

"He means that those who experience the scarab, master, have no more time for points of view. They are interested in one thing only: when will they experience the scarab again?"

It was past midnight when they came rustling through the syrupy-warm kif fields to the makeshift encampment of the Nazarenes. The sky was purple, the same color as old-fashioned typewriter ribbons; and the moon hung in it like a mirror. The Ahl-el-beit, the people of the tent, used to believe that the moon reflected the Sahara Desert, a map suspended in the sky.

A haze of kif smoke hung over the tents. They heard voices and breathy pipes. Grant took hold of Suzanna's hand and squeezed it to reassure her; or maybe to reassure himself. Hakim and Hassan were walking slightly ahead of them, all wound up in their turbans and djellabas. Every step they took crushed blossoms beneath their sandaled feet, and Grant could smell dew and the rotten-sweet fragrance of flowers.

It's like a dream.

They opened the largest of the tents. Inside, around a loudly hissing pressure lamp, sat eight or nine wild-looking travelers in ragged djellabas and shirts. A gray-haired man of fifty or so, with eyes like pebbles; three or four young men with dirty cheeks and sulky expressions; a Sudanese boy of sixteen or seventeen wearing

Graham Masterton

nothing but a belted shirt, so that his long, bare penis rested openly against his thigh; an older woman, with her face covered; two young women, with uncovered faces, in thin muslin dresses.

Uncle Hassan sat next to the gray-haired man and began to speak in his ear, emphasizing his conversation now and again by tapping two fingers into the palm of his hand. The gray-haired man nodded, and nodded, and nodded again. Hakim whispered into Grant's ear, with breath that smelled strongly of oranges, "Hassan is asking for the repayment of a favor. Last year the Nazarenes were caught trespassing into the fields of the Adepts, and Hassan saved them from certain punishment."

After twenty minutes of murmuring and nodding, the gray-haired man beckoned to one of the young sulky men, who disappeared from the tent and then, two minutes later, returned. He gave the gray-haired man two small boxes carved out of olivewood and inlaid with tarnished silver. Hassan took hold of Grant's sleeve and said, "In these boxes, the Nazarene has two scarabs. They will bring him ten thousand dollars in Tangier, enough for his people to live for a year."

The gray-haired man unscrewed the top of one of the boxes and passed it to Grant to look at. The bottom of the box was entirely filled with hashish resin, which gave off a strong, distinctive odor. On top of the resin, scurrying quickly from one side of the box to the other and back again, was a tiny black humpbacked beetle, very similar in appearance to a dung beetle, only very much smaller.

Grant and Suzanna watched it in fascination. "You know what this is like?" said Grant to Hassan. "This is like discovering the source of the Nile, only more so."

The gray-haired man leaned over to Uncle Hassan and murmured something in his ear. This time it was Hassan's turn to nod.

"He asks if you would like a demonstration of the way in which the beetle is used."

"I don't understand."

Hassan pointed to one of the girls, and then to one of the sulky young men. "They will show you, if you wish it."

"What do you think?" Grant asked Suzanna. "You want to see what they do with this thing, or what?"

Suzanna grasped his arm. "It's what we came for, isn't it?"

Grant thought for a moment, then turned and nodded. The

pressure lamp hissed and hissed, and moths pattered against it and spun dusty to the blankets on the ground.

The gray-haired man spoke. One of the girls argued, but then he snapped sharply at her, *"Tais-toi!"*

She stood up and lifted her djellaba over her head. It dropped onto the cushions beside her. She was black-haired, with skin the color of fresh dates. Her eyes were slanted and defiant. She was small, only two or three inches over five feet, and glossy with good feeding. Her breasts were huge: two enormous globes with areolas as wide as the circle that you would draw around a wineglass, veined with blue. Her navel was buried deep in her rounded stomach, but it was pierced with a golden ring. Her thighs were heavy, and between her thighs, her hairless vulva swelled like a plump and clefted fruit. Although these were Nazarenes, which was Hassan's derisory way of calling them Christians, they followed the Muslim way of shaving all their body hair, so that they were smooth and clean.

The girl knelt down on the blankets. She tossed back her hair with her hands and her breasts swayed. Her vulva opened like a sticky kif flower, and Grant could see her clitoris and her inner lips with the odd microscopic detail that he felt as if he were peering at the moon.

The gray-haired man spoke again, and waved his hand, and one of the young men stood up, and stripped off his robes. He was curly-haired and very lean, much paler than the girl. He too was completely shaved of all his body hair, so that his penis looked even longer. It was slowly rising, its wedge-shaped circumcised head swelling up with every beat of his heart, his bare balls tightening. He knelt in front of the girl, and by then his penis was fully erect, a hardened sculpture of veins and silky-shining skin. A single drop of clear fluid appeared in the opening of his penis like a magician producing a diamond from the palm of his hand, and quivered there.

The gray-haired man passed one of the olivewood boxes to the naked girl. Then he snapped his fingers, and one of his assistants gave him a thin lacquered pipe, even thinner than a *sebi* pipe, and he passed that across to her too.

The naked boy leaned his head back, closing his eyes. He grasped his own testicles in his hand, squeezing them so that they bulged. The girl placed the pipe between her lips and gently started to suck.

She probed the other end of it into the olivewood box, and kept on sucking until she had trapped the tiny beetle on the end of it.

"Watch now," Hakim told Grant and Suzanna. "This is how the Jajouka scarab is used to give you ecstasy."

The girl took the pipe out of her mouth and capped it with her thumb, so that the beetle was held against the other end by pressure alone. Then she grasped the boy's erect penis with her left hand, stretching apart the urethral opening with her finger and thumb, and slid the pipe right down the length of his erection. The boy gritted his teeth and clenched the blankets with his fists, but didn't cry out. The girl pushed the pipe right down until less than a quarter-inch of it was protruding from his penis. Then she released her thumb, so that the beetle was freed, right inside his urethral bulb, where his semen would collect in the last few seconds before he ejaculated.

She drew out the pipe, and a few drops of blood came with it. She leaned forward so that her erect nipples brushed the blankets, and licked off the blood with the tip of her tongue.

The gray-haired man went into a long, gesticulating explanation, which Hakim translated. "The scarab is inside the boy's body. It will remain there until he reaches the moment of climax. At that instant, his seed will propel it to the very tip of his penis, but it will react in a negative way to the female juices. It will cling to the opening of his penis, and instantly produce an irritating chemical, which will give both boy and woman excruciating pleasure and excruciating pain."

Hakim said, "I have never tried it myself, master. Perhaps I am a coward. But I know many people who have, and they say that it is heaven and hell, combined."

The gray-haired man impatiently clapped his hands. The naked boy lay back on the blankets, holding his erection in his hand. The girl climbed over him, her thighs wide apart. "Here, here," said the gray-haired man. He leaned forward and opened the girl's vulva with his fingers. Grant saw juicy pink flesh like a freshly cut pomegranate. The gray-haired man grasped the boy's penis and lasciviously rubbed it once or twice. Then he fitted it between the girl's inner lips. The girl sat on it, and the plum-shaped head disappeared deep inside her, until the smooth hairless pout of her vulva was pressed against the smooth hairless curves of the boy's penis root.

Suzanna reached over and clutched Grant's hand. He could see by the look in her eyes that she was frightened, but aroused too. This was the sort of shameless sexual exhibition that would have made anybody want to rush out to the nearest private place they could find and fuck themselves into a rage.

Usually, the Little Hills were filled with music. Flutes, drums, *raitas.* But all they could hear now was the wet kissing of a plump vulva against a bone-hard erection; and the conspiratorial hissing of a pressure lamp. Everybody watched transfixed as the girl and the boy began to thrust more quickly. The girl sat up straighter and clasped both of her sweaty, pillowy breasts in her hands and started to squeeze them, so that her dark nipples stuck out stiff between her fingers. Everybody watched as the boy's scrotum began to wrinkle and tighten, and the girl's juices slid down the dark divide between his testicles, and dripped across his puckered, hairless anus. Everybody watched with tautly held breath, mesmerized by the shluk, shluk, shluk of cock sliding deep into slippery cunt; thoughts that grew dirtier and dirtier; fantasies that grew wilder and wilder; and all the time that beetle was nestling, deep in his shaft, in the very place where semen and sperm would flood together, and tauten, and tighten, and then pump irresistibly into her body.

Grant didn't even realize that he was clutching Suzanna's fingers so fiercely; and neither did she. But then the boy tensed, and tensed even harder, and screamed. The girl screamed too. Only in anticipation, to begin with, because she must have known what was coming. But then the two of them were clenched together, rolling from one side of the blankets to the other, screaming and screaming and thrashing their legs, but never letting go of each other, thrusting closer together if anything, hips bucking, buttocks hard, fucking and screaming with their eyeballs white and their teeth clenched.

They were like *bouhanis;* they were like dogs baying at the moon. They were like ululating women and Aissaoua, the trance dancers, who would kiss snakes and throw live sheep into the air and devour them before they hit the ground. Grant thought for one long moment that they were going to die. "Jesus," Suzanna whispered. "Eat your heart out, Dr. Ruth."

It was over five minutes before the boy and the girl stopped quaking and climaxing and rolling around. At last they fell back on the blankets, eyes closed, gasping for air, their naked bodies shining with sweat. Sperm dripped from the girl's open vagina, but the men in the tent watched it with nothing but dispassion, as if she were nothing more than a she-goat who needed milking and had overflowed. The gray-haired Nazarene knelt beside the boy, lifted his wet, softening penis, and probed inside the opening with the narrow pipe. At last he smiled and picked out the scarab, which he carefully returned to its olivewood box.

He said something to Hakim, and Hakim translated. "These two will sleep for three or four hours. When they awake, they will want to do the same again, but much more urgently this time. The scarab is worse than kif when it comes to addiction. Once you have experienced it, you will always desire more. But perhaps that is the truth that you have come here to find."

He smiled. "You may take two of the scarabs. They are both male, so they will not breed, and besides, they cannot breed anywhere but here, in the kif fields."

He handed two olivewood boxes to Uncle Hassan, who secreted them someplace inside his woollen djellaba.

"One warning," he said. "Never place two male scarabs in the same box; and never try to insert more than one scarab into your penis. Male scarabs are small, but they are more aggressive than scorpions. They will fight each other to the death."

Uncle Hassan placed his hand on the Nazarene's shoulder. *"Mektoub,"* he said. "It is written."

They returned to Fes on the same train that wound its way down through hills. The morning was overcast, and the flowers smelled even more sickly decayed than they had before. Grant was restless and excited, and scribbled endless notes about *Scarabaeidae Jajoukae* on a legal pad balanced on his knee; but Suzanna seemed curiously listless and tired, and watched the hills rotating past the window as if she were dreaming about them. Hakim had smoked too much kif the previous night and slept with his chin against his shoulder.

The first thing she said when they returned to their hotel room was, "I think we ought to try it."

"What?" Grant asked. He was opening a bottle of Oasis Gazeuse.

She came up to him and stood very close, even though she didn't touch him. "I think we ought to try it. The scarab, I mean. There's no point in giving lectures about it if we don't know what it can do."

"You're talking about you and me?"

She nodded. There was a look in her eyes that he had first seen when she described to him the way in which she had made love to five men at once, but had rarely seen since. He was suddenly conscious of the way that her white djellaba was open at the front, revealing the curve of her breast, and he was sure that he could feel the radiated warmth of her body.

He swallowed salty-tasting mineral water out of the neck of the bottle. "You're not frightened?" he asked her.

She shook her head. "I've never been frightened of passion. Have you?"

"Sometimes. But this is chemical passion, rather than natural passion. It's my guess the scarab reacts to the protein content of male semen by giving off a substance rather like cantharides, or Spanish fly."

"We could take samples," Suzanna suggested, but her smile was very much less than scientific.

Grant walked across the tiled floor and stood by the billowing net curtains, looking down at the courtyard and the splashing blue-painted fountain. A man with one eye was standing in the corner of the courtyard, holding a large live toad in each hand.

"I don't know," Grant said. "All of our equipment's packed already."

She came up close again, and this time she stroked the sun-bleached wing of hair behind his ear. "You're frightened," she said.

He turned and stared directly into her eyes. Yes, he was frightened. But he couldn't decide which frightened him more: the tiny scarab in its olivewood box, or Suzanna.

They showered and soaped each other all over in the echoing bathroom with its antiquated plumbing. Then, with their loins white-lathered, they shaved off all of their pubic hair with Grant's Gillette razor. Grant stood drying himself while Suzanna rubbed herself with jasmine-scented oil which she had bought in the Socco. Her hair was wound up in a turban towel. Her breasts were high and rounded and very firm, with nipples that stood up knurled and hard. She was very slim, with narrow hips and very long legs. Her vulva had neat, closed lips, as if it was a secret in itself.

Grant came out of the bathroom with his heart beating in a slow, pronounced rhythm, like the drums of the trance dancers who dance and spin and break earthenware pots on their heads until their faces stream with blood.

"Do you think we should have music?" Suzanna asked him.

He went across to the radio and tuned in to an Algerian music station. Suzanna climbed onto the red-and-green-striped *durry* that covered the bed, and sat with her legs crossed, her wrists resting on her knees. Grant went to the bureau and picked up one of the olivewood boxes and the narrow laquered pipe. His hairless penis was half erect, and Suzanna smiled at him, that unscientific smile. "You look like Michelangelo's *David.*"

He climbed onto the bed facing her. He handed her the pipe and then carefully opened the box. The scarab was motionless in one corner.

"It's not dead, is it?" Suzanna frowned.

"High, more like. There's enough hashish resin in this box to keep you flying for a month."

Suzanna leaned forward and prodded the scarab with the tip of the pipe. Grant watched the way her breasts swung, the way her vulva opened as if the secret was soon to be revealed. He felt hot, almost feverish. The radio was playing some endless wailing music. The net curtains billowed, and their transparent shadow blew across Suzanna's face as if it were trying to show Grant that she was somebody else. Her nipple, the color of a heat-exhausted rose petal, brushing her suntanned thigh. He could see her actual clitoris protruding from her lips like a shiny pink canary's beak.

She sucked gently on the pipe. The scarab clung onto the hashish resin at first, resisting her gentle, insistent suction. But then it clung to the end of the pipe, and she was able to lift it out of its box, trapped by the tiny vacuum she had created. She raised her eyes. "You don't have to do this, you know."

"I know . . . but as you so rightly say, how can we pretend to know what we're talking about if we don't try it for ourselves?"

Suzanna took hold of his half-erect penis in her left hand and slowly rubbed it until it stiffened and swelled. They had never made love like this before, not in such a ritualistic way. On most occasions they had been drunk, happy, exhausted, or just plain horny. This morning everything seemed to be slowed down, as if they too were stuck in hashish resin.

Grant watched with detached fascination as Suzanna squeezed his plump purple cock head so that his opening widened. Without raising her head, as careful as a seamstress or a surgeon, she slid the lacquered pipe into his urethra, all the way down the length of his erection. Instantly, it burned. He felt as if she were filling up his urethra with boiling fat. He flinched, but Suzanna clasped his shoulder to steady him, and pushed the pipe the last inch into his urethral bulb. Then she took her thumb off the end, and slid it out again. Blood welled from the end of his penis and ran down between his legs.

"Christ that hurts."

She kissed him and tenderly rubbed him. "It hurts, but it's inside you. Now we can see what it feels like."

She pushed him back onto the *durry*. He felt the coarse-woven fabric against his naked back. She climbed on top of him like a hairless animal. She kissed his face, nuzzled his lips, nipped at his ears. His penis blazed, because she had penetrated the delicate membranes of his urethra, but he felt something more. An itch, an irritation, deep between his legs, like a cinder that flies in your eye. His penis stopped bleeding and started to drip with clear sexual lubricant, much more than he had ever experienced before, and quivering bright. She massaged his testicles and pulled at his shaft, and he began to feel that something terrible was just about to happen to him.

At last she sat astride him with her thighs farther apart than he thought it was possible for any woman to kneel. He could see right up inside her; a glistening cave. She took hold of his erection with both hands and guided it up between her hairless lips. He closed his eyes. He heard a long ululation, music. He heard arguing and prayers. He felt as if his penis were being sucked by a fire-eater in the Socco Chico. Then she slowly sat down on him, and he slid right up inside her warm wetness, right up to the moment when bare skin kissed bare skin.

They made love slowly at first. His eyes remained closed. He could still feel that irritant deep between his legs. Then she rode him faster and faster, swaying her hips, her wide-flared bottom, her breasts swinging from side to side. Their juices made a lascivious smacking sound against their hairless skin. Suzanna clutched him, and Grant clutched her back. They were out in the desert where the sand endlessly slides in a whispering glissando. They were out in the desert, alone, on the Great Erg of the Northern Sahara, beneath a shadowless dune. The mid-morning sky rippled over their heads like a sheet of azure silk.

Grant could feel his muscles tensing, his climax rising. But this was more than an ordinary climax. The blood began to hammer in his head like the drums of the Black Brotherhood. He started to gasp. The irritation was almost more than he could bear. It felt as if somebody had inserted barbed wire into his urethra and was slowly dragging it out.

Then—a startling explosion. He screamed; or he imagined that he screamed. His whole erection was ablaze with white-hot pain and unimaginable ecstasy. He felt as if he had plunged it into molten steel. He rammed his hips up, so that Suzanna's juices would put out the fire, but they didn't. She was screaming too, and both of them were locked together in spasm after spasm.

It was more than he could stand. His whole life was flying out of his penis. He was hurtling through doors and walls, through walls and alleyways and sordid souks. He burst through courtyards and poured down zigzagging corridors. He detonated with a howl through the shrine of Sidi Bou Galeb, where the mad people are all chained up. He rose up over the desert where the heat ripples and the voices call *"Houwa! Houwa! Houwa!"*

At last he atomized like a French hydrogen bomb fifteen miles over Sidi Ben Hassid, blinding everybody who looked at him.

Suzanna touched his cheek. He opened his eyes and was amazed to find that it was twilight, the color of washable ink. A warm breeze blew from the courtyard, and he could smell the water from the fountain.

"What happened?" he asked her. "Am I dead?"

Her voice was low and trembly and lustful like the Pan pipes from the Little Hills.

She lifted his wet, reddened penis and probed inside his urethra to retrieve the beetle. *"Scarabaeidae Jajoukae,"* she breathed. "That's what happened to you."

They ate a supper of highly spiced lamb kebabs in a little restaurant opposite the hotel. Moths whacked against the lightbulbs. They could scarcely speak to each other. They both felt as if their souls had been drained. They didn't look at each other either, but they kept intertwining their fingers and thinking of the beetles in their olivewood boxes. The gray-haired man had been right: *Once you have experienced it, you will always desire more.*

They were still finishing their meal when an unexpected figure appeared out of the darkness.

"Hakim," said Grant. "What are you doing in Kebir?"

Hakim dragged up a chair and they ordered more tea. "I thought I could resist it," he said. Grant offered him a Casa Sport, which he deftly disemboweled and filled up with hairy green marijuana.

"You thought that you could resist what?" asked Suzanna, sensing that she had the upper edge.

"I used the scarab many years ago, master. I never forgot it."

"So . . . what are you suggesting?"

Hakim's eyes glittered. "You have already tried it for yourselves, is this not true? I knew it when the railroad called me to ask where you were. Nobody misses their train back to their homeland for kif; or for any other drug. But they would miss it for the Jajouka beetle. Is this not true, master? You would miss the end of the world for the Jajouka beetle."

Grant and Suzanna said nothing, but their fingers intertwined and intertwined. Hakim watched them and knew that he was right.

"You may not think that I am a worthy man," said Hakim. "But my father and mother were of good birth, and I have always observed the true ways."

He took out a match, a brown twist of paper with its head dipped in turquoise sulfur, and struck one up against the gritty little desert on the side of the box. He lit his joint. Pea-soup smell on a warm North African evening: *When, brother?*

"Well, you're right," Grant admitted. "We did try the scarab."

"And you wish for more?"

Both of them nodded.

"Then may I ask to join you?"

"A threesome?" Grant asked aggressively.

But Suzanna squeezed his hand. "Why not? Our last night in Morocco. Tomorrow we can fly Air France and drink champagne and be professional and pure. The day after we can have lunch at the Commonwealth Brewery. But tonight . . . why not?"

"I have no diseases, master," said Hakim. "I have always been a man of the utmost scruples."

Grant looked at him with his angular Cubist face and his eyes that seemed to float in the evening air, and he was jealous and resentful. But there were Jajouka beetles up in their hotel room, feeding stickily on hashish resin. And he could still remember what it was like to atomize.

Hakim appeared in the bedroom door naked. The room was shadowy except for the light cast by a small pierced lamp, in which an oil wick dipped and deliriously floated. Hakim was very lean and muscular, with nipples like almonds. He had no body hair whatsoever, he shaved all over for cleanliness. His penis was circumcised and very long, with a head shaped like the head of a cobra.

Grant and Suzanna were waiting for him on the rumpled bed, already naked. Between them, the two olivewood boxes lay side by side. In spite of himself, Grant felt his penis rising when Hakim appeared; and when Hakim politely climbed onto the *durry* beside them, and Suzanna took hold of Hakim's penis in her left hand and rubbed it up and down, smiling and looking excited, Grant's erection rose bigger than it ever had before.

"Here . . ." Suzanna said, and took hold of Grant's hand and drew it down between Hakim's legs. Grant found himself squeezing and manipulating Hakim's smooth coffee-colored penis, rolling his hairless balls between his fingers. He had never touched another man like this before, and he found it so arousing that he was breathless.

Suzanna opened the first olivewood box and used the lacquered pipe to suck out the first beetle.

"For you, Hakim," she said, and gripped his erection tightly. Grant watched his thin stomach flinching as Suzanna pushed the pipe into his penis and then released her thumb, so that the scarab would be dropped deep inside him. Hakim dripped blood and Suzanna leaned forward and licked it. Grant waited in jealousy and rising excitement.

Suzanna slid the second beetle into Grant's penis. This was the second time that his urethra had been penetrated today, and it was agony. His hands gripped the *durry* tightly and he could have shouted out, but he stopped himself. He didn't want to show weakness in front of Hakim.

Music from Radio Cairo warbled through the room. The lamp threw black shadowy lace onto the ceiling. Suzanna pushed Hakim flat onto his back, and then she lay on top of him, her back against his chest, turning her head around so that she could nuzzle him and kiss him.

She reached down between her legs, took hold of his wedge-shaped penis and positioned it between the cheeks of her bottom. Then—with the most extraordinary pushing and twisting and panting that Grant had ever seen—she forced herself downward, downward and downward, until Hakim's erection was completely submerged, right up to his mocha-colored scrotum.

Suzanna's vagina dripped juice like a broken comb drips honey. She didn't have to beckon for Grant to know that this was the time for him to climb on top of her—on top of them both. He found a place to kneel between the tangle of four legs, and then he slid his itching erection into Suzanna's body. His balls bounced against Hakim's balls, and Suzanna couldn't resist groping between their thighs and mixing all their balls together, as if she were being fucked by a double-cocked, four-testicled monster.

The two of them pushed harder and harder. They sweated, and gasped, and the radio music wailed and exhorted them. Hakim made Suzanna sore to begin with; but then she relaxed her bottom and he was able to push himself into her deeper and deeper. Grant felt slippery breasts and urging thighs and his balls knocking against Hakim's balls like the English are coming! the English are coming! He could feel Hakim's cock through the thin slippery membrane that separated her vagina and her rectum, and they were fighting each other, Nazarene cock against Muslim cock, with only the thinnest stretchy skin to separate them.

At some point Suzanna climaxed and trembled and shook like the Agadir earthquake. The men's joint balls were anointed with juice. But they kept on thrusting; until Hakim ejaculated, and Grant ejaculated, and all three of them were locked together in utter chemical spasm, pumping and thrusting and (maybe) screaming or (maybe) silent. It was a world inside another world inside another world.

But the two scarabs were male. The one that clung to the end of Grant's penis, and the one that clung to the end of Hakim's penis. And there was less than a half inch between them. And they detected each other's presence not by smell or by sound, but by the high vibration of their wing casings as they gave off their stimulating chemicals. And they were blindly ferocious adversaries.

Grant thrust and thrust, and his head went through heaven. Hakim thrust too, dreaming of dances and pipes and suns that burst over the desert. They went through climax after climax. And all the time the scarabs were furiously burrowing through

Suzanna's flesh, mad for each other, giving off more and more of
their stimulating chemicals as they did so.

Suzanna reached another huge climax as the scarabs ripped
through the walls of her vagina and grappled each other. Blood
gushed out of her vagina and flooded the *durry,* but neither she nor
Grant nor Hakim were conscious of what was happening. The
fiercer the scarabs fought, the stronger the chemicals they gave off,
and the three of them rocked and shook and bounced on the bed,
locked together in never-ending orgasm.

The scarabs pursued each other for hour after hour, burrowing
their way through womb and kidney and bowel. They clawed
through arteries; they shredded mucus membranes; they scratched
through liver and lung tissue. Blood welled in cavity after cavity.
Suzanna climaxed one more time, and then the pain suddenly
flared up. Her stomach and her bowels felt as if they had burst into
flame, as if she had swallowed a quart of gasoline and set it alight.
Every nerve ending shriveled; every ganglion screamed.

Suzanna screamed too, but even as she screamed she climaxed
again.

The scarabs were tiny, but their madness was the madness of the
desert, the madness of total survival. The bed grew thicker and
squelchier with blood, while Grant and Hakim thought they were
hydrogen bombs.

Suzanna's arms flopped from side to side, and her legs gradually
stiffened.

The owner of the Hotel Africanus opened the door and showed
Captain Hamid what had happened. There was so much blood on
the bed that it looked as if somebody had carried a whole bucketful
from a nearby abattoir and sloshed it over the *durry* and the three
people who lay on it as if they were dead. The girl was white-faced
and *really* dead. The two men were hideously bloodied, but slept
with beatific smiles on their faces. The net curtains rose and fell in
the morning breeze.

Captain Hamid touched the girl's ankle. Her skin was cold. The
blood was already dry. He picked up one of the open olivewood
boxes and smelt it, and then passed it across to his sergeant, who
smelt it too.

"Hashish," he nodded.

* * *

Later, in the police station, under a tirelessly-revolving fan, Captain Hamid carefully opened the olivewood box and set it down on the table.

"That's right—that was one of the boxes we kept the scarabs in," said Grant. *"Scarabaeidae Jajoukae.* Professor Hemmer will tell you, at the Tangier Institute."

Captain Hamid had a very meticulously clipped mustache. It reminded Grant of a little hedge he had seen in the gardens of the Koutoubia Mosque in Marrakesh. "I regret that there is no such professor, and no such institute."

"I don't understand. We went to the Little Hills, to Jajouka."

"Jajouka? I regret that there is no such place."

"But we went there. We found the scarabs for ourselves, and brought them back."

"I regret that there is no such thing."

"But I saw it with my own eyes. They killed Suzanna, for Christ's sake!"

Captain Hamid pushed a pack of Casa Sport toward him, and a box of brown-paper matches. "Your lady friend died from a perforated bowel, because of violent anal intercourse. A scarab, my friend? There is no such thing. Somebody has been telling you lies."

The man in the white suit replaced his hat. He had obviously seen something of the shadows that had passed across Grant's face, like cloud shadows passing across the Sahara.

"I apologize, Dr. Donnelly, for my discourtesy."

"No, no," said Grant. "You don't have to apologize. Here—" he added, and took out his address card.

The man took the card and held it uncertainly between finger and thumb. "You wish me to call on you, when you are back in Boston?" he asked.

"I wish you to keep in touch. Just in case you find what you're looking for."

He gave the man one last, intent look. Then he walked across the shiny tiled lobby of the Hotel Splendid to join his wife. He was filled with such craving that he could scarcely speak.

BEACHED

Wendy Rathbone

*T*here are times Cecily listens to the wind outside her bedroom window and imagines it is the color of gold dust washing the world in glitter. She smells the seasons distinctly: peach-dust summers, autumn's barbecue of leaf and mold, winters like a man's tears, bee-filled honey springs. She barely remembers what the outside world is really like and yet misses it. Her books tell her what is going on, how the ocean washes sand into perfect ridges, how the forests burn in October, how silver clouds gather into shrouds of mist just before a storm. Sometimes the books have pictures. She will stare for long minutes at a scene, then glance up and stare out the window, where all she can see are the topmost branches of a granny apple tree and one triangle of sky that turns from black to purple to blue to gray.

The scene she stares at right now is the cover of a new book her mother brought her. A man with long dark hair holds a woman bent back almost double. He has a square chin and pink, lush lips. His eyes glow the blue of sapphire. A ripped white shirt exposes dark, muscled arms that keep the woman, who is blond and slender, from tumbling to the ground. The woman's waist-length hair fills nearly half the cover, windblown and curled just right, as if to make a cape for her. The man's lips are close to hers. He's smiling. She is not, but her eyes in profile are gazing obsessively into his.

The cover title promises: SAVAGE PASSION, by Domina Dupree. Romances are her favorites.

Cecily imagines real people like this exist, and that they are the luckiest people in the world. They have beauty. They have lust and love. They have freedom.

Cecily puts the book aside, fondling it with her left hand as if she can feel the warmth of its secrets, and a little thrill tingles through her body at the anticipation of becoming lost within its five hundred soft, rectangular pages. She already knows the heroine is named Priscilla, Pris for short. The dark hero is Damian Knight.

Beneath her, the bed is saggy and soft. Just before she closes her eyes to savor the anticipation longer, her gaze sweeps over her form, half covered by the sheet. She is a mound of hills and rises. The heat in the room—for it is a humid week in mid-August, the month she hates most—is nearly unbearable, and she wears nothing but the sheet. Her breasts are massive flesh mountains capped with pinkish purple nipples the size of her fists. They pull to the sides, making a valley where she can see her stomach, huge, distended and white, a bloated ball upon the sweaty sheets, except where it's partially deflated where the thick skin folds in on itself. Beyond her belly, which she cannot see over, she knows that, hiding in the flesh pile, there are her overripe genitals, virgin, untouched though she is now thirty years old. They steam with an all too human need, though she has long stopped thinking of herself as human. Her legs are squat trunks, the fat on them so out of place that it, too, sags, making her ankles look like bags out of which her wide feet have grown.

Cecily does not know how much she weighs. No scales, save those at a truck stop, will hold her. She can no longer walk. Mother, who is thin and gray, but who loves Cecily-her-baby with all her heart, can do nothing more for her than bring her books and food and the bedpan. It is hopeless. Cecily has been trapped here for two years.

She started putting on the excess pounds just after graduating from high school. She stopped going out of the house five years after that, when walking, or simply moving about, became too difficult. Up until age twenty-eight she'd been able to get to the bathroom herself, but that was about it. Now her body has become her unearned prison.

She closes her eyes and tries to forget the sight of her own gelatinous bulk. That mass isn't the real Cecily. It isn't the true definition of who she is. Cecily is about what she thinks and imagines and believes. Nothing else matters.

She leans against the pillows, a fan Mother brought into the room blowing across her damp skin; she dreams.

The hero of *Savage Passion*, Damian Knight, has found her and will kiss her out of her old life, break the evil spell and take her away to a villa in Italy. She will let her hair grow until it surrounds her. Until it is so long and beautiful and thick that it has a life and wind of its own. Damian will bend her over backward. The waves will break on the sand in perfect ridges where they take their honeymoon.

Cecily's arms are weighted by thick blobs of flesh, but she can still reach, if she tries hard, around her side and over her huge thigh to the still-human part of her that steams and aches. She can touch there just right and pretend it is Damian, and his dark head is between her legs, and his lush lips know what to do. Her left hand clutches the book. Her right teases and opens her swollen vulva. This is how it feels to be loved, she tells herself. Possessed fully. Appreciated.

The sensation of pleasure is all she has left in her world, apart from food, that can take her away from what she has become. The book helps form the world, but Cecily does the rest. She is reborn. The new person she is can run and swim and climb mountains.

Her orgasm showers her with little hot and cold drops of sweat, hints of hope. Hope of a thinner, blonder Cecily unshackled and free.

Mother brings her mashed potatoes with gravy, steak smothered in A-1, just as Cecily likes it, three hot rolls in a towel-covered basket, a half a stick of butter and a bowl of fresh-made chocolate pudding. "The kind that you boil on the stove," Mother tells her proudly. "None of that instant stuff for my baby girl."

Cecily eats it all. The full feeling in her belly makes her feel secure and sated. This, too, she thinks, is what love is like. In this form, and in the form of her fantasies, it is all the love she has ever known. She thrives on it. She is addicted to her situation despite her hatred of it.

Cecily loves her mother, but she also feels sorry for her. Mother has worn the same old clothes for many years, plaid skirts with pastel pink or blue blouses. She has no life outside of the house, where she also takes care of her husband, Cecily's stepfather, in a downstairs bedroom. Ron, whom Mother married when Cecily was sixteen, had a stroke a few years back. Cecily has not seen him since that illness. She wonders if he too is now a blob of flesh aching for a different world, for a new body, for a female Damian to take him to a better place.

Now, as Mother leaves with her empty tray, devoured of all the luscious foods she cooked, Cecily says, "Mother, wait." Her voice is low and breathy. She has trouble breathing sometimes, especially when it's hot like today. It's as if her mouth and tongue and cheeks and throat have grown too fat for air to pass into her lungs. As if her lungs are constricted by weight, and by their own thickening.

"Yes?" Mother turns. Her eyes are gray. But maybe once, Cecily thinks, they were sapphire-blue. And she was young and had a man who loved her offer to take her to a foreign land. She is too shy to ask.

Instead she says, "Do you ever dream of leaving here?"

Mother's eyebrows make a deep crease above the bridge of her nose. Her mouth is wrinkled so much it must hurt. "How can I? I have responsibilities."

"But don't you ever dream?"

"It does no good to dream." She looks genuinely confused.

Maybe Mother is afraid to dream, Cecily thinks. Afraid because dreams always end. Cecily knows this, and often cries when she is alone and out of ideas for her own fantasies. It is a very scary feeling to acknowledge day in and day out that you are miserable and the misery will never change.

Cecily has thought often about change. She has thought about not eating what Mother brings. About making herself starve and starve until she is as thin as those girls in her books who wear bikinis to the beach or pool without ever once worrying about being fat. But she can't. The food is too consoling. She is not strong enough to give it up.

It makes her mad.

Suddenly, Cecily feels an anger toward Mother. Dreamless Mother. Mother who never yells or lays boundaries for her, who never suggests anything other than the routine they've followed since Cecily got too fat to leave the house.

Hot tears pool in Cecily's eyes. "Why do you keep bringing me all that food?" Her voice quivers, but still comes out strong, accusing.

"What kind of question is that? You need to eat. I take care of you, don't I? You should be grateful!"

"Look at me, Mother! I don't need to eat!"

"But you enjoy it so." Now, are there tears in those gray, old, tired eyes? In those depths that Cecily could never, even as a little girl, plumb? "There's so little enjoyment left for you. What else am I to do?"

Cecily can't hope to fight her own longings, her own needs, if Mother won't even help. It's useless.

Cecily turns her head away. The old wallpaper on her bedroom wall, patterned with little hyacinths and primroses, seems to sag against her vision. It is ugly. Faded. Used up and disintegrating. She looks down and sees strands of listless hair across the pillow, her hair, once golden, now mouse-brown and dull with dirt.

Mother says, "I love you, dear. I do everything I can for you. You know that."

"Yes, Mother," Cecily says. Tears fall against her temples and into her hair.

At supper, Mother brings her lasagna, garlic bread drenched in butter, and the rest of the chocolate pudding that was cooked, not instant. Cecily eats it all.

After dinner, she reads several chapters of *Savage Passion* before falling into a moist and humid sleep.

Cecily wakes in the middle of the night. A breeze is blowing in from the window, apple-blossom scented. There is a noise on the stairs, a creaking. Mother must be up late, insomnia again.

Cecily sighs and tries to turn in the bed into a more comfortable position. It is nearly impossible. On her sides, she has trouble breathing. She rests that way sometimes, but usually falls onto her back again. Because she has so much trouble shifting in the bed, her back is covered with sores. She bends her knees and lets her fat legs fall open. With the sheet pushed down, the apple breeze caresses her intimately.

She closes her eyes and imagines herself light and airy, floating on the breeze like a tiny fairy creature made of gauze and silk. She hears a truck pass by on the dark highway half a block away. A highway she hasn't seen in over five years.

Again the stairs creak.

She hears a moan. Or perhaps it is simply Ron snoring. Sound travels well at night.

Something scrapes downstairs. The sound is alien. Cecily wonders dreamily what Mother is up to. Does she have a project down there that gives her pleasure? What does Mother do during her spare time? Does Mother have spare time?

When there are no more sounds to try to identify, Cecily drifts into a hazy doze. The breeze on her body feels like magic. She dreams a man with dark hair and muscled arms is standing by the side of her bed. He is staring at her with wonder, with pity, with awe. His hand, long-fingered, with nails that are chipped and rimmed with black dirt, reaches out and touches the huge mountain of her stomach. The hand is warm and strange.

Cecily, who has learned to let herself be free only in her dreams, allows the touch. She is not pleased that she is dreaming herself fat, but it doesn't matter. The man is all that matters. She wants him.

Slowly, the man's hand moves up to cup the huge, purple nipple of her right breast. The breast lies to the side and he lifts its weight, pushing it more toward the center of her body. His palm is smooth, hotter than the rest of his hand, and her nipple hardens.

"Oh," the man says. His voice is whispery, reverent. "My God."

His free hand comes up, touching her other breast. He has to reach all the way across her wide body to accomplish this. This puts him in closer contact with her, and Cecily can smell him. Engine oil. Grass. Sweat.

Man.

She wants to pull him to her, but her arms are heavy. The effort, even in dream, is too much.

The man fondles her breasts for a few more minutes. They are hard on the tips. Her genitals burn.

Just when she thinks she can't wait any longer, the man moves his hand over her belly, up and over, and down the long incline and folds of her abdomen to the place that heats and aches between her legs. He touches her there, fumbling, spreading her, his own breathing coming now in rapid, heaving sighs.

His heat is summery. He speaks again, voice of desperation, of hushed need. "Oh God. I don't believe . . ."

Cecily does not move, but in her mind she smiles. He has assessed her. And now he wants her.

She hears the snap and slide of his belt, the hiss of zipper teeth opening. He climbs up onto the bed, and she can see in partial shadow and starlight through the open curtains that he is kneeling by her hip. He throws one leg over her thick trunk thigh, and she sees a silhouette of his erection jutting up, dark and thick. His balls brush her leg and his other leg lifts, goes over. He is now between her thighs, and with a grunt he pushes himself against her, bracing his hands on her tall belly. The head of his penis brushes the opening to her body. She knows. There can be no other feeling that would be mistaken for this. He is hot, pushing hard against her. Something gives and then she can feel the movement. He is inside her. She has accepted him. Taken him in. The thrusts are liquid heat melting her into a real woman, a human who wants, who needs.

It does not last long. He cries out and falls against her. She comes, believing the dream is over.

But it's not. Because it repeats. Again and again until she is raw and hurting.

She doesn't mind. But by dawn, when the triangle of sky she can see is as purple as her swollen, round nipples, she is exhausted. She falls into a noisy, snoring sleep.

It's late when Cecily wakes, and the heat is smothering, hellish. She has wet the bed, and tries to move away from the spot on the sheet. She succeeds only in rolling to her side, her flab folding and wrinkling and dimpling as it follows, like a parasitic creature. Immediately, her shoulder begins to ache with the weight of her upper body.

There is a small clock on the bed stand. It reads 10:47. Late morning. Cecily wonders why Mother has not been up with her breakfast. Maybe the talk they had the night before had upset Mother more than she let on. Maybe Mother took her advice and left to chase a dream.

For an hour Cecily lies in bed and waits. She does not call out. Like a good girl, she waits for Mother, who knows best, to come when she sees fit. Cecily is too shy to bellow. Patience and time are things she has a lot of. She would never consider yelling for Mother.

Besides, insomnia may have kept Mother up late. Perhaps she is still sleeping, exhausted from caring for two people, from her age, from simple motherhood, which Cecily thinks is the greatest of humanity's burdens.

Cecily once wondered, when she was younger and still in school, if she would ever make a good mother. She had even considered names for her children. Holland for a boy. Devon for a girl. Now, children are the furthest considerations from her mind.

The room heats up quickly as the August humidity condenses on the windows, on the walls, on the folds of her flesh. The air is sticky. It smells of sewage which overwhelms the apple tree scent.

The room seems to sparkle with hotness and liquid light. The triangle of sky Cecily can see is like melted white glass.

She moves onto her back again, and her sores sting when they hit the damp sheet. She can no longer feel where she wet the bed. Everything is damp; every scent is rancid.

Cecily dozes off and on. She tries to read *Savage Passion,* but the print blurs too small and she has trouble concentrating because she is hungry. She loves Paris and Damian as they plumb international intrigue while sunning on Italian beaches, but the allure of her Damian fantasy can only go so far to alleviate her growing physical discomfort. Where is her lunch? Her dinner?

As the hands on the clock by her bedside approach five P.M., Cecily's patience wanes. She finds the strength, then, to call out, softly at first. "Mother."

No answer.

"Mother, are you there?"

Silence.

"Mother!" Louder now. Her voice is thick and rich, but wavers with fear. Her pulse climbs. It beats in small explosions in her oversized chest, a hand pounding to be released. Everything wants freedom. Even Cecily's heart. She breathes deep, the air coating her with more heat and sweat. Tears dot her eyes.

Cecily begins to fear the worst, yet she can't quite accept what common sense tells her. Mother could be sleeping still. Could be out at the store, or talking with a neighbor. Perhaps Ron fell deathly ill and Mother had to take him to the emergency room. All these things are possible. But Cecily knows somehow these scenarios are not the truth. Deep inside, something tells her Mother is the one who is sick or dying, that Mother hasn't been up to feed her because Mother is unable to come.

She knows what she has to do. And it will take all her effort. Cecily leans back onto the pillow, preparing herself mentally for what comes next.

When she has caught her breath from her anxiety, after her tears are dried and she is able to think more clearly, Cecily moves. Her bulk shudders, wiggles and shifts as she rolls slowly to her side once again. The sores stick to the sheets, parts of her skin pulling free as she forces herself to the edge of the bed.

Now comes the hard part. She tries to sit up, but all she can do is move onto her elbow, which immediately begins to ache from the weight. Her thick legs bend and she pushes them to the side, dangling her feet over the sagging edge of the mattress. If she can get those legs under her, there is a chance her muscles will still work well enough to catch her and make the fall she must endure more cushioned. She pushes her legs out farther, feels the weight redistribute itself, but at the same time feels her hip begin to slip against the mattress edge where her weight has squashed it nearly flat.

She is falling.

The floor is hardwood, and the thump she makes as her entire body slides from the bed is sickening. She lands on her left arm, partially on her side, partially on her stomach. Her body jarred, she groans, trying to catch her breath, to stave off the pain. Her arm might be broken. She can't tell. Too much is happening for her to assess each pain individually. Her knees hurt. Her hip aches. The sores on her back burn like fresh-lit fires. The arm she has landed on, as well as the shoulder, feels completely smashed.

Cecily forces her body to move until she is all the way on her stomach on the hardwood floor. With great effort, she finally wrenches her trapped arm free. It flops to one side, the wrist bent at a funny angle, useless.

For a while she lies on her stomach and cries with big, heaving sobs. With one arm useless, she must make do with the other alone, and her legs. The broken wrist will hinder her progress, but she is not about to quit.

When she has rested and feels stronger, she pushes against the floor, using her legs. Her damp body sticks to the hardwood, but she manages to move a couple of squeaky inches. She hoists herself up with her good hand, then pushes with both feet, moves another inch, and flops down again. It is slow progress. She feels naked and exposed at first, but all modesty fades after a few hours, when she has finally reached the door. If she can reach a phone, she can call for help. And she knows there is a phone on a little table at the top of the stairs, plus two phones downstairs; one in the kitchen, one on the living room coffee table.

Cecily raises herself, pushes, flops, then repeats the exercise again and again. She is a fish out of water. An angel with severed wings. She is exhausted. Her lungs surge like swollen fireballs in her chest. Singeing every breath.

In the hall outside her room, Cecily can see little but the runner rug with maroon, paisley designs.

It is dark outside again, night cascading through the house like something secretive and evil. It envelopes her with hot, slimy hands. It reminds her that this spell of imprisonment is strong, too strong to ever be easily broken.

Through the shadows, at the end of the hall, she spies the phone stand. It is about twelve feet away. The distance seems like miles.

Cecily stops to rest only when she must, drifts into agitated napping, only to wake with a start and begin her routine all over again. The rug in the hall is coarse against her belly, and she can feel little rug burns on her breasts, her stomach, her knees, her toes. She ignores the pain. She must get to the phone.

She has no sense of time anymore. It is still dark when she reaches the little stand at the top of the stairs. She groans, a grunt of pain mixed with the elation of finally reaching a goal. She positions the arm of her useless hand out from her body for some balance, winces as she raises herself up on the elbow, still favoring the broken wrist. But it is worth it. She grabs the phone, pulling it on top of her. It clatters against her back and neck, then falls with a little ring to the floor.

Half laughing, half crying, Cecily uses her good hand to lift the receiver to her ear. There is no sound. She checks the phone's base, pushing down on the cradle, but still no dial tone comes out. She checks to see that the phone is plugged in. It is. But it still doesn't work.

"Mother?" she calls. "Mother?"

Now she is crying, big jagged sobs swollen with pain, with desolation. Her belly growls in hunger. Her stringy hair falls in her eyes in clumps. Her bladder lets go.

The traitor phone becomes her pillow while she rests yet again.

When she wakes, there is a soft gold light filtering throughout the house. The glitter of the outside world. The allure. At first she thinks she's still in bed. The Damian dream comes back to her, and she remembers how he touched her, how his body joined to hers. She becomes aroused just thinking about him. Then Cecily remembers her night-long journey. The dead phone. Her hunger pangs.

Her body stinks. She's never smelled such a stench before, and wonders if her sores are festering. Plus, she is filthy. She's had only sponge baths for two years, and the last one was too long ago for her to remember.

She tries not to think of all that. It's too much for her lonely mind. If only she could be on a beach somewhere in a foreign city, Damian lying next to her, the sea breeze blowing cool against her taut, tan skin.

Cecily maneuvers herself up and forward again, trying to position herself at the top of the stairs so she can assess how to best climb down to the first floor. Despite the golden light, the shadows in the hall and on the stairs are still thick. As her head crests the stairwell, she can barely see down the incline. She crawls forward, squinting. There is a dark puddle of shade at the bottom of the stairs. Slowly, she inches along, squeezing herself down the angles of stairs. With her head downward, all the blood rushes to her face. Her ears ring. She becomes dizzy. The only plus to this position is she can use gravity as an aid. Her progress is quicker.

She imagines her body is gliding across ridges of perfect, white sand. She can almost hear the waves break, smell their salt spray.

As she nears the bottom of the stairs, the shadow puddled there takes shape, but her vision is blurred. The smell of her own sweat is nauseating. The air spins with little dots and shapes of white light. The waves, she thinks frantically. The beach!

She desperately pictures a blue-green sea, dunes of powdered silk, a sky the color of Damian's eyes.

There is a bile taste in Cecily's throat. The bitterness is distracting. It threatens the fantasy. It's the first time her hunger has abated since she awoke yesterday morning. But this new sickness is worse.

As she nears the stairwell bottom, she bumps into something soft. Furry. Like an animal. She stretches her good hand forward and feels further, then draws back abruptly. A screech escapes her chapped lips.

Skin. She felt skin. And something sticky on the skin.

Cecily's breath heaves. No. No. No.

It's only seaweed, she tells herself. Only litter along the foreign beach.

She reaches out again, trying not to breathe because the smell is like rotting potatoes now and she is already almost too ill to move.

As her good hand probes, she immediately recognizes Mother's coarse hair, the conservative, clip-on metal earrings she always wears, the silver cross at her throat. It would all be so normal except for the fact that Mother isn't moving, and the stickiness on Mother's head, face, and throat is, Cecily knows, blood. The stickiness is also all over the stairs.

There is no more energy left for tears, but Cecily's moans fill the house, dry, hoarse, inconsolable. For the first time in her isolated life, Cecily bellows.

"Help!" Her voice vibrates the stairs. The air moves in her large breath. "Help!" She calls out over and over. Bile courses over her lips, down her chin and into Mother's messed hair.

Hours pass. The bellowing has stopped but Cecily has not moved. As the house darkens again, the smell seems to ease up, or Cecily is simply getting used to it. She is no longer thinking about that, or anything. It is as if her mind has stopped, frozen and folded in on itself, small and sharp and cold. She is a thing lying among other things that do not move. She is a shell along a tropical beach, waiting to be found, to be brought to someone's eyes or ears and freed.

Hunger returns slowly, and the Cecily-thing opens her mouth, suckles on air, chews on tendrils of hair that catch in her teeth. Her open eyes are wet and squishy, bulbs of kelp caught in a jellyfish face. They see nothing.

A crack sounds from the house, startling her. It is only the roof settling, as it always does come night, but she doesn't remember that. Her eyes blink. Vision returns slowly, shadows undulating around her like people in a circle. A party circle. The hand that hurts her reaches up, trying to touch one of them. She thinks she can hear the waves crash against each other, splash and roar.

"Damian?" she asks.

She pulls herself forward with her hands, ignoring the pain. Her feet push. Her huge body slithers over Mother, squashing her into the stairs, becoming damp and sticky again. She doesn't feel it, or notice. She can see better and tries not to notice all the red, how it gets on her hands and the rest of her body. What does it mean when the sea runs red? It must be sunset, she thinks, when the light burnishes everything with scarlet. It's everywhere.

When she tries to brush the dirty strands of hair from her face, the red gets in it and on her own face. She can taste it on her mouth. Salt. Rancid. Ocean.

Where's Damian now?

After she has cleared the dampness, she finds herself flat on the floor by a door. Where can it lead, this door on the beach? And whoever heard of such a thing?

She smiles. If she opens the door, what will she find? She can already taste freedom. The real beach with the sun and the people and the bigger waves is on the other side. Compared to all that, she has been in only the smallest of ponds.

Her body squishes and squeaks along the floor, making sucking sounds as she moves inch by inch. The red has dried and is now caked under her fingernails and toenails. She shudders from the reality of it. Her mind goes numb again, but still she crawls.

The beach awaits her. It is silken; it is rippled sand. She will lie in the breeze off the cool waves that will tickle her body. Sea foam will salt her lips. Damian will be beyond her, frolicking in the waves, his lean, tan body catching them full on, glistening in the bright sun. She can hear the breaking swells, the cry of a gull. Seaweed brushes her feet.

It is difficult to open the door. To get close enough to lift her hand to the knob, she must maneuver her bulk in front of the door, blocking it. Finally, she manages to get it ajar, move back, and swing it farther open. She is wider than the frame, but sideways she fits through. Moving onto her side hurts. But as she inches across the threshold, her body mutates, transforms foot by foot. All the fat melts away. A lean Cecily emerges onto a porch that leads to an outer world: deep rich sky, air like sweet fizz, voices and people and, oh, the peach summer sun!

Damian is with her. They lie side by side. His hands brush her breasts.

The porch creaks. It is dusty, and the dust sticks to her body, creating a coagulating slime on her skin. Her perfect skin. Her tan, lean, tight skin. Damian is so pleased. "You're all right," he says, again and again. She knows "all right" translates to "beautiful" in man-speech. She remembers her dream of how he came to her like a hero, up in her dusky, humid room. How he touched her, how he shuddered against her when she was huge. He didn't say anything bad about her weight, saint that he is, but she can tell he's so pleased now that she's thin.

Down the porch steps, Cecily rolls. Into Damian's arms.

There is a sparse, damp grass on the beach. Soft blades of sandy leaf. They bend under her perfect, Malibu Barbie body. She holds her arms upward to embrace Damian full on.

People surround them. "Oh my God," they say. They are obviously jealous.

Some run up onto the porch and through the door of no return. There are screams from beyond that door. Low voices that say words such as "murder," "rape," and "robbery." It's a good thing she is here, at the beach, safe on the other side. Though Damian does not have sapphire eyes—they are brown—and his attire is a bit too uniform for the beach—police blue with bright, glittering badges on the breast and lapel—she doesn't mind. He smells like Damian, cool sweat, sun, bleach and salt. He is gentle, and his voice is of the sand and surf.

"Lie still," he says. "You're safe now."

Cecily smiles, and runs a hand seductively through her long, blond, windblown hair. Yes, she thinks. Safe. And finally free.

HOT PHOSPHOR

John B. Rosenman

*R*ex Stud: Hi, Teddy.

Reddy Teddy: Hi, Rex.

Rex Stud: I've been thinking of you, baby, since our last time.

Reddy Teddy: Oh?

Rex Stud: Yeah, I've been thinking we ought to try it a new way.

Reddy Teddy: Oh, really. That sounds interesting! Maybe you want ME on top this time?

Rex Stud: Yeah. I get hard just thinking about it. See?

Reddy Teddy: Oh YES, Stud, it's bigger than I ever saw it before. And you see how wide and juicy I am for you.

Rex Stud: Sure do, you ARE ready, aren't you? Now let's just move into our private room here and I'll lie down on my back on our bed. . . .

Reddy Teddy: And I'll just ease down on top of you, my legs straddling you on both sides as I guide you in. . . .

Rex Stud: Ooooh, that feels so good, baby!

Reddy Teddy: Like my tight wet pussy, Rex? Like the way it strokes and holds you deep inside me?

Rex Stud: Oh, Teddy, it's . . .

Arthur Gruber, alias Rex Stud, paused with his fingers on the keyboard. For some reason, reality had intruded, and he was suddenly aware that he sat naked before his monitor, typing make-believe sex to a woman he had met only three times before, and then only on this same network. This was their fourth on-line tryst, and though each had gotten steadily hotter, he had abruptly remembered that it was all a lie—and a sick, pathetic one at that.

Reddy Teddy: You all right, Stud? Your cock's starting to go limp on me.

Arthur Gruber swallowed and adjusted his glasses. He had to make it with the keystrokes fast, pick up the action where he left it.

Reddy Teddy: Rex, you haven't gone faggy on me, have you?

He swallowed, lifted his fingers onto the keyboard again. *No, babe, something just came up for a minute. As you can tell, I'm hard as ever and raring to go. Feel how I thrust? There! Does that FEEL like I've got a limp dick?*

Reddy Teddy: God, no. It's splittin' me apart. Let me lower my swollen tits to your face. Like my erect nipples? Do you want to suck 'em?

Rex Stud: I'm licking and sucking them both, taking them deep in my mouth, rolling them around on my tongue and tasting your milk.

Reddy Teddy: Your tongue feels so good. Bite my nipples, baby, hurt me a little.

Rex Stud: Like the way I thrust up my hips, my manhood going all the way inside you?

Reddy Teddy: Hard against my clit . . .

Rex Stud: Your little love button . . .

Reddy Teddy: Ha! Not so little now. Oh, grind it into me, all your hard sweaty meat! I'm about to come. . . .

Rex Stud: So am I, you always Reddy Teddy. Gonna come now, the hot white pounding sea surging right up into you!!! Ohhhh . . .

Reddy Teddy: Oh Jesus, I can feel you spurting! Spurting, spurting, spurting into me filling me and here I come joining you. Ahhhh . . . Oh, I'm EXPLODING!

Rex Stud: Ah! Ah! Ah! Ah!

Reddy Teddy: Just keep keep keep it comin', babe! Let's neither of us stop!

Finally, silence. Arthur Gruber swallowed. Removing his hand from his wet, subsiding crotch, he looked at the phosphor symbols of lust on the monitor. Had sex really taken place, or was it just an illusion? It was a common question concerning on-line sex. Some writers he'd read said no, because there was no physical union, no exchange of real—as opposed to digital—bodily fluids. For all you knew, your partner was a three-hundred-pound, eighty-year-old queen who was hung better than you. On the other hand, this last experience with Teddy had been more erotic and exciting than anything Gruber could remember, and he *had* climaxed in his hand like a ton of TNT. If the woman at the other end hadn't "faked" it, then who was to say real sex hadn't happened?

He smiled. Maybe we both oughta light up cigarettes, he thought. Savor the afterglow.

Wait a minute, she was typing again. And it didn't look like "Good-bye till next time," as he expected. No, this time . . .

Reddy Teddy: I want to meet you for REAL, Rex. In the flesh. What do you say, honey?

Arthur Gruber rubbed his fingers and placed them on the keyboard. Then he rubbed them again.

He sat staring at the monitor.

It was December, and business was brisk at the Seven Seas Travel Service. Sitting before a different monitor this time, Gruber arranged a weekend trip for a handsome young man and his girlfriend to the French Riviera. There was no doubt in his mind that she was turned on by the guy. The way she smiled at him, the way her blue eyes lit up . . . His lips tight with envy, Gruber thought of the last time *he* had had a date, which had been over a year ago. It had been an unqualified disaster. The girl had been easily forty pounds overweight, with a healthy start on a mustache. And yet *she* had treated *him* like a doormat, as if he weren't even worthy to worship at her feet. Why, just the memory—

"Could you give me a window seat, please? I like to have a view."

He looked up into the girl's blue eyes. Slim and blond, a knockout. Why couldn't *he* have a girl like this just once?

"Sure," he said, "no problem." As his fingers moved over the keyboard, he wondered how it would feel to run them across her naked skin instead.

After the couple left, he glanced about the agency, seeing the familiar posters of beautiful people in exotic places. Mexico. Spain. Bermuda. Here, a fairy-tale couple shared daiquiris on a broad terrace overlooking moonlit waves. There, lean, hard, almost naked lovers held hands as they leapt into a sun-kissed surf. Everywhere, from four walls, romance in distant lands looked down on him. "Warning to nerds," the pictures seemed to shout. "Stay out! Only the photogenic need apply."

I want to meet you for REAL, Rex. In the flesh.

He closed his eyes, leaned back in his chair.

What do you say, honey?

He sighed. What he had eventually said was Maybe. Sometime. He had hemmed and hawed. When he had finally found the nerve to overcome his monumental shyness and log onto USA Ultraline, he had been told that people rarely wanted to meet in person. It was all fantasy—safe, anonymous sex. Even if they checked the files, all they would know was the city you lived in, and you could have even that omitted. One hand diddled the keyboard and the other hand diddled yourself. That was the extent of your involvement.

Now she wanted to meet him.

He could have said no, of course. Why hadn't he? But then he would have run the risk of offending her, of *losing* her and all their "relationship" represented. On that monitor he was not simply a five-foot-seven-inch, 130-pound wimp with thick glasses. With Reddy Teddy, he was a six-foot-three-inch, 220-pound stud. He was *Rex Stud,* handsome and virile and athletic, always ready and able. What if he couldn't find another girl? He had heard stories of men roaming the network, forever trying to make a connection. No, he did not want to run the risk of rubbing her the wrong way (bad pun!) and have her walk out on him just like all the other women had in real life. Yet, at the same time, he was terrified of meeting her in person, for he knew she would only be disappointed. Rather than endure her scorn, he preferred to meet her in cyberspace, where he could hide behind his persona.

"Excuse me?"

Gruber opened his eyes. A young, fat woman stood before his desk, looking down at him.

"Oh, I'm sorry!" He sat up. "May I help you?"

For some reason, she didn't answer, only stared.

He forced himself to smile. "May I help you?" he repeated.

Why can't we meet, Rex? It's so hot when we're together here, just imagine how much better it would be if we did it in PERSON!

Gruber stared at the words. This was the third time they had "met" in Eros' Hideaway, their private room on the network, since she had begun asking for a real meeting. It was also the first time ever that they had not gotten hot together. In fact, he had barely placed his verbal hand on her thigh before she had started pestering him again about their meeting "for real." As she persisted, he found that sex became secondary to the need to explain why they couldn't meet, at least not yet.

Yet why *shouldn't* he meet her? he wondered. Maybe this time a woman wouldn't be disgusted or disappointed in him. Maybe she would actually like him. In his gut, though, he knew that even with the most optimistic scenario, she would not like him half as much as she did the incomparable Rex Stud, who didn't even exist.

Are you there, Rex? Please SAY something.

What could he say? Against his better judgment, he stroked the keys.

What if you don't like me? If you want to know the truth, I'm not exactly a handsome lover boy like Rex.

I don't care. I'm interested in YOU, the REAL you. Please let's meet. Say you will!

He licked his lip. *In a couple weeks . . .*

But even as he paused, trying to decide what to say next, her words ambushed him. *I know. You NEVER want to meet me. You don't think I'm GOOD enough for you, do you?*

Not good enough? He blinked at the screen. That was what *he* was supposed to think. Confused, he started to type, but it was too late.

You don't think I'm good enough, but I'm going to MAKE you meet me! You forget: I live in Elizabeth City, less than fifty miles from Virginia Beach. And I have ways of FINDING OUT EXACTLY WHO YOU ARE!!!

He stiffened in his chair, feeling a biting chill. All-caps mode. She sounded . . . sick, driven. How could anyone become so obsessed with mere rows of phosphor on a monitor? With poor, unattractive Arthur Gruber? It was unthinkable that such a thing could happen to *him,* that a woman could want him so much. But then, he thought, it wasn't really Arthur Gruber that she wanted, was it? She wanted rugged Rex Stud, who was a sexual superman that any woman might find difficult to resist. The kind of man that *any* woman might be driven, despite her better judgment, to pursue.

No, even that did not wash. He *wasn't* Rex Stud at all. It was just a fantasy, and she MUST know that!

Well? she pressed, her words corrosive, etched in acid. *Are you going to meet me or not? Say YES or be prepared to pay the price.*

Price? He swallowed. *What* price? The price for being dumb enough to come on this net to begin with? Or the price for choosing a private relationship instead of going for one of the public sex channels or "hot tubs" that featured everyone's boldest and kinkiest fantasy? But he had been too shy for group sex and the handcuff/leather/S&M crowd. Suddenly, he found that he didn't want anything to do with cyberspace anymore. Suddenly it scared the hell out of him.

He looked down at his fingers, watched them slowly stroke out a final word: *Good-bye.*

Then he quickly logged off the computer, made a phone call to the network, and cancelled his membership.

Two days later, as he left work, he realized that he had cancelled it too late. Despite the heavy mist, he could tell that someone was following him. She stayed a block back, and whenever he turned around, he saw her duck behind something. Still, he wasn't sure. Maybe it was just his imagination. Jittery as he was, he was likely to see anything. How did he even know it was a "she"? For all he knew, it was only another Christmas shopper.

Reaching the parking lot, he paused beside his car and looked back. Nothing. But who could tell in this mist? It had crept in during the night, transforming the city into a surreal landscape that concealed familiar buildings and objects. Nothing was quite what it seemed. In the dense cover, anything was possible.

Nervously, he got into his car and drove toward Lynnhaven Mall. Tonight, he felt that he needed people around him, the more the better. After entering the toll road, he kept checking the rearview mirror, recalling spy and detective movies. The bitch really had him spooked! He shook his head and gripped the wheel, knowing he should stop running and confront her. But he was shy and scared, used to feeling inadequate. When it came to challenges, he avoided them, especially if they involved women. Yes, his life was lonely and empty, but wasn't that preferable to being humiliated and rejected all over again?

He swallowed. How had it come to this? She had seemed so safe, so healthily lusty. He had thought she wanted the same thing he did. Now he was skulking about, looking over his shoulder as if the mist were alive!

Behind him, in the rearview mirror, a police car suddenly emerged from the whiteness and switched into the other lane, speeding toward him. He caught his breath, then forced himself to relax. Why should he fear the *police?* He checked his speed, confident that he was going barely twenty-five, and watched the patrol car rush past him, going far too fast in this poor visibility. If the cop wasn't careful, he could get hurt.

Turning off onto Lynnhaven Parkway, Gruber managed to laugh. What was he getting himself worked up for? No one had been following him. It was just his imag—

Suddenly, a horn blared right behind him. He gasped and checked the mirror, seeing bright lights. Turning his head, he was just in time to see a car swerve out into the left lane and roar past him. As it did, the driver held up his finger.

"Stop blockin' the road, you fuckin'—"

Then he was gone, while Gruber almost collapsed in relief. The bastard had just been impatient and wanted him to speed up! Other times, he would have been angry, but today he wiped his sweating face and grinned. Hey, he'd better take it easy himself before *he* caused an accident.

Reaching the mall, he parked and, forcing himself not to look back, entered a department store. Instantly, he was surrounded by Christmas shoppers. Thank God. Usually he didn't like crowds, but today he felt like having a party! He giggled, feeling giddy. Who knows, maybe he'd call the network back and log on again, try crashing one of the public sex clubs. Yeah, he'd become Mr. Modem Sex himself. He smothered a laugh, seeing people look at him, and left the store to enter the mall's vast concourse. What was happening to him? He seemed to be changing, spinning like a top from mood to mood.

Far from calming him, the sprawling mall only excited him further. His heart raced. Looking about, he saw flash and glitter. On the second level, stores seemed to flaunt their wares with even more vigor, as if to lure him. Clothes, books, toys. Buy Buy Buy!

Oops, his shoelace was untied. Stopping by a bench, he sat down to fix it. As he did, he glanced at a shoe store a hundred feet away, just in time to see a woman pull back into it. *It was her!*

He leaped up, guts churning. She was *here*—she had *followed* him! Whirling, he half ran down the concourse toward the escalator, which seemed to recede as he approached. At last he reached it and boarded, only to feel it was frozen in amber. Trembling, he started to climb, shoving past annoyed shoppers. He ignored their looks and complaints, eyes trained on his goal.

Finally, he reached the upper level and looked down, clutching the rail that ran along the edge. He couldn't see anybody, but then, his glasses had suddenly clouded over, as if he'd brought the mist inside! Tearing his glasses off, he wiped them hurriedly on his shirt, only to find that they were worse than before when he put them back on.

Get moving. Get moving NOW!

He turned and plunged on, darting between shoppers to lengthen his lead. Then, seeing a policeman, he slowed himself down. He mustn't get arrested, and that was sure to happen if he kept acting like a thief! Inhaling deeply, he concentrated on steadying his racing heart. A glance behind, though, only set it pounding again as he spotted a woman turning her back to him at a store window. Ha! She didn't fool him!

Turning down another concourse, he almost collided with a jolly Santa in a flame-red suit. "Ho, Ho, Ho!" the man laughed, pealing a bell and thrusting out a pot for contributions. Salvation Army! But who would *save* him?

Relax, damnit, he thought. *No one's following you, and even if they were, they could hardly do anything to you here. Besides, ol' Reddy Teddy was bluffing. How could she have even found out your name? The network assured you that your identity would remain confidential!*

The last thought finally calmed him. He slowed, then proceeded more sensibly, even glancing behind him with a smile. See? No one was there. It was just—

"Excuse me."

He halted, seeing a fat woman standing directly before him. Somehow, she looked familiar.

He wiped his mouth. "Yes?"

She swallowed. "You probably don't even remember me, but you sold me a ticket to Fort Lauderdale last week."

"So?"

A plump hand rose and timidly touched his sleeve. "The truth is, I didn't even want it. I work at the coffee shop across the street, and . . . find you attractive."

Her voice died, and she stood gazing at him with a beaten, desperate look he sensed he himself had worn many times. It was an expression that said: *I know I don't deserve it, but PLEASE like me.* Slowly, he raised his finger.

"You . . . You've been following me, haven't you?" He hesitated, feeling his anger rise. "Do you know you almost scared me
to death?"

She glanced in embarrassment at passing shoppers. "I . . . I'm
sorry."

He leaned toward her, part of him wanting to comfort her as one
loser to another. But it was the anger, bright and hard, that
prevailed. "Leave me alone," he said. "I wouldn't give you a
chance if you were the last woman alive."

He spun and marched away.

It wasn't till he was halfway home that he realized there were *two*
women involved: Reddy Teddy and the fat woman.

The revelation astounded him. How could he have missed that
fact? And with that, he found himself confronted by an even
greater realization: For someone who was so unattractive to the
opposite sex, he was in the unprecedented situation of having *two*
women pursue him.

But he found little satisfaction in being chased. Yes, the fat
woman liked him and was harmless. If he dated her, he'd have
someone to see and would no longer be alone. But she *was*
unattractive. As for Reddy Teddy, only the Dark Lord of
Cyberspace knew what she looked like. At the very least, he had to
assume she was dangerous. After all, what kind of sicko acted that
way?

He was still mulling it over when he entered his apartment.
Oddly, though his old life had been shattered, he found he did not
miss it. If he didn't like the feeling of being helpless, of having lost
control, neither did he like his empty and hopeless existence,
especially since he knew he would soon return to it.

Entering his bedroom, he removed his tie and jacket in the dim
light. What he needed was a good, stiff drink—

"Hello, Rex."

He turned, seeing a form emerge from his closet. In the shadows,
he could see little.

"What's the matter," a voice said softly, "cat got your tongue?
That's too bad. You're glib as hell on the net."

He parted his lips. "W-What are you d-doing here? How did you
get in?"

"You didn't pay attention, did you?" she said in the darkness. "I told you I was coming to see you. I have contacts, Rex. A friend in Records provided me with your name. As for your apartment . . . well, let's just say I'm good with locks."

He swallowed. "What—do you want?"

"You. I want *you,* Rex. And I want you *now.*"

His mind was chaos. He couldn't even think. This was impossible, so totally beyond his experience it wouldn't even register. Somehow, though, he heard his voice respond.

"You must be mad. I'm not Rex Stud. My name's Arthur Gruber."

"Rex Stud, Gruber, I don't care. What's in a name, anyway? It's what's in your *pants* that counts, Rex. That and whether or not you want *me* as much as I want you. Isn't that *right?*"

Numbly, he raised his hand. "Look, I don't know how you can—" He stopped. "It's . . . out of the question. If you just think about it—"

Suddenly a gun appeared, glinting in a pale hand. "You're not going to reject me *again,* Rex. Not after I came all the way out here to see you. Not after all we've been through together, all we've shared." The gun made a sharp gesture. "Move back toward the bed," she ordered.

He retreated on wooden legs, stopping when he felt the bed. Briefly, he thought of running, but before he could, the figure moved forward. He saw her enter the faint beam of light that filtered through the blinds. Now it sliced across the top of her head, and now her eyes moved into the light. Now he could see her nose, her cheeks. Her mouth.

He stood staring at a woman who was plain except for her eyes. Even in the poor light, they glowed like balls of phosphor, seeming to devour his face. He trembled. What was she doing here in his bedroom? What did she *want?*

She crept forward and pushed his chest, sending him backward onto the bed. He drove himself desperately toward the headboard by ramming his heels and elbows into the mattress, but she only laughed and leapt onto the bed, catching him easily.

The gun barrel pressed against his temple. Cold. "Take off the *rest* of your clothes, Rex. Complete the striptease."

"What?" he croaked.

The gun rose, brutally struck his forehead, bringing searing pain. "I won't tell you again," she said.

Numbly, he undid his belt, tugged at his shirt while she deftly stripped him of his shoes and socks. "I want you naked," she said. "All of you for me alone, just like before."

Before? But we've never been together! his mind screamed. He watched her move and straddle him, caress his penis with silken fingers. "No one ever made me feel the way you did," she said. "Never once in all my life. No one ever knew just how to treat me, or just what I liked." She gazed down at him, her features serene with lust. "No one can make your Teddy Reddy like you, Rex Stud. You're the *only* man for me."

He wanted to scream, but the barrel dug into his temple. "Raise your hands," she ordered.

He licked his lips. "Why?"

"Just *do* it."

Slowly, he obeyed. With one hand, she secured both of his to the headboard with a rope, twisting it tight. He moaned and tried to move his hands. No good. He was trapped, like a fly in a spider net.

"That's better," she said huskily, her eyes molten in the shadows. *"Much* better. Now to *really* put you in the mood."

Expert fingers coaxed him, stroking the underside of his cock and caressing his balls. Before, he had always scoffed at the notion that danger could excite a man, that fearing for his life could even make him hard as a rock. Now, as her sharp nails slid up and down his shaft, he discovered how stimulating terror could be. Heart pounding, chest trembling, he felt himself surge erect and throb painfully in her hand.

Hating his traitorous body, he opened his mouth to protest, but she was already moving and sliding him inside her. He barely had time to realize that she wore no panties beneath her dress before the gun barrel gouged his temple again. "You'd better be good, Rex," she warned. "That is, if you know what's good for you."

She moved against him, the channel of her sex tight and wet, fitting him like a glove. To his surprise, he found himself moving too.

"Isn't this good, Rex?" she moaned. "It's just like we did it before. Remember? It was the first time I asked to see you. I was on top, and you were on fire below."

She did something with her buttons, and her dress seemed to dissolve and slip away on both sides. "I did this too," she said, lowering her breasts to his lips.

Kissing them, taking the taut, erect nipples in his mouth, he wanted to tell her that on the net, she had never tied his hands to a headboard. But he sensed that to tell her would be dangerous, for it could spoil the illusion she had woven for herself and push her over the edge. And there was no guarantee that she wouldn't go over it anyway. After all, she had already tied him up and placed a gun to his head. How could he be sure she didn't plan to use it?

Suddenly, he found that his right hand was freer than his left— not much, but a little. Straining, he twisted it back and forth.

Laboring above him, she raised her eyes toward the ceiling. "Oh, Rex," she sobbed, holding the gun against his temple, "no one does it like you." She strained, her face looking as if she had found heaven. "I'm almost there," she gasped. *"Please* take me all the way."

"I *will,* Teddy," he answered, twisting his hand against the rope as he pounded back and forth inside her. He saw her smile at the use of her name and felt his storm of seed gather and then erupt inside her. He shot off deeply as she joined him, the bedsprings singing, a flush of warm sweat coating both their bodies in a union he longed for even as he spurned it. Again and again he felt their bodies throb in mutual release, until at last they were still.

Slowly, the barrel slid from his temple to the pillow, and she sagged till she lay full-length on top of him, the soft fire of her hair against his cheek. Her breasts rose and fell against his chest. "I love you, Rex," she whispered.

Twisting, twisting. And at last his hand was free. He flexed his fingers as something new stirred within him, a rage toward this woman that was even greater than he'd felt toward the fat one in the mall. How the bitch had used . . . dared to humiliate him! It wasn't right that she be allowed to get away with it!

His lips parted in a silent snarl, then a new thought occurred. What would it be like if *he* were the stalker and predator? How would it feel if *he* were the one in control, the one who toyed with her and caused *her* misery?

His breath quickened. Was it possible it would feel good? Was *that* the reason she did it?

Taking a deep breath, he braced himself, then shoved up and away, turned and spilled her off. Forcing himself onto one knee, he seized the gun in his free hand and started to lift it, only to feel her hand grasp his own.

They struggled for the gun, his one hand against her two. Despite her advantage, he knew he would win if he only had some leverage. But his other hand was bound fast to the headboard.

"Let go," she hissed. "Give it back!"

His knee wobbled on the bed, and for a moment he thought he was going to lose his balance and fall over. It would all be over for him then. She would have the advantage and finish him off. But he stiffened his spine and somehow stayed upright. He fought on, turning his head when one of her hands clawed out for his eyes, leaving deep grooves in his face instead. He struggled, his breath wheezing through his nostrils and blending with her fevered pants. Blood trickled down his face, and he felt its warm, salty taste cross his lips.

Then, slowly, he felt the gun twist back toward her face and her mad, mad eyes. They burned at him as he focused all his remaining strength on his pain-seared hand and wrist, turning the weapon inch by agonizing inch until finally the barrel pointed directly between her eyes.

"Rex," she gasped, her breath hot against his face. "You *wouldn't*. You feel the same way that I do about you—don't you, Rex? We were *meant* to be together."

He gazed down at her, and despite his pain, he felt himself harden again, grow erect against her body. She did not look so confident now, did she? No, now *he* was the one in control, and he would make her pay for her offense, for every single indignity she had put him through.

Twisted against her, he drank in her fear, tasting the rich, musky flavor of her terror. He hardened even more, stiffened like steel, feeling pleasure such as he had never known. It surged through his body, throbbed in his blood. For the first time in his life, he felt truly complete and whole, absolutely confident and certain of who he was.

"Rex," she moaned, eyes bulging at the gun. "Please!"

He smiled, and his finger tightened on the trigger. "My name's *not* Rex," he said.

When the gun went off, it took half her brains with it. He came like he never came before, in seemingly endless spasms, the weapon clattering to the floor. Gazing down at her blood-spattered face, he shuddered in ecstasy and reached out to caress her wet cheek, to dip his fingers in the wells of her eyes.

* * *

King Arthur: Get right down on your knees before me and take it in your mouth.

Passion Slave: But it's so big and hard, Your Majesty. I can't take it all.

King Arthur: Just relax. Think of the largest, juiciest banana in the whole world.

Passion Slave: Yum, that's better. You taste so good! My lips are sliding up and down it, taking it all the way in, letting it bruise the back of my throat.

King Arthur: Easy . . . don't suck too hard or your king will come. Now—get up and lie down on the bed. . . .

Arthur Gruber, now King Arthur, sat before the monitor, waiting for his new partner to obey. After the police had asked their million questions, he had returned to work bearing the battle scars on his face like ornaments. Oddly, he had been proud of them, and found himself actually enjoying the media's attention. One of his very first acts after the excitement died down had been to renew his membership in USA Ultraline.

It had taken him just a few days to find a new partner and establish a relationship on his terms.

Passion Slave: How's this, sire? Your loyal subject is lying here all hot and obedient for you.

But he didn't answer, for he had remembered the intense, shattering orgasm he'd felt when he had pulled the trigger and seen the woman's head explode. He had discovered a whole new man inside his skin, one he had never even suspected. Even as the gunshot echoed in his ears, he had known what he would do with the rest of his life, and how he would fill the endless void.

My liege, are you still there? Why don't you answer?

Yes, he thought, still not seeing her words. A whole new world had been opened to him when he had pulled that trigger. It was a world where *he* controlled, where *he* meted out the pleasure and pain. He remembered the fat woman who had dared to stalk him all the way to the mall, and smiled. He would be sure to return the favor and make her pay just like Reddy Teddy. Since she worked near him, it would be easy to ask her out. He chuckled, already imagining how it would feel when he stripped the bitch naked and strapped her hands to a headboard.

KING ARTHUR, ARE YOU THERE?

Finally, Arthur Gruber remembered the woman who lay spread
before him on an imaginary bed. Touching the wound on his
cheek, he grinned and briefly picked up the knife on his desk. Then
he leaned forward to answer her.

Your king's still here, he typed. *Don't you think it's time we
actually met?*

MALE-CALL

Lucy Taylor

I want a young, long-haired blond, blue or green eyes, a full-body tan," said Beth Dobbs, gazing at the ad in her hand as she spoke to the suspicious-sounding woman who had answered the phone. "No chest hair, great pecs, and, of course, well-endowed. Yes, I'm sure they all are. You've got someone blond and blue-eyed, and hung? What's his name? Corky? Yes, he sounds like he'll do. Yes, I'll wait."

There was a pause while the operator conferred with someone. Beth could almost feel the tension simmering across the line. The good folks at Male-Call were afraid she was Vice. And why not? How many women phoned up a male outcall service, even in a hell-raising, dick-sucking, cum-shooting town like Las Vegas?

The operator returned. Did Beth understand *exactly* what she was buying?

"Yes, I know he's just coming over to strip. No sex, just a show. The striptease for a hundred, anything extra we work out ourselves. Yes, I understand. This is not a sex service."

Not a sex service. Right. And Caesar's Palace doesn't have slot machines.

Beth gave her first name, the name of the motel, and her room number. No address needed—they probably sent "strippers" over here all the time. She hung up the phone and started to laugh, until her laughter fragmented and burst into dry, soundless sobs and her chest hurt like a line of chorus girls had high-kicked across her ribs.

"Corky," she murmured when she got herself under control, "blond, buff Corky. I think I'm going to like you just fine."

Beth gazed at the Male-Call ad that had been torn out of a copy

of *Nightline,* a tabloid-style sleaze sheet that catered to those Vegas
residents and visitors who gambled more with their dicks than
their dollars. The name "Corky" was scrawled in pen across the
bottom of the ad, which featured a photo of a 'roided up blond
with a Johnny Depp curl to his lip and a torn T-shirt exposing a
male tit with a nipple erect enough to suckle a babe. Or a grown
man.

Or a nervous, thirty-something, married woman, looking for
action on a hot Vegas night.

Beth looked at her Piaget watch. An hour and a half, the
operator had said. Busy Saturday night. Hustlers out turning
tricks, transsexuals in garter belts and push-up bras swinging their
dicks under tight leather skirts, cocksmen rendezvousing with
perverse and shady ladies in tacky trysting sites.

Well, at least one perverse lady.

Beth Dobbs dried her eyes and set about cleaning up the shabby
motel room, whose blandness, unmarred by one iota of decorative
touch, reminded her of the hospital rooms she used to work in
back in her nursing days, gray rooms where the only touch of color
had been blood. She wanted everything about the room to look
perfect, to be just right. Just like Corky expected it to be.

She thought about him, wet her lips.

Corky.

Paying cash to fuck a pretty man hadn't always been one of Beth
Dobbs's fantasies. Not too many years earlier, just about the time
she met Charlie, her idea of romance verged on prim and bor-
rowed heavily from the lush and purple prose of bodice rippers—
in her daydreams she was made love to, ravished, possessed,
seduced, never fucked, reamed, dicked, boinked, or corn-holed.
And she was always just herself, Beth Conners (then), not some
costumed cliché from a dirty movie: a porn star, schoolgirl,
headmistress, whore.

Not that Charlie's sexual proclivities were confined to role-
playing. He was enamored of a host of inventive humiliations,
from forcing her to sip his cum, deposited in a crystal goblet with a
cherry at the rim (he called it a "cocktail") to his current favorite,
having her pretend to be a call girl and meet him in some seedy
motel like the one she was in now.

Charlie should have been a porn producer, Beth thought as she
fitted fresh sheets—the gold silk ones she'd brought from home—

onto the splotchy mattress. Instead he'd found another calling—financial guru to the gullible and greedy who never understood that, yes, the money moguls of late night TV *did* know how to make a fortune—not by investing in real estate, but by persuading the suckers to plunk down $500 for a "How to Make a Million Dollars" weekend, and don't forget to buy the inspirational cassettes on your way out, by the way, or a sixty-dollar year's subscription to the monthly *Dobbs Report*.

And hadn't she herself been just as greedy, just as naive and dumb as any of the rest? Beth thought. She'd left a barely-make-ends-meet life as a nurse's aid to become Mrs. Charles R. Dobbs and to experience all that Charlie's wealth could give her—twelve years of late-model luxury cars, designer dresses, spa weekends. Twelve years, too, of being just another one of Charlie Dobbs's possessions, of having her self-esteem eroded, her self-respect siphoned out, not to mention the countless shiners and split lips.

Twelve years of learning what kind of pleasures Charlie Dobbs enjoyed when he *wasn't* sweeping up to hotels in rented limos, grinning his Good Ol' Boy grin as he glad-handed the adoring marks, teeth flashing ivory caps, dyed hair combed just so to make sure you couldn't see the plugs where his hair implants had been put in, his cunning eyes always focused inward, planning, scheming, doing mental masturbation with his two personal icons: dollar signs and cum. And when she'd asked him for a divorce, thinking she could take him for everything he had, or at least a substantial part of it, Charlie'd told her she wouldn't have time to pick out an attorney before he'd have her killed.

"There are plenty of people willing to kill for enough money," Charlie had said. "It's just a matter of finding the right one."

Too bad *she'd* never found one of those people, Beth thought. Because if she had, she'd certainly have had good reason to engage their services.

There were the other women, for one thing. A lot of them were hookers, for Charlie relished bought sex. He also enjoyed stashing away little mementos of his flings—to the point where Beth had wondered if he was planning to publish a pornographic autobiography someday. With Charlie's ego, anything was possible. She'd become adept at searching for and finding the cutesy love notes, motel receipts, even dirty photos of Charlie and his playmates hidden away in the rat's nest that passed for his office. The only good thing was that Charlie never seemed to fall in love with any of them, never spent any serious time or money on his tarts. And he always came back to *her*. So she hadn't worried too much about anyone replacing her. Until lately . . .

"It's power," Charlie'd told her once, a few years into their marriage, when she'd caught him with a Korean hooker and a boy who claimed to be her younger brother in their king-sized bed at the Chicago Hyatt. "To rent another human being's mouth or ass or pussy for a set amount of time, make use of them as you will, and not give a thought to what they think of you, to whether you brushed your teeth that morning or break wind when you bend over to put on your shoes, that's a feeling of power you never can imagine."

Oh no, Charlie?

Guess again.

She was going to find out what that kind of power felt like, how it felt to be in control, dominant, on "top." She was going to find out soon.

"You Bess?"

The young man from the Male-Call ad stood in the doorway, Rapunzel-golden and teakwood tan, a surfer dude who pumped iron in the off-season, she'd have taken him for. Crotch-defining Calvins, loose blue silk shirt open to a sleek V of solar plexus, diamond rings twinkling on both hands.

She started to correct him about the "Bess," then decided it was better if he didn't have her first name right.

In the bleak box of the motel room, he seemed to fill up every inch of space. His energy, all coiled muscle and testosterone, sizzled forth, surrounded him in a halo of hormones and heat.

And horniness. Hers.

Beth hadn't expected it would be this exciting. Maybe Charlie had been right about bought sex. Or maybe just the circumstances under which she was buying it . . . at any rate, she felt her clit throbbing with its pea-sized hard-on, her nipples getting stiff and pebbly underneath her top. Her breasts, enhanced so many years ago she'd forgotten they were ever modestly proportioned, jutted out in D-cup splendor. Her hair, dyed just that morning from blond to auburn for the new look she was cultivating, flowed full and wavy past her shoulders. She'd painted up her face and put in tinted contact lenses that transformed her azure eyes to smoldering gray.

Whether Corky was gay or bi or just your standard hustler, she didn't care. She wanted him to want her. That would be another little vengeance against Charlie.

"It'll be a hundred dollars for the strip," he said. Bourbon breath and ice-water eyes. All business.

Beth handed him the bill, then counted out three more.

Suspicion warred with greed in his eyes. "What's this for?"

"I was told we could negotiate for . . . more than just the strip. There're some other things I'd like to do. Things my husband likes to do to me that I'd like to try myself."

"Your husband, where's he at now?"

"Relax," said Beth, "he isn't hiding in the closet watching, if that's what you think."

"S'okay if he is," said Corky, and he glided, jaguar smooth, to check the closet, "only it'll cost extra if he's in here."

Watching him peer in among the hangers, Beth suddenly felt annoyed as well as nervous. She didn't want him snooping around. She wanted to get *started.*

"So for enough money, will you do anything I want?"

"Honey, you don't have that kind of money."

She smiled. "Don't bet your ass."

She pulled out a roll of bills, peeled off another two hundred and put it in his hand.

"Okay," he said, "for the right amount of money, whatever floats your boat. Just tell me what you want."

She did—or some of it, at least. A queer expression, part distaste, part sour mirth, crossed his face. For what she asked, he said he'd need three hundred more.

Beth paid him.

It was Charlie's money, after all.

Moments later, Corky's clothes lay in a pile on the floor.

Beth stood back, appraising her purchase. Sculpted abs, grapefruit-sized biceps, cock a lolling eight-incher. She could see why any woman—any man, if he were so inclined—could be quite smitten with him. Yet her hands were as clammy as if she'd just emerged from a steam room, her heart yoyoing crazily inside her chest.

Could she go through with this?

Hell, why not? She'd come this far. Since meeting Charlie, she'd already done things she'd never dreamed she was capable of doing.

He was looking at her, awaiting further instruction. "Well?"

Beth reached beneath the mattress and took out the hunting knife she'd hidden there, watched Corky's eyes go briefly cold. Turning the knife by its blade, she put it in his hand.

"My clothes," she said. "Cut them off."

"Whatever you say."

She shut her eyes, felt the blade whisper through the thin fabric of her tee, her short wraparound skirt. Then the sound of it ripping through her bra straps and her panties as they too slithered to the floor.

"I hope you got some extra clothes," he said, looking her up and down. He might like men, but it was his hetero inclinations causing his dick to swell to prize-winning zucchini size.

"I brought extra clothes," Beth said, indicating the tote bag on the floor.

"What position do you want to fuck in?"

"Doggie style."

"Fine."

He waited for her to assume the pose.

"Not me, sweetie. You."

She smiled.

The power of it all. You're right, Charlie, this is fun.

He waited for her on the bed with his dimpled ass in the air.

While he was holding that ungainly pose, she strapped on the object she'd been practicing with ever since the shopping trip to My Mistress's Toys, leather and latex for the dyke who has everything. A rubber phallus fitted to her groin by a harness contraption that went around the hips.

"Hang on, honey, let's go for a ride."

Spoken just like Charlie. Maybe this could be habit-forming.

In the privacy of her home earlier today, she'd wondered if she could do this, but—like so many other things—crossing the line between fucker and fuckee proved less difficult than she'd expected.

She seized Corky's hips, positioned herself, and visualizing how Charlie would do this, rammed it home.

Corky's sphincter muscle had obviously seen some action— she'd had more trouble popping a straw through the plastic lid on a soft drink. He grunted and took it like a pro.

"I know it hurts," she said, mock-soothing, "but think of all that lovely money that you're earning. Think what it can buy. That's what I do when my husband does this to me. I shut my eyes and think of three-hundred-dollar Ferragamo pumps, and weekends at the Broadmoor, and two-hour shiatsu massages. I remember what I can do with all his money."

As she spoke, she imitated Charlie—timed the rhythm of the thrusts to the syllables so that the words came out sounding like rap music. Sex-rap, set to the atonal music of cheap creaky bedsprings, punctuated by Corky's harsh grunts.

"You know what else my husband likes to do?"

When he didn't respond, she yanked his head back by the hair and looped the belt she'd taken from his trousers around his neck.

"You love it, don't you? You love every minute of it."

He wheezed out some type of assent. Grunt and bear it, as they say. She was that kind herself.

"Am I the best, Corky? Am I the fucking best?"

"Yes."

"Say it. Am I the world's greatest fuck or what?"

"Yes! Yes, you're the world's greatest fuck!"

She got into the thrust and the pull of it, the meaty suction. She heard Corky swear under his breath.

Was this what Charlie liked? Did it lie in the fact that he knew their union was just another financial transaction, that she was bought and paid for? And did he guess that, even though she didn't love him, still she searched his briefcase, closet, desk drawers when he wasn't home, obsessed with the idea that he might find someone prettier, hotter in the sack, someone to replace her in spending all that money?

She pulled out, eyed Corky's upraised rump. An idea came.

"How limber are you?"

"Why?"

"Have you ever seen a yoga position called the plow?"

He hadn't, so she explained it to him. "With a dick as long as yours is, it shouldn't be a problem."

His brow rumpled with irritation, but he lay back on the bed, swung his hips up as she'd instructed and let his feet and legs fall back behind his head. His cock now angled down dead center with his mouth.

"A little closer, come on, *try*."

He flexed his buttocks, scrunched his belly in, took the head of his own penis in his mouth and lapped with practiced tongue action.

Beth clapped her hands, delighted.

"That's wonderful, Corky. Now's the most special part of all."

She fished in her tote bag and brought out a cheap tourist mug shaped like a woman's breast. Corky was sitting up in bed. She handed him the mug.

"Jerk off while I watch."

"Do what?"

"Jerk off in it. I want to watch you drink your cum."

He gave a wry smile. "You are one seriously fucked-up bitch."

"I paid you well enough, didn't I?"

"Not for sicko shit like this."

She smiled and reached for her purse. "Open your mouth wide, honey."

He did. She stuffed in three hundred-dollar bills.

After he removed them, he seemed to have become a good deal thirstier.

"Your husband makes you do this shit?"

"And worse."

"But he's got a lot of money?"

"Tons."

"Sounds like a guy the world could do without."

"Amen," said Beth.

While he stroked himself, Beth leaned behind him, pillowing his head against her tits, reaching down to knead his nipples, tug on his ear with her teeth.

When he came, she lifted up the mug with its inch of creamy, musky-smelling jism and put it to her lips, pretended she was sipping. "The rest's for you," she said, "but because you've been so good, I'm going to make it tasty."

She went into the bathroom, where she added some rum-spiked banana daiquiri mix she'd bought at the liquor mart up the street, and blended it and the ejaculate to a smooth consistency.

"Here," she said, handing the drink to Corky, remembering all the times Charlie had played this game with her.

He took a sip. "Hell, there's so much rum in this I can't even taste . . . the rest of it."

"Just think of it as a cocktail," Beth said. "Right out of the original container."

He canted an eyebrow at her as he finished drinking. "Anything else you'd like for me to do?"

"Nothing difficult. Just chat awhile."

"Yeah? 'Bout what?"

"Those are nice rings you're wearing."

He smiled, clearly pleased that she was noticing. "Real stuff too. And this is nothing—I got bracelets, necklaces, a new Jag."

"One of your clients?"

"Yeah. He thinks I'm really special."

"That's nice," said Beth. She reached over, stroked Corky's blond mane. "But why do you have to work? Sounds like he'd support you."

"Oh, he will, he will," said Corky. "Just as soon as he gets rid of . . ."

"His wife?"

Corky got a strange, sick look. "How much rum did you put in this anyway?"

"Just a jigger or two. The rest's . . ."

He tried to sit up, but fell back, gazing up at her with a silly, inebriated scowl.

". . . chloral hydrate. I found out about it when I was a nurse and it . . ."

His eyes closed.

". . . puts people to sleep quite quickly . . . especially when you mix it with alcohol."

Moving quickly now, Beth gathered up her ruined clothing and dropped it in her tote bag, then put on the extra jeans and sweater that she'd brought. Kneeling beside the bed, she dragged her husband's bloodied body out from where she'd shoved it a few hours earlier.

Next she used a pillowcase to pick up the hunting knife and drop it onto Charlie's chest. It had proved good for cutting clothes, but even better for slashing Charlie's throat, which she'd done a couple of hours earlier while they were playing his favorite game of call-girl-comes-to-meet-man-in-his-motel-room. The bloodied sheets, she'd already gathered up and stuffed into the tote bag, to dispose of later.

Her final touch was to leave on the bureau a couple of the photos that she'd found in Charlie's desk along with the ad for Male-Call and Corky's name. Those hadn't bothered her so much—it was the receipts for all those expensive gifts, the steamy, fuck-buddiesin-love letters planning how they would get rid of her, that had really turned her stomach.

You were right, Charlie, she thought. *For enough money, there are plenty of people who will kill—I just never realized I was one of them.*

She tossed the key onto the bed and slipped out into the dry heat of the desert night, heading for a phone booth to call in her tip to 911 about a hustler who'd murdered his john.

FIVE CARD STUD

Michael Newton

*N*ice place," said Tommy Hardwick.

"We enjoy it," Amy or Amanda said.

"Sit down and make yourself at home."

Which one was that? What difference did it make?

If Tommy had to tell the truth, he would have said the flat was small, a little on the shabby side, but what the hell, he wasn't shopping for a new apartment. And he knew from past experience that truth got in the way with women.

Twins, for Christ's sake. The fulfillment of a lifelong fantasy. He didn't plan on blowing it because their place turned out to be a smallish walk-up in a shitty neighborhood. He had been looking at the Strip and all its neon for the past three days and nights. Now, it was time to see some skin. Not up on stage, like at the dinner show, but close enough to touch . . . or taste.

"You want some wine?"

"Sounds good."

He didn't need it, but the more they drank, the better Tommy's chances were of pulling off a doubleheader. Two for one, goddammit, and they weren't just twins, they were *identical.* Both knockouts. Honey-blond, with bodies that reminded him of *Playboy*'s Miss September.

He was running movies in his head, imagining the two of them together, cutting to a shot with both of them on top of him, when Amy or Amanda brought the wine.

"Is red all right?"

"My favorite," Tommy said.

They sat on either side of him, a little crowded on the sofa, but he wasn't bitching. Nice and warm, the way they pressed against him. Tits, hips, thighs. He felt like the bologna in a happy sandwich.

"So, I still don't know your names," he said.

"We told you at the club. I'm Amy," coming from his left.

"And I'm Amanda." On his right.

"I mean your *last* name."

They exchanged a glance and smiled at one another, mellow and seductivelike.

"Let's keep it friendly," said Amanda.

"Casual," said Amy.

"Fine by me. I figured, since you knew my name and all . . ." He left the comment dangling, didn't want to push it.

"Tommy Hardwick," said Amanda, stretching out his surname so that it became two words. "I hope there's truth in advertising."

"No complaints so far," he told her, shifting slightly to accommodate the swelling in his shorts.

"You been in Vegas long?"

"Since Thursday," Tommy said. "I come out three, four times a year. On business."

"Monkey business, I expect," Amanda said.

"Well, now . . ."

"Are you a gambler, Tommy?"

Am I ever. Putting on a big smile, nice and casual. "I do all right," he said.

"I'll bet you do."

"Let's play a game," said Amy.

"Hey, I'm up for that." His best cool grin, just making sure they got it.

"Poker," Amy said.

"Right now?"

"The *card* game," Amy told him, giggling.

"You *do* know how to play?" Amanda asked him.

"Sure. It wasn't what I had in mind, is all."

"*Strip* poker," Amy said.

"Hey, now you're talking."

"Get the cards," Amanda told her sister.

Tommy watched her go and felt an urge to follow, maybe see the rest of the apartment. Find out what the bedrooms looked like. He restrained himself by concentrating on Amanda, looking forward to the game.

You play strip poker properly, nobody loses.

"So," he said, "you hang out on the Strip a lot?"

"Depends," Amanda said. "Sometimes we just get in the mood, you know?"

It crossed his mind that maybe they were working girls, the way they picked him out in the Sahara's cocktail lounge, but at the moment Tommy didn't care. He had been smoking at the blackjack table, up two grand from Friday afternoon. He could afford a fantasy. And, if the twins were giving it away . . .

"My lucky day," he said.

"Could be."

She had her left hand on his thigh, about six inches from the mother lode, when Amy brought the cards back.

"We can play right here," said Amy, bending low to pull the glass-topped coffee table out. A glimpse of ample cleavage in the process. Tommy smiled at the preview of coming attractions.

"We're sitting on the floor?" he asked.

Amanda nudged him in the ribs. "You don't like roughing it?"

"Rough, smooth," he said, "it's all the same to me. I like it, period."

"That's good to know."

They sat around the table, yoga style, and Tommy clicked to the advantage right away. Glass tabletop, you couldn't hide a thing.

"You deal," said Amy, passing him the deck.

He pulled the jokers out and shuffled quickly, twice, to keep it fair. Amanda made the cut on Tommy's right and handed back the cards. They waited, luscious mirror images of one another.

"Five card stud, okay?"

"It sounds appropriate," Amanda said.

"More wine before you deal?" said Amy.

"Great."

She brought the bottle back and topped their glasses. Tommy took a sip and started dealing to his left, hole cards facedown, the next round showing. Amy had a deuce of clubs, Amanda drew a jack of diamonds, and the dealer wound up with an ace of hearts. He set the deck aside and checked his hole card.

Ace of clubs.

"You're high," Amanda said.

"Not yet. Left shoe."

The sisters saw his bet, and Tommy dealt another round of cards: the six of spades to Amy, three of diamonds to Amanda, nine of diamonds to himself.

"Possible flush to my right."

"I'll bet the other shoe," Amanda said.

"I call," said Tommy.

"Call," from Amy, on his left.

He dealt the next round. Three of hearts to Amy. Jack of hearts to blow her sister's flush but leave a good pair showing. Eight of spades for Tommy.

"Pair of jacks."

Amanda didn't check her hole card. Playing cool.

"Left stocking."

"See you."

"Call," said Amy. Still on target for a straight?

It could be anybody's hand.

The last round seemed to strengthen Amy, with a five of diamonds. On his right, Amanda got the three of spades, with two pair showing. Tommy drew the nine of clubs. Two pair, with aces over nines.

"Your bet," he told Amanda, wondering if Amy's hole card was a four, prepared to smoke them both.

"Right stocking," said Amanda.

"Call."

"I fold," said Amy, tossing in her hand. No straight.

"Two pair," said Tommy. "Aces over nines."

Amanda turned her hole card over, letting Tommy see the jack of clubs. "Full house."

"Amazing."

Tommy kicked his shoes off, followed with his socks. His eyes were locked on Amy. Peeling off one stocking, she was forced to hike the miniskirt above her hips. Her panties were translucent, baby blue.

"Your deal."

He passed the deck to Amy, watched her shuffle with a serious expression on her face, pink tongue just showing at the corner of her mouth. He wondered what that tongue would feel like on his cock.

"Same game?"

"Suits me," Amanda said.

"I'm in," said Tommy. *Or I will be, soon.*

She dealt the hole cards nice and easy, followed with the second round faceup. A ten of hearts went to Amanda, Tommy got a rotten deuce of clubs, and Amy drew the ace of spades. He checked his hole card, all that he could do to keep from scowling at the ten of diamonds.

Nothing.

"Dealer's high," said Amy, just in case they hadn't noticed. "Bet my belt."

"I call," Amanda told her sister.

"Call that belt," said Tommy.

Three more cards around the circle. King of hearts went to Amanda. Ten of clubs for Tommy, giving him a pair. The five of hearts to Amy.

"Working on a flush. Your bet, Amanda."

"Skirts," she said.

"I guess that's slacks, to me," said Tommy. "Call."

"I'll stick," said Amy, dealing three more cards.

The four of diamonds killed Amanda's flush, but Tommy had to settle for a six of spades. The jack of clubs that Amy drew would be no good unless she had its brother in the hole, but she was back on top with what was showing on the table.

"Bet my blouse," she said, directing the remark to Tommy, giving him a Cheshire smile.

"I call," Amanda said.

"I'll see you." *Any minute now.*

She dealt the last three cards: a king of spades to give Amanda two old men; a lousy three of hearts that finished Tommy off; an ace of hearts that put the dealer back on top.

"I'll bet . . . my bra."

"I call," Amanda said.

"Too rich for me."

"You're folding?"

Tommy shrugged. "I didn't wear a bra."

"Let's see 'em, little sister."

Amy had a five of diamonds in the hole. "Two pair."

Her sister faced a king of clubs. "Three of a kind."

"Well, *damn* it!"

Tommy stood to take his slacks off, sat back down before unbuttoning his shirt. All eyes on Amy as she dropped the miniskirt and kicked it over to the growing pile of clothes beside Amanda, spent a moment grappling with her clingy top.

The bra and panties were a perfect match, dark nipples clearly outlined through the sheer material. And Tommy felt his hard wick straining at the fabric of his jockeys when she slipped the bra off, tossed it to her sister, round breasts wobbling slightly with the effort.

Tommy caught a glimpse of it as she was sitting down.

"What's that?" he asked her. Leaning closer, pointing. "This?"

She spread her legs to show him, unembarrassed by the see-through panties. High up, near the juncture of her hip and thigh, two words. Ten letters.

Daddy's girl.

"That doesn't look like a tattoo."

"It's not," said Amy.

"It's a brand," Amanda told him, busy shuffling.

"Hey, that musta hurt."

"I don't remember." Amy had a wide-eyed, dreamy look about her, like a little girl. Her stunning body and Amanda's voice put Tommy back in focus.

"One more hand," she said.

He glanced down at his bulging shorts. "I haven't got much left."

"Don't underestimate yourself," Amanda said. "We'll think of something."

Amy bounded to her feet. "We're out of wine," she said, and headed for the kitchen with the empty bottle. "Be right back."

No wonder his head was spinning. Christ, how many glasses had he finished, sitting there? He definitely had a buzz on, but the flagpole jutting from his groin was ample evidence he hadn't drunk *too* much.

When Amy came back with the wine, she stood above him, bending down to fill his glass. Her nipple grazed his cheek, and Tommy turned his head to get a taste, tongue darting out and back before she could retreat. She giggled, stroking Tommy's hair.

"He's getting anxious," Amy told her sister.

"One more hand."

"You really love your dad, I guess, to brand yourself like that." His lips felt thick and rubbery. The wine was really kicking in.

"I didn't," Amy told him. "Brand myself."

"Oh, yeah?"

"It's a forget-me-not," Amanda told him, dealing out the hole cards. "Each of us has one. Identical."

"Identical," said Tommy, grinning like an idiot when he received a three of hearts faceup. His hole card was a jack, or possibly a king. He couldn't really tell, the way his head was swimming from the wine.

What did it matter, anyway? The object of the game was getting naked. Getting laid.

"I bet my panties," Amy said.

Amanda called the bet.

"Awright."

Another round of cards he couldn't read, Amanda telling him, "Our father liked to mark his property, so everybody knew exactly what was his. No trespassers. I guess you know how that goes, Tommy Hard Wick. Big old stud like you."

"You've marked some women in your time, I bet," said Amy.

"Hell, yes." He could barely see the *table* now, much less the cards. The conversation made no fucking sense to him at all. "Hey, what's the bet?"

"What have you got?"

He tugged at the elastic of his jockeys, showing her. "How's this?"

"I'll cover it," Amanda said.

With what? he wondered, drifting. Maybe with her lips, for starters. Finish with a double-team event. He had a flash of Amy sitting on his face, the legend *Daddy's girl* mashed right against his lips, and he could almost taste her.

Her *father* did that. Did them both, for Christ's sake.

Jesus, she was suffocating him!

He toppled over backward, moaning as his skull bounced on the floor. Somebody pulling on his shorts, and Tommy raised his hips to make it easy for them. Hell, he hadn't come this far to fight them off. No fucking way.

Warm fingers wrapped around him, stroking. One hand on his shaft, another cupped around his scrotum. Tommy craned his neck and saw the sisters kneeling, one on either side of him, both staring at his face. Both smiling, but their eyes were cold.

As cold and sharp as the straight razor in Amanda's hand.

"Straight flush," she told him in a husky bedroom voice. "You shouldn't bet with anything you can't afford to lose."

VIDEO DATE

Jeff Gelb

*A*ngela Matthews watched as George Brenner brought his latest pile of video tags to her register. She knew his name because he always brought them to her, never Bob or Joel or Christina. Maybe George thought she was turned on by the video titles he rented. If so, he was certainly mistaken. Or maybe, she figured, he just liked her breasts. They were, she felt, her best feature.

"Hi, Angela." His voice was just above a whisper, an outward indication of the man's shyness and almost certainly his loneliness as well. He gave Angela the creeps.

He placed the numbered tags on the counter in front of her. Angela nodded without smiling, picked up the tags and turned to locate the matching numbered videos from the shelves behind her. As she did so, she swore she could feel his eyes scanning her up and down, first locating the bra strap that was barely visible through the white T-shirt, then on her tight jeans. She sighed. She'd be damned if she'd let a customer make her dress more conservatively. These were just the clothes she felt most comfortable in, and one reason she'd taken the job at Movies 'N More was because there was no dress code. The other reason was because she was flat broke.

As she retrieved the videos, her attention was diverted by the nearby TV screen. Store employees were supposed to use the TV to show new videos, but it was Angela's turn to choose, and she'd been too busy to pick one.

A TV newscast was on-screen, an attractive yuppie newscaster giving more sordid details of the latest in the sexual serial killings that had plagued Milwaukee for months now, with the police no closer to catching the killer than when they'd found the bloodied, tattered remains of his first victim.

George tilted his head toward the TV and clucked his tongue. "Did you hear? They found another girl dead, not two miles from here. Terrible thing—I heard she had no—" He stopped short, unable to say the word. "You know," he said, finishing his sentence with his eyes, which dropped to Angela's young, perky breasts, cupped by a push-up bra in the V-neck T-shirt.

She ignored him. "Are these your titles?" She pushed the videos toward him.

He smiled sweetly, showing the gap between his two front teeth that made his *s*'s whistle. "Sorry, I forgot my glasses. Can you read them to me?"

Angela rolled her eyes. This was some sick game George insisted on playing with her. It seemed George never wore his glasses and always had her read the titles to him. It was cheap thrills for him, and becoming downright annoying to her. "George, I'm busy. There's a line of people behind you. . . ."

"Oh Angela, please? I left my glasses at home and my wife and I just had a big fight, and if I go back there now, she won't let me come back to the store, and besides, I'd hate to tell your boss you weren't being cooperative—"

"Oh fer chrissake," she interrupted him. If she didn't need this gig to pay her bills, she'd have told him where to stuff his precious porn videos. But she was in between boyfriends, and not talking to her parents, so she put on a relatively happy face and announced loudly, so the others in line could hear, "Tonight you're going to be watching *Big Tittie Committee, My Double D Cup Runneth Over,* and *Leave it to Cleavage.*"

He clapped a hand to his mouth as his whiter than white face colored. "Please, Angela, not so loud. What do I owe you?"

She rang him up, noting the wads of cash in his wallet. She could swear she'd seen several hundreds in there. He certainly didn't seem the type to make that kind of money: he was overweight, white as a dead fish, with thinning hair, dirty and outdated clothes. In short, a real nerd. On the other hand, she reasoned, with the advent of the computer age, the nerds were taking over the world. So maybe he was rich. Well, if that's who she had to fuck to have a boyfriend, she'd rather cozy up with her vibrator.

She watched George Brenner waddle out of the store, muttering as he gathered a soiled winter coat around him, and then turned her attention back to the TV newscaster's horrifying details of the latest serial killing.

"Nobody's safe anymore," she noted to her next customer. "Or sane."

She came up with the idea that night, as she was paying her bills and coming up short again, as usual. She weighed all the potential problems, decided it was worth the risks, and rehearsed what she would say the next time George Brenner came into the store.

She sucked in her breath when she saw him enter the store two nights later to return the videos. Was she really going to go through with it? Suddenly the whole idea seemed ludicrous, like something out of one of the straight-to-video B movies the store stocked. And was she daring enough to try it right here, right in the store? What if a customer came in?

He placed the videos on the counter and smiled shyly at her. "Hi, Angela," he said, displaying coffee-stained teeth. She smiled sweetly, and he blinked, unused to any sign of interest from her. That's good, she thought, keep him off balance.

He turned away from her and went into the adult section. She glanced around the store. It was an unusually quiet night; only one other customer during the last hour. She figured they were all staying home, behind locked doors, afraid the serial killer boogeyman was gonna get them. Well, so much the better for her plan. Suddenly, as he approached with a fresh stack of video tags, she knew she was going for it, no matter what. She had too many bills, and besides, he was such a jerk, he deserved it.

"How are things at home, George?"

"Uh—what?"

Perfect, Angela thought. He's not used to me being nice. He's already off balance.

"I mean, are you and your wife fighting again? Usually, that's when you come in to rent videos, isn't it?"

He hesitated, pawing the tight collar of his dirty white shirt. "I guess so." He was plainly uncomfortable having to explain himself, Angela thought. Everything was going just as she'd planned.

"Let me get these for you, George. Four tonight, huh? Gee, it must have been a hell of a ruckus." She took a video off the shelf and read its title aloud: *"Big Bouncing Boobs.* Does your wife know you watch these, George?"

"Hell no," he burst out, with more volume and speed than the question deserved. "Why, she'd kill me if she knew. . . ."

Angela nodded. Just as she'd hoped. She returned with the rest of the videos and put them on the countertop. George started to reach for them, and she placed her hand atop his. He reacted with a start and quickly withdrew his hand. "Angela—"

"No George, tonight I'm going to talk. Did you know that we keep a list of all the videos our customers rent? Why, let me pull up your rental history. It'll just take a second."

"Angela, no. I . . . I've changed my mind. I think I'll rent these some other time."

"George!" The power behind her voice surprised even her. She was in control of this jerk, and it felt *great*. "Check this out first."

The computer list was already printing out. George and Angela both watched as it consumed three sheets of paper before the printer stopped clacking. She tore off the bottom sheet and looked at the list, whistling at its length.

"Well, George, according to this, you've rented 194 videos from us in the past four months. At three dollars per, that makes it over—let's see—six hundred dollars, including tax, that you've spent on your dirty little habit. What do you think your wife would have to say about that, George?"

He angrily pulled the list out of her hands and started shredding it. She laughed, punched a key on her computer, and the printer sprang back to life. "Hey, George, I can print these out all night."

"What . . . why are you doing this to me? It's a free country. . . ."

"Yeah, George, but my apartment isn't free. My food isn't free. My car isn't free. And I don't have a nerdy sugar daddy pornhead hubby to boss around and spend his money as I see fit."

She leaned in toward him and watched his eyes involuntarily roam down to her cleavage. "Naughty naughty, George," she said. "You don't spend nearly enough money in here to even think about my tits, let alone see 'em. But that's all about to change."

He backed away from the counter, looking right and left. Angela noted with relief that it was almost closing time on a cold, rainy night, so chances were in her favor that no one would walk in on them.

She took a deep breath and said the words she'd been rehearsing for two days: "I want money, George. In return for my promise to delete your computer file and never call your wife and tell her your dirty little secret."

"I don't understand. How much money?"

"You pay me fifteen hundred dollars and promise not to step one foot in this store again, George, and I'll be out of your life forever."

He shook his head. "I'll tell your boss, he'll fire you. You . . . you can't do this."

"George, you're pissing me off here. You want me to call your wife right now and start reading her this list of titles?"

"No! No! I—I don't have the money."

"Bullshit. I saw tons of money in your wallet last time you were in the store."

Sweat was pouring down his face, making him blink rapidly. "That was payday. I always cash my checks and bring them home to Marge, because she pays the bills, and she doesn't believe in charge cards, and—"

"George, I don't want your life story. I want your money. Go home and get it."

"What do I tell her?" She could see that he was almost in tears. "Oh, Angela, don't do this to me! I promise I won't come in the store anymore."

She poked at his chest with a fingertip that sunk a half inch into flab. "It's too late, fucker. Your kind doesn't deserve a break. You guys come in here, leer at my tits, and then rent the most disgusting filth ever created, to fulfill some sick need.

"And you—you're the worst of the lot—you're ugly, twisted, and pathetic. I can't believe you even found a woman to marry you. She must be quite a vision. A real double-bagger." She laughed as she poked him again, noting with glee that each time she did, he winced, as if her touch caused him physical pain. Well, I hope it does, she thought.

"Now you go home," she hissed, "get the money, and be back in fifteen minutes, or I'll call your wife. Your phone number's in our computer file too, you know. Now *get!*"

George's mouth moved up and down silently for a full ten seconds before he turned on his heel and left the store at a near gallop. Angela let out a huge rush of air and started chuckling, then laughing until tears ran down her cheeks. It had *worked!* The jerk was actually running home to double-bag wifey Marge, and somehow he'd think of some excuse to get the money and get back here.

She shook her head at a sudden thought: this was so easy, she should have asked for more money.

She was supremely relieved that no one had interrupted them while she was making her blackmail demands. Well, maybe my luck is changing, she thought as she cleaned up the counter and replaced tags on the video shelves.

Her gaze alternated between the wall clock and the store entrance. He'd been gone nearly twenty-five minutes and the store was closing in less than ten. Finally she saw a shape approaching in the gathering darkness outside. *It's about time.* Her heart pounded in anticipation of the money she was about to receive. She was disappointed instead to see a woman in an exercise outfit, carrying a gym bag at her side. "Shit," Angela muttered.

"We're closed," she said.

The woman stood at the entrance. "But—your sign says you don't close till nine. I still have ten minutes."

"Well, make it fast. I've got a hot date tonight."

"Aren't you lucky?" The woman smiled as she stepped past Angela into the store.

Angela sighed. What the hell, she had to wait for George anyway. She casually perused her new customer: about thirty and relatively attractive, with close-cropped dark brown hair and bangs that fell just above her eyebrows, good legs in the tight spandex pants. And just about no tits at all.

Angela noted the gloves on the woman's hands as the woman handed her a tag. The woman caught Angela's gaze. "It's cold out there," she explained.

Angela nodded. "Winter's coming early this year." She took the tag and started to retrieve the video. "Yeah, leavin' this godforsaken town real soon."

"Oh, really?"

"Yeah—I'm coming in to some money. Think I'll move to California." She returned with the video, setting it on the counter.

"I hear it's real nice out there. Um, do you have a—well, you know, an adult section here?"

"Listen, I've really gotta close the register now."

"Oh please, I have nothing to do tonight. And, well, you know how it is for us single girls—life can get pretty lonely sometimes."

Angela sighed and nodded. Despite the situation, she felt her heart going out to the woman; she *did* know how she felt. Maybe that was really why she was blackmailing George: to get back at all the men who'd ever screwed her, physically or otherwise. And there had been many. But all of that was going to be over now, thanks to George and his taste in womens' tits.

"Okay," she agreed. "It's just to my left—you have to go through that door," she said, tilting her head in the direction of the adult video room.

"Thanks." The woman walked into the adjoining room. Angela could see her in the store's video monitor, walking slowly, looking at titles, picking up videos and then replacing them. *Hurry up—you're taking too fucking long. Where's George, anyway?*

"Anything in particular you're looking for?" Angela shouted.

"Yeah," the woman yelled back. "Could you help me find something not too offensive, but—you know, titillating." She laughed nervously.

"Be right there," Angela said as she stepped out from behind the counter. She could appreciate the lady's predicament; no matter how pretty the face, men always preferred women with big tits. Life for this lady was probably less than thrilling, or she wouldn't be in the back of a video store, checking out the porn. For good reason, Angela thought, store employees called the adult section "No Woman's Land."

"I've heard this one isn't too gross," Angela suggested as she pulled a title off the shelf and turned to hand it to the woman, who suddenly pushed Angela's face into the wall of videos, shoving tags and tape boxes off the shelves and onto the floor with a clatter of noise.

Angela fell to her hands and knees, her face bruised, the wind knocked out of her. *What the fuck?*

"Got any with big tits, like yours?" she heard the woman screech. She jumped on Angela's back, and Angela felt a blinding pain in her chest. She looked down in a sickened haze and saw the woman's hand holding a knife that was embedded between her own breasts. Blood splattered from the end of the knife and gathered in a pool on the floor, staining the carpeting, tags, and boxes alike a deep crimson.

"You think you're so fucking perfect, don't you? Don't you?"

Angela gasped in pain as she struggled to regain her footing. She clawed at her attacker's hand wielding the knife, till she let it go. Angela rose to shaky feet, turned to meet her attacker, and swung at her. The woman laughed at Angela's drunken-looking attempt to strike her, missing by at least a foot.

"You ain't shit, sister," the woman screamed as Angela backed out of the adult section on less than steady feet. "And the only date you have tonight is with the county coroner!"

Angela flashed on the TV news reports she'd been watching all day. "Oh my God, you're the . . ." She turned and ran out of the adult section of the store, spilling shelves of video boxes in her wake in a last-ditch attempt to keep the madwoman from striking her again.

But Angela could feel her strength fading with each drop of blood emerging from her chest wound. If only I can make it outside, she thought, maybe someone will see me.

She lurched for the back door, barely able to see it, and fell into the arms of George Brenner as he stepped into the shop.

"Oh my God, George," she gasped, "help me! Help me! There's a woman in here—she's the killer, George, the one on the TV."

George studied the knife embedded in Angela's chest. "That's no killer," he announced, "that's my wife!" He pushed the knife blade farther in, twisted it, and pulled it out.

Angela twitched uncontrollably and fell to the floor, the last of her life's blood spurting through the open cavity in her chest.

"George," Marge shouted. "What are you doing here? You're supposed to be watching for cars."

"You were taking too long—I got worried."

"Well, get your ass outside and get the car started. I'll be out in a minute. I've got to . . . clean up."

"Right!"

A minute later she exited the store, the gym bag held tightly against her chest. She jumped into the passenger seat of the blue Chevy Camaro and they drove away silently, as Marge caught her breath.

Finally, George asked, "Did you remember the disk?"

She pulled the computer disk from the bag, along with several copies of George's rental list.

"How about the computer? Sometimes this stuff is stored on the internal memory."

Marge laughed. "Listen to Mr. Wizard. Yes, honey, Humpty Dumpty had a great fall, and even Super Glue won't put him together again."

George smiled. "So—what'd you think? Can I pick 'em or what?"

Marge nodded. "Yup. She had all the physical attributes, as you know. And just like you said, she was a cunt. Her kind gives women a bad reputation!" She laughed.

George's smile faded. "I wasn't sure whether she was gonna be our next victim till she pulled that blackmail shit on me. Imagine the nerve of her!" He shook his head.

"It was a first all right. Still, George, you were an idiot to go to the same store every time for so long. Thank God the bitch didn't put two and two together." She shook her head. "I swear, sometimes I wonder what attracted me to you in the first place. I mean, a tit man with a woman with no tits?"

George kept one hand on the steering wheel as he reached over and playfully grabbed Marge's left breast. "She certainly had great tits, didn't she?"

"Yeah, she did," Marge agreed as she reached inside her gym bag and gave one of them a squeeze.

IMPULSE

Yvonne Navarro

*W*hen Gabriel opened his eyes, a strange woman was sitting on the passenger side of his Puma convertible and smiling at him.

"I've always wanted to meet you," she said.

Gabe struggled up from his slouch within the space between the steering wheel and the snug bucket seat. He'd been dozing, and it took him a couple of blinks to figure out what was going on—at least, what was *supposed* to be going on. At the same time he remembered he was at the Schaumburg train station to pick up his girlfriend, Audrey, came the mental flash—*duh*—that she was horrifically jealous, and if she saw him in the lot with an unknown woman perched on the other cream-colored bucket seat of this two-seater, he was in really deep shit.

"Yeah, well," Gabe managed, "thanks for the compliment, but now you'll have to get out." The train had just pulled in, and his gaze flicked nervously around the horde of people disembarking. The only thing that might save him from getting his head chewed off was Audrey's refusal to search for a seat in the more crowded front cars by the drop-off lanes; she'd have to walk nearly the length of the Metra commuter train before she spotted the Puma. Still, Gabe needed to get rid of his unexpected visitor right away.

She made no move to get out of his car.

He stared at her and she stared back. He couldn't think of anything to say—would he have to go around and physically *pull* her out, drag her from the front seat? The notion made him cringe. "Look . . ." he began, but his voice faded when she just smiled wider. Gabe forgot the rest of his sentence; she was very pretty, much prettier than Audrey, in a way that made it clear there was very little stress in her life. She might be Audrey's age or younger, but there was a translucence to her skin and a relaxed flow to her muscles that he envied. Her hair was so blond that the strong western sunlight of late afternoon turned it nearly platinum over sun-pinkened skin and eyes the color of old jade. That she was in the wrong car—or the *right* car, if she was nervy enough—called to mind a hundred dumb blonde jokes. But there was nothing at all vapid about the level gaze directed at him, or the way the tip of her tongue slid smoothly across the underside of her upper lip.

"Drive away," she said.

Gabriel groaned. He and Audrey were going off for a long weekend; he'd planned the whole thing as a semi-surprise—"semi" because although she knew they were going *some*where, he'd refused to tell her the exact location. His overnight bag—stuffed so full he couldn't close the zipper all the way—was in the trunk, alongside the space he'd saved for Audrey's bag. The plane tickets were tucked inside the pocket of his jacket; all he had to do was pick up Audrey and transfer her suitcase from the trunk of her car to his. They were even going to leave her car in the train parking lot. It was that simple.

Or so it had seemed.

"My girlfriend is getting off this train," Gabe told the stranger. Something about her presence made him feel like he was caught in a heat flash, or maybe the wash of steam that came when you opened the bathroom door and someone inside was taking a hot shower. It didn't take a master's degree to know this would be an abysmal way to start the weekend trip, and he was starting to feel desperate. "Please—she'll be here any second."

"So drive away," his passenger said again.

For the first time it occurred to Gabe that this woman might have a gun aimed at him, and his eyesight dropped to her lap—nothing—before it flicked back to her face. He glanced at the train and thought he saw Audrey's taller-than-average figure at the back of the small crowd headed in the direction of the waiting cars. "Oh, man," he whispered to himself.

"Go for it," the woman said. "Before she gets here. I *dare* you."

Gabriel tried to glare at her, and opened his mouth to demand that she just get the hell *out*, right *now,* but she was smiling at him still, and the funny thing was, her humor was . . . *infectious.* He couldn't remember the last time Audrey had looked at him like that, even though he loved her and they were supposed to get married in that vaguely assumed mode that attaches itself to people who've been dating for years and simply have no other plans. But *did* he love Audrey? Really? He told her so regularly and he supposed he did—in that same, nebulous way that made his future kind of foggy and uninspired. She was what his mother always called a "good, stable woman," the type who'd never break his heart or let him down by cheating on him after five years of marriage, a rock of security who would raise his children to be hardworking pillars of society just like she was. And he was the same: stable, dependable, a man who could be counted on to be there for someone.

And as boring and monotonous as a drive across Nebraska's interstate on a bland summer midnight.

When he looked again, Audrey had seen them. She was frozen, her mouth open in an O of confusion that would quickly turn to anger. Right on the mark, her expression darkened and she began striding toward the car. Gabe could see the play of emotions across her face: indignation, forced calm as she told herself to wait for an explanation, a little fear.

"Last chance," the woman beside him said softly.

Gabriel thought of the way the setting sun sparkled on the fine strands of the stranger's hair, the way her sun-kissed complexion looked soft and just a touch moist from the heat and humidity. Her smile was framed by full lips covered in bubble-gum-flavored lip gloss that he could, incredibly, smell from here.

He swallowed and put the car in gear. He revved the engine once, then left his girlfriend of ten years standing with a stunned look on her face as he drove away with a woman whose name he didn't know.

They were halfway to O'Hare Airport before he thought to ask her if she had a driver's license. They hadn't spoken a word since he'd steered the car into the traffic flowing out of the parking lot and onto the Elgin-O'Hare extension leading to 53 north and eventually the airport. Gabe had expected his passenger to start asking questions, but the way she sat wordlessly letting the miles and exits crawl by at rush-hour speed unnerved him almost as much as what he'd done. But he couldn't think about that, or about Monday and all the repercussions that would come—and oh, there would be *many*—when he tried to pick up his life again four days from now.

"Yes," she said in response to his question about the driver's license. She said nothing else, and finally, as he took the ramp that would lead them to the long-term parking lot at O'Hare, Gabriel could handle the silence no longer.

"What's your name?" he asked. It seemed a good way to start.

"Lilah," she said softly. "With an *h* on the end."

"Lilah," he repeated. "That's pretty. Mine is Gabriel. Gabriel Zantowitz."

"So you were always last."

"Pardon me?" he asked, puzzled.

"I said, you were always last. You know, because of your last name."

He had to smile. "I suppose I was," he said. He hadn't thought about that in years, but it had certainly been true. "But I did have a teacher in sixth grade who called attendance in reverse alphabetical order every other month. I guess she thought like you do."

Lilah gazed at him without blinking for a moment, then looked away. "I doubt it."

Gabriel cleared his throat awkwardly. "So," he said. He was already in the lane leading to the gate into the parking lot. There were six cars in front of him and another ten plus behind him. No place to turn around, and it suddenly occurred to him how foolish he was to think that this woman would go on a trip to Cancún with him for the weekend, out of the *country,* for Christ's sake. What had he been thinking? Sweat began to trickle down his chest, following the line of his muscles and pulling the fabric of his shirt against his skin like glue.

"Where are we going?"

Finally, the Question. Good timing too; it would be awkward but not impossible—forgotten tickets would do it—to convince the parking lot attendant to let him go in, turn around, and come back out. "Cancún," he said as nonchalantly as he could. "Do you like Mexican food?"

"Yes."

Paying the attendant and collecting the ticket was like watching something done in a dream by someone else, turning him into an absurdly somnambulistic voyeur. He drove to the first available space and they both got out; she helped him pull the top up on the Puma without being asked, and waited patiently as he went to the trunk—which was actually the hood, since the Puma's engine compartment was in the rear—to get his overnight bag. Before he pulled it out, he dumped half the contents, most of it stuff he'd packed because Audrey would expect it to be there: a carefully folded dress shirt and tie, a pair of khaki slacks rolled in a towel to keep them from wrinkling, a bottle of hair gel and cologne he'd never really liked. Audrey wasn't a bad woman, just a . . . *stable* one who came with all the stodgy expectations of an adult whose feet were as firmly planted as an oak tree. This weekend was his chance to be a sapling. When Gabe lifted it clear, the bag was considerably lighter.

"I'm ready," he announced, then immediately felt foolish. This woman—Lilah—didn't have so much as a change of clothes. Whatever she carried in her small beige pocketbook was it.

"Yes." Gabe started to take a step toward her and hesitated, still thinking about the clothes thing and suddenly wondering if he could touch her—what would Lilah do if he put his hand on her arm? He had no idea. She cocked her head to the side and looked at him expectantly, then smiled. "Don't worry. I don't need a bag. I'll pick up the essentials when we get there. What time is the flight?"

Gabriel glanced at his watch. "We have forty-five minutes," he said hoarsely. "The traffic—"

"It's not much time," she agreed. "Shall we get going?"

He nodded and took a tentative step, then another, and another. She fell smoothly into stride next to him, long legs clad in slightly shimmery stockings, easily matching his pace. She was taller than Audrey by a good three inches—taller than him—and the thought unnerved him slightly. When they danced in the hotel lounge tonight—*would* they?—she would be looking down at him. He tried to imagine how she would feel in his arms, and felt himself start to sweat again as they crossed the parking lot and waited for the shuttle bus, unpleasant moisture snaking from under his arms to dribble down his rib cage. She was slender to the point of being bony, and he hadn't held a woman like that in years, not since a girl in high school whose name he couldn't remember. He wanted to drape his arm around her shoulders and hug her just to find out if his impression was true, but he resisted.

The terminal was as crowded as Gabe expected, and he stepped to the luggage check-in with the woman at his side in a sort of customized fog, clear but warped vision graying out slightly at the edges, as if the world beyond the two of them didn't exist. Check-in stalled momentarily when the ticket agent looked at Lilah suspiciously and asked for luggage; Gabriel waited for the axe to fall, wielded by this mousy airline employee and her malicious sense of being able to play God over helpless, harried travelers. But Lilah surprised him again with her smoothness, a simple chuckled story about being late for the flight and leaving it in the taxi. "We've already called the cab company," she told the agent with a serene expression. "They promised to be on the lookout, but we"—here she shot a compan ionly glance in Gabriel's direction—"know we'll never get it back." She shrugged prettily. "I'll just buy what I need there. A few T-shirts, shorts, and jeans— it's not the end of the world." Mollified, the agent stamped the airplane ticket and waved them toward the security checkpoint. Not even a hitch here for Lilah, while every bell in the unit went off for Gabriel and they nearly made him strip before they were satisfied he wasn't carrying a concealed weapon. At last the couple walked side by side up the boarding ramp and found their seats.

He let Lilah have the window.

Things started getting scary as soon as they stepped out of the airport and into the hot, dry air of sunny Mexico.

Gabriel couldn't have said why or what it was about Lilah that changed, but it was something in her eyes as she looked around the crowds of light-complected tourists and darker-skinned natives scurrying among taxis and vendors and little boys who wanted to play packhorse for an American dollar. Lilah's eyes were an intriguing shade of green to begin with, but the Mexican sun . . . *did* something to them, deepened them and cleared them out. Gone was any resemblance to the antique pieces of jade jewelry Gabriel had thought of when he'd first seen her; instead the gaze fixing him now left him feeling as if he were drowning, falling deep into a bottomless, tropical lake overlooked by impossibly luxuriant plant life. He might have passed it off as excitement or interest, except that when her gaze made the circuit and returned to him, it darkened even more and made him feel like a baby antelope frozen in the killing view of a hungry lioness.

"So," he said lamely. "Here we are." It was the best he could do, given the overwhelming sense of dread that inexplicably bled through his nerve endings.

"Yes."

Lilah smiled at him, and for a moment the brash woman in the parking lot returned and Gabriel told himself to relax. Of course he would be afraid; he was a couple thousand miles from home with a total stranger—and no one knew where he was, although Lilah didn't know that. It occurred to him that he still didn't know her last name, but instinct told him now was not the time to ask; over dinner maybe, after a cocktail or two. In the meantime, there was the matter of the hotel room. "Let's grab a taxi," he suggested. "We'll check in at the hotel and get settled, then see what we can line up for the evening."

"Sounds wonderful." She made no move to do or say anything else, so he stepped toward the first taxi in line at the curb. The driver was out in an instant, chattering so rapidly that Gabriel, whose Spanish was confined to long-ago high school courses and occasional vacations, had to struggle to understand. He kept his overnight bag with him and held the door for Lilah as she climbed into the back. "The Hyatt," he directed the driver as he slid in next to her. "And go *slow*. They drive like maniacs here," he said to Lilah by way of explanation. He expected her to say something back, but she didn't; he wondered when and if she was going to start talking. She would talk, wouldn't she? About Cancún, the weather here or back in the States, herself—

"Why did you want to meet me?" he asked suddenly. He couldn't stand it anymore. Their flight might have been a nonstop but it was still a big chunk of time in which he'd naively thought she would spill everything, *explain* it all. If she thought he was prying, then so be it. She'd just come into the resort on a six-hundred-dollar airplane ticket he'd paid for . . . nope, scratch that. *Audrey* had paid for her own mystery ticket, not him. Jesus, he thought and not for the first time in the last few hours, I must be out of my ever-loving mind. How the hell am I going to fix this when I get back?

If I get back.

The niggling little sentence zinged in from the outfield of his brain, without reason or basis for suspicion. That, Gabriel decided, was what bothered him about this . . . *feeling* he was having—that there *was* no reason for it, just primitive intuition. He was still waiting for her answer, and he glanced over at her now, noticing her outfit for the first time. It was a business suit—lightweight tan and cream tweed—that had been so conservative and well-matched to his car's interior that he'd hardly registered it back in the parking lot or on the flight. It no longer seemed conservative; as a matter of fact, the fabric, color, even the *fit,* had gone through some odd and not-at-all subtle shift, and suddenly Gabriel couldn't stop himself from openly staring. The nearly colorless shell top she'd worn underneath the jacket had disappeared, and any resemblance to tweed had likewise vanished; the silky, slightly iridescent two-piece suit dress that encased Lilah now looked more like a shimmering golden snakeskin that was difficult to see against the smudged yellowish fabric of the taxi's backseat.

"You haven't answered my question," he said hoarsely. "Why me?"

Lilah never actually turned her head, but Gabriel could feel her gaze slide toward him, saw the motion under the finely veined skin of her eyelids. "Because you needed me."

Gabe frowned. "I needed you? But that doesn't make any sense. I don't even *know* you."

"Here we are *señor y señora,"* the driver interrupted. "La Hotel Hyatt." His movements strained, Gabe reached into his pocket and pulled out pesos as the driver came around to open the back door for them. Lilah gave Gabriel another of her smooth smiles but didn't elaborate further.

He didn't have time to think about how they looked coming into the hotel. The place was fabulous, more opulent than his travel agent had promised. Tropical plants crowded every available niche of the cavernous lobby amid plush, royal-blue chairs and settees. The floor was made of thick, multicolored tiles that swirled in a dizzying pattern starting at the registration desk and continuing outward to the thick carpeting that divided the lobby from the lounging area. Gabriel had already gotten the attention of one of the clerks when he realized how awkward it would be for Lilah; while the weekend had been a planned surprise, he'd included Audrey's name on the registration.

"Buenos tardes, señor." The clerk wore a name tag that said *Lupe;* she looked like a teenager, and Gabe felt his cheeks start to redden. He glanced sideways at Lilah, then jerked. A quick glance over his shoulder placed her across the lobby, settled onto a heavily cushioned couch in front of a planter stuffed with huge, leafy ferns. Gabriel turned back to the registration clerk, then stuttered and had to swallow as his brain processed what his eyes had seen. That damned suit dress was gone, replaced by a satin sundress with thin

straps and huge, golden sunflowers against a backdrop of deep green, the same color as the foliage behind her. He heard the clerk clear her throat politely. *"Señor?"*

Gabriel whipped his head around. "Uh—yes!" The clerk winced at his too-loud voice, and he gritted his teeth, found a steel fist somewhere inside himself and let it come down and close around his frazzled nerves, the latest in mental get-a-grip methods. When Gabe spoke again, his voice was calm and even. "I have a reservation for two under the names Onwei and Zantowitz."

A few taps into her computer terminal and the clerk nodded. *"Sí.* And your *señora* is in the lounge area?"

"There's been a change in plans," he said. He hoped he didn't sound too stiff. "The other party couldn't make it. Miss Lilah—" Here he nearly did stumble, then abruptly made something up. "—Johnson should be substituted."

"Ah." A quick nod accompanied by a sly glance at Lilah sprawled sexily on the couch across the lobby. "We will change the name, *sí?"*

"Yes," Gabriel agreed. He suddenly felt very tired. "Do you have a room with two double beds in it?"

"Don't be silly, darling." The voice slid over his left shoulder like warm syrup, left the words hanging in the air between him and the hotel clerk like an invisible sweet treat. "Why on earth would we want separate beds?" Lupe blinked and looked uncomfortable, as though she'd been both abruptly outclassed and had interrupted an intimate couple in a private room. She wasn't the only one; Gabriel knew he was beyond blushing now, he must be downright *scarlet.* Lilah decided to take pity on him and smiled gently at Lupe. "He thinks I need an entire bed just for my luggage. Men are so silly sometimes, don't you think?"

Lupe smiled back, and Gabriel marveled at how cleverly Lilah had put her at ease, wondered how the clerk could fall for that line when there was no pile of suitcases to be seen. It didn't matter; he was sure Lilah would have another answer ready if Lupe asked. *"Sí."* Lupe nodded her head and her voice dropped confidentially. "My—how do you say it—*boyfriend,* he is the same way." The two women chuckled together as if they were old friends, and Gabriel suppressed a snide comment; he felt oddly left out, *jealous* of this sudden camaraderie. "Here are your keys, *sí?* The busboy, he will help you with . . ." Her voice trailed off and Gabriel had a short—

very short—moment of vindication when Lupe realized there *was* no luggage other than the nylon bag Gabriel clutched in one sweaty fist. ". . . your luggage?" She looked at Lilah in confusion.

"The concierge already has it," Lilah said suavely. "We didn't want to leave it outside or somewhere in the lobby."

"Of course. Enjoy your stay, *por favor.*" Lupe smiled and looked strangely relieved. Gabriel wondered if she was expected to do something if she caught a guest in the hotel in a lie. Perhaps make them stand in the corner, he thought absurdly. He fought the bray of laughter that wanted to explode from his mouth, and won, at least for now, by realizing he was on the edge of hysteria, and yes, it was his own fucking fault.

Lilah's fingers left trails of heat when her hand wormed between his rib cage and arm, then settled comfortably into the crook of his elbow. "Let's go to the room, shall we?" Gabriel opened his mouth, ready to let the words spill out so that Lupe, *someone,* would rescue him—*No, I don't want to. I don't know you and we shouldn't be here. I've never seen this woman before this afternoon. May I go home now?*—and Lilah's mouth covered his in a kiss that nearly sent him reeling. He didn't know how she'd gone from holding onto his arm to standing in front of him, and he didn't care; there was nothing in the world but the feeling of her lips against his, fiery but weirdly cool, like jalapeño ice cream melting across his mouth in this hot, hot climate. For an instant her tongue slipped past the threshold of his mouth and branded his own with that cold, spicy taste; then it was gone and she was staring up at him. Had her eyes been almond-shaped on the plane? He couldn't remember, he couldn't *breathe,* where the hell did he find the air he needed to speak the words of agreement? Maybe he'd only nodded.

The room was a paradise that seemed to be decorated solely to match the flamboyant sundress Lilah now wore. He had time, but only briefly, to wonder if what she wore would have been different had the room's colors been something else—red, or perhaps shades of gray and black. The first thing she did was duck into the bathroom, and when she came out, Gabriel's jumbled mind finally offered up the word he'd been searching for to describe her: *chameleon.* He felt a flash of triumph, then realized she was changing faster now, and was it a thing of conscious willpower or did Lilah simply respond to her environment, to the emotions that were happening around her? The stranger who stood in front of him and slipped her fingers expertly down the row of buttons on his shirtfront wore something that might have been silk or might have been satin, or maybe a little of both—emerald-green shot through with gold filigree threads, and Jesus Christ, Gabriel thought, I don't think there's more than a yard of fabric to the whole thing.

"Come lie with me," Lilah whispered into his ear.

Wordlessly, Gabriel looked down as her hand darted inside his open shirtfront and her fingers did a peculiar hot/cold dance across the muscles of his chest, raising a trail of chill bumps behind them. Sudden heat blossomed in his midsection, then blasted into the rest of his body with so much intensity his knees nearly gave out. For a few seconds he wobbled like a drunk, then Lilah sidestepped and turned him, in one uninterrupted movement, in the direction of the king-sized bed sprawling beneath a huge window that gave a panoramic view of the Caribbean Sea. The last of his protests seemed to have been left at the registration desk, and it didn't take much of a push to make him go down.

Lilah glided next to him, the shiny, scalloped fabric of the teddy she now wore hugging the exquisite contours of her breasts and hips with such perfection that it could have been body paint, or maybe an iridescent snakeskin with all the hues of a stained-glass window. Gabriel reached for her hungrily and she let him, never played coy or shy, guiding his hands to her most intimate spaces when he hesitated. At one point he felt like he was touching hot oil, slick and sensuous against his skin, inescapable; at another he felt like there was no substance to her skin, nothing at all, like wild, white smoke rather than flesh surrounding his body.

Usually so quiet and conservative, Gabriel screamed when he came.

They'd been here too long. Gabriel couldn't exactly calculate *time* anymore; he'd lost his watch somewhere, and while he could have sworn there had been a clock or two in the room, at least a digital alarm clock on the bedside table, Lilah seemed to have disposed of them sometime during their stay. The room and all their meals were taken care of by the credit card he'd presented at the registration desk—they hadn't eaten anywhere but the hotel restaurants, and he'd been charging it all to their room. His mind was so fogged he couldn't even recall how many times he'd opened his eyes to find morning sun slanting off the waves of the ocean. It might have been two . . . but it might've been ten—*weeks*, not

days. Surely by now he'd lost his job, his girlfriend, his *life,* all
because of a crazy impulse. It wasn't Lilah's fault that he'd gone for
it and left . . . what on earth was her *name?* Jesus, he couldn't
remember that either. Climbing into his car had been the same
thing for Lilah, an impulse, and while she might be a little strange,
moody and uncommunicative, Gabriel had begun to believe that
the thing with her wardrobe, the way her skin just sort of . . .
melted into whatever she wanted, was nothing more than his
heated imagination. He was out of his mind, of course. Why else
would he even be here?

Audrey.

Well, at least he wasn't totally daft. What was Audrey doing
now? Calling his apartment? His job? Probably, and beyond—by
now his mother and father knew he had simply chucked it all and
disappeared with an unknown woman. Maybe they thought he was
kidnapped and were waiting for a ransom note, checking their mail
and answering machines daily, even forcing his landlord to let
them into his apartment to see what they could see. Like three
blind mice, running in useless circles, while he was trapped here
with Lilah.

He couldn't leave, he simply didn't have the strength. It was as
though she was some sort of female spider that had wrapped him
in a cocoon of physical ecstasy from which he could not, *would not,*
pull free. Lilah was the one who made him eat, made him bathe,
made him dress—he cared about none of those things anymore.
All he wanted was her touch on his skin, her mouth against his, her
smoky oil flesh encircling his center. He wanted to live that way, he
wanted to die that way. He wanted to *be* that way.

He would never leave her.

"You're getting old." Lilah's voice was a whisper in the dark
room, the edges of each word stretching out and out and out like
the hiss of a snake. Gabriel could remember almost nothing before
Cancún and Lilah and this room, but the memories since then
were sharp and fresh, like ice fragments dropped into a glass by an
ice crusher. Their first time together, that was it, when the sexy
teddy she'd worn had looked like the shimmering skin of a snake.
That's what her voice reminded him of now.

"I am?" Something in her tone scared him inexplicably. They
couldn't have been together *that* long, not for the years it would
take for him to be considered *old.* Could they? He was only on his

third credit card, for Christ's sake, and it had taken . . . how long? Months, maybe, not so long in the scheme of a life, to push the amount on the first two to where the companies denied him further credit. Hell, he had a whole walletful to use before they'd have anything to worry about. "Why do you say that?"

Next to him, Lilah stretched. She looked like a painted cat, with her arms reaching gracefully above her head and her legs, long and sleek, pulling out behind her. Gabriel could think of no way to describe the scrap of material she wore, other than that it was white, like the sheets on which she languished, not-quite-shiny and as soft as Lilah's own flesh. It covered just enough to make her more enticing. They'd been in bed since last night, and there were spots on her skin that he didn't remember seeing before, freckles that matched his own, as if she were trying to mirror his flesh.

"You should look in the mirror." Her tone of voice was unaccountably cruel, and for some reason it hit Gabriel that she'd never, *ever* used his name. He grabbed for her arm, impressed with his own quick movement, but it wasn't fast enough. She twisted away before his fingertips could barely brush her wrist. "What's my name?" he demanded.

For the first time in their short—or was it long?—relationship, Lilah looked confused. Perhaps no one had ever caught her before. "What?"

"What's my name?" he repeated. "You have no idea, do you? You don't remember—no, you never even *listened* when I told you!"

"Don't be absurd," she snapped. She was up and off the bed nearly too fast for his eyes to track. "Your mind doesn't even work right anymore. You've had it." She headed toward the bathroom, and Gabriel blinked. For a stupid moment he thought her clothes were changing with her as she hurried across the room.

"Lilah, wait," he pleaded. Fear, unfounded, inexplicable terror, rose in him. "Let's not fight—"

She paused at the bathroom door and turned to stare at him. He'd finally gotten used to the way her eyes changed to match her clothes and her surroundings, but today they were black and hellish, like nothing they'd been before. "Forget it," she said coldly. "You're all used up and I'm through with you." She slammed the door.

Gabriel tried to run to the bathroom door, tangled himself in the sheets and fell on his face, literally, was glad later that he hadn't broken his nose when he saw the yellow and purple bruise that covered his right cheekbone. He clawed his way free and heard the spread rip, and when he got his feet to finally carry him forward, he felt like an old man who needed a cane as he lurched between the bed and the bathroom door and started pounding on it. "Lilah!" he shouted. "Open the door and talk to me, damn it!" The only response was the start of the shower, and it was useless to try and compete.

After three hours Gabriel started crying and pounding on the door again.

Eventually one of the housekeeping staff came to see if he was all right. The dark-haired maid didn't speak much English, but understood enough to use a key and unlock the bathroom door. Gabriel's fit of rage went into hysteria when the bathroom was empty and the maid called the front desk, which called the local *policía*. Before long the room was filled with dark-eyed Mexicans who told Gabriel with their eyes that the girlfriend whose last name he'd never known had simply left him for greener pastures. None of them could explain how the bathroom came to be locked from the inside, and none of them tried. It wasn't until Gabriel was on the airplane back to O'Hare that he remembered the bathroom's wildly colored shower curtain that hadn't seemed quite as bright the day before.

Gabriel's life in the States was a mess. His parents were at first worried, then furious; he was nearly twenty thousand dollars in debt on his credit cards; and his job was gone. He managed to get another one to keep his bills at bay, though he had to take a thirty percent pay cut and every month was a tap dance of minimum payments. His old boss had taken only one call from Gabriel—the first one—specifically to tell him there was no room in Jaynerson Electronics for someone prone to irrational behavior. Predictably, perhaps justifiably, Audrey had covered all the bases. He still had his apartment, but only by sheer luck; the landlord had used his security deposit to cover the delinquent months, and he had to push his last available credit card to its limit for a cash advance to replenish the deposit and pay a bunch of trumped-up late and interest charges.

The biggest loss, of course, was Audrey. He thought of her constantly, a mishmash of memories tinged with longing and anger, sometimes blaming himself for throwing it all away on an impulse, often blaming her as he decided if she'd kept things more interesting none of it would have happened, he would've never been tempted to drive away with Lilah—a sorry cop-out if there ever was one. His mind was working again, the mental filing cabinet back in order. Available on demand were memories of any number of wonderful evenings and years, family gatherings, immensely satisfying lovemaking, a future forever gone. No amount of begging or calls or flowers could fix the damage; she would have nothing to do with him, and in fact was already dating someone else. He'd never even had to think up a story to explain his actions; she wouldn't stay on the telephone once she heard his voice.

All those years wasted, and where would he find another woman like Audrey?

Or like Lilah?

Gabriel thought a lot about her, too, and the way her skin and body tasted, and the way she had melded into her surroundings and fit his body like her skin covered her own frame. His new job was still in sales, but in engineering and tool manufacturing, and now his hours ran with the shop's. He quit for the day at three-thirty and had plenty of time to make the drive from Elk Grove Village to the Schaumburg train station, and he spent at least two days a week—sometimes four, when he was feeling more desperate—just parked there, watching the trains and the people coming home from their downtown commute. He told himself that he did this in the hope that Audrey would see him and break down, decide to listen to what he had to say and try and pick up the pieces, or at least talk about it. In reality, he always parked where Audrey wouldn't see him when she disembarked; he was too afraid she'd think he was stalking her and get a restraining order. And what would he look like if he did try to speak with her? An old fool chasing her across the parking lot with tears dripping down his face and no shame in front of anyone. And he *was* old; Lilah hadn't been running at the mouth when she'd said that. He looked as if Lilah had taken something indefinable out of him, a couple of years of his life, or ten to be exact, if he considered the loss of the ten years he'd spent with Audrey.

The day Gabriel finally saw Lilah again was as different from the day she'd climbed into his car as South America was from the Arctic Circle. The temperature had been in the teens for two weeks and the trees were dry and bare, like thin, unwrapped mummies.

There was no snow, not yet, but everyone agreed that when it did come, the city and surrounding suburbs were in for a helluva load. Gabriel didn't care; he had chains in the trunk if he needed them, and was dressed to fit the cold interior of the Puma since the makers of the Brazilian convertible car hadn't really had a northern climate in mind when they designed it. Coming here had become such a habit, waiting one more routine in his empty life, that when Lilah walked across the corner of his vision, Gabriel did nothing. He'd always gotten drowsy just sitting in a car; his eyelids were open only to slits and he was burrowed into his parka and thinking more about his cold feet than Lilah or Audrey. Lilah was climbing into the passenger side of a forest-green Ford Explorer before he finally sat up.

He was out of the car too late.

"Wait!" he screamed at the Explorer. "Don't take her with you—*wait!*" He must have made enough noise to be heard through the rolled-up window, because the driver, a young man with a frightened but determined face, jerked his head around to stare as Gabriel pounded across the parking lot. The wind was picking up, determined to bring the snow it'd been holding for so long, and the feel of it on the uncovered skin of Gabriel's face was like being slapped with cold barbed wire. He was almost to the vehicle and he could see Lilah saying something to the driver, that exquisitely lipsticked mouth moving quickly, whatever she was saying punctuated by fluid, sensuous motions of her hand. He was close, so *close,* reaching for the handle of the driver's door when he met Lilah's gaze, old jade again. The smile she sent him was dark and instantaneous and made something white shimmer in front of Gabriel's eyes . . . the long-awaited snow? A sudden burst of it, a louder blast of heat and motion, and the driver of the Ford stomped the accelerator and left Gabriel breathing exhaust and speckled with bits of loose gravel.

A car chase was for people who wrote movies, and in the real world there was nothing Gabriel could do but walk back to the Puma and think about the look on the young man's face. There had been an odd expression on it, a mixture of triumph and erotic adventure, with a huge dose of hope thrown in. Had Gabriel looked like that to Audrey when he'd left her standing in this same parking lot? Or had he looked like that *before* Lilah had climbed into his car? Perhaps that expression had been the very thing that had drawn Lilah to him, a beacon for her. He'd never considered it, but maybe it wasn't *his* impulse that had destroyed his life, but *Lilah's*.

He would never know.

Funny, Gabriel thought as he stared bitterly after the vanished Ford Explorer, how things had come full circle. If the expression on his face so many months ago had matched that of the man who now captivated the elusive Lilah . . .

. . . then surely the look on his face today was a memorial to Audrey's.

DEAD GIRLS IN LOVE

Edward Lee and Gary Bowen

*W*ho's to say that the dead can't want the same things as the living? Melanie and Stephanie? That's all they wanted—they wanted love.

Was that so bad?

Love?

"The son of a bitch . . ."

"Stop dwelling on it."

"I—I *can't!* That prick! That lying, two-faced jock piece of shit!"

"Jesus Christ, Steph. It's been two months now. Can't you get over it?"

"No," Stephanie blurted. "I'm pissed, I can't help it! I can't believe how bad that prick pulled the wool over our eyes! The nutcase!"

They both had their moods; they both had their bad days. When it wasn't Melanie blubbering like a spoiled tot, it was Steph, cussing it up worse than a longshoreman. Melanie was the good little girl, the prim and proper, LSU Here I Come. Steph, on the other hand, had long since proved herself the family firebrand, one step up from black sheep status.

And for two months now the sisters had both lain dead in their graves.

At least the coffin liners were nice. White satin. Padded. Comfortable stuff. Certainly, eternity could be spent in worse ways—for instance, they could be in hell!

But the question never ceased to dumbfound them.

Why?

"Why?" Melanie queried. "Why are we like this? We're supposed to be dead."

"We *are* dead, oysterbrain," Steph replied. "We're in fucking coffins, for Christ's sake."

"Sure, smart-mouth, but if we're dead, how come we've been talking to each other for all this time? How come we can hear each other?"

Stephanie never had an answer for that one. What did it matter, though? Could anything matter when you're dead?

But feelings were power, weren't they? And Melanie and Stephanie Brown had *a lot* of feelings. So maybe that's what kept them talking in their tombs, enabling them to even hear one another through the soil that separated them. Their emotions. The subcorporeal remnants of their hearts.

And now here they were, side by side in the family plot. They'd both been seniors at Largo High. Melanie had turned eighteen last fall, Stephanie was nineteen, held back a year due to a certain lack of academic motivation. After the accident, their parents had them dressed up nice for their interment: matching white sequin evening gowns. Tacky, Steph thought. Melanie didn't mind, though. She liked dressing up, even when she was dead. One of the pathology technicians had squeezed Steph's breast on the morgue slab. "At least it was a good squeeze," she'd said later, underground.

"Stephanie! You're impossible!"

"Hey, it was a better squeeze than Willy ever gave me!"

They both laughed like what they were: dead high school girls.

But here arrived the sore point. Willy. Willy Parks. Good-looking. Cool. Star halfback on the varsity football team. Every girl in school had the hots for him, and Melanie and Steph were two of the lucky ones. They'd both actually dated him.

But the problem was they'd dated him at the same time, and didn't know it.

"You're *horrible!*" Melanie wailed when she'd first found out. It had taken them a month of casual chitchat in their graves before they realized what had happened. "I can't believe you could do something like that to your own sister!"

"How did I know he was fucking you the same time he was fucking me!" Steph objected. "I'm not too happy about it either, you know!"

For a full week Melanie scarcely spoke. She'll get over it, Steph figured. And what was she mad about anyway? This was all her fault to begin with.

"Talk about women drivers!" Stephanie had raged.

Melanie pouted. "You're blaming me? It was an accident! You heard the policeman! It was brake failure!"

"Yeah, Melanie, and maybe you didn't know this, but when you own a car, you're supposed to check the brakes." Another sore point, which Steph took, literally, to her grave. When Melanie made the honor roll, Mom and Dad gave her a brand-new red Miata convertible for her birthday. All Steph got was a pair of goddamn rollerblades, but of course, she'd never made the honor roll in her life.

"You did check the brakes, didn't you?"

"What do I look like? Mr. Goodwrench? How do I know how to check *brakes,* for God's sake?" Melanie had griped right back. "Don't try to blame me by saying I didn't take care of the car, because I did!"

"You did, huh? How?"

"I put gas in it whenever the tank got low."

Great. And she drove like a maniac to boot. Hadn't been paying the least bit attention. They'd been on their way to cheerleader tryouts. Melanie hadn't seen the flatbed truck in front of them, too busy changing the radio station. BANG! That's what it sounded like. Too bad neither had been wearing their seat belts. Steph's head smacked the windshield; her neck broke. Melanie, on the other hand, had fared a bit worse: the back of that truck was loaded with steel roofing girders, one of which plowed right into her pretty face. The morticians didn't even try. At least my coffin was open at the wake, Stephanie thought. My sister is such a dick!

"I blame Willy," Melanie cited once she started talking again. "The only reason we were trying out for cheerleaders is because we wanted to impress him."

Good point, even from a dead girl. "I just hate him *so much,*" Steph seethed. "When I think back to all the times he told me he loved me, I could puke. He'd always say I was the most beautiful girl he'd ever been with."

Melanie started crying. "Oh, Stephanie! He told me the same exact thing!"

"That two-timing, double-dipping piece of shit. Boy, was I stupid."

"We both were."

Steph shook her head in her casket, her eyes narrowed to slits in percolating rancor. "I just . . . hate him . . . so much. . . ."

Hence, their underground lament. All I ever wanted was to be in love, Steph thought, though that would be too sappy to actually say out loud. But Melanie felt similarly. What they wanted more than anything—love—was something they'd never have now. How could they? They were six feet under!

They weren't bad girls. Perhaps Melanie was a trifle inept, and maybe a little pretentious. And Stephanie, of course, had a predilection for profanity. But they weren't *bad,* were they? They weren't selfish and malicious and greedy like so many people these days. What? For wanting *love?*

So here came the alchemy of their honest desires; with nowhere for their love to go, it could only revert, ferment, and change. To hatred.

One strong emotion transposing to another . . .

Melanie was sniffling again. "How many, I mean, how many . . ."

"How many *what?*" Steph griped, frowning. At least she still had a face to frown with. She supposed she shouldn't be so inconsiderate: the accident hadn't left Melanie with much more than a plop of ground chuck for a visage. But she hated it when her sister whined and sniffled.

"How many times . . . did you—you know."

"No, I don't know, Melanie. Jesus Christ. And quit sniffling. Quit being such a baby."

"How many times did you do it with him!" the more refined sister finally blurted.

Steph's thoughts ticked back. "I don't know. A bunch. Couple of dozen, I guess."

"A couple of *dozen!*"

"Yeah, what's the big deal? How many times did he do you?"

A pause, another sniffle. "Three times . . ."

"That's all? Jeeze. Hey, did he ever go down on you?"

Melanie would've blushed, were her ruined face capable. "No . . ."

"Me either. He ever get you off?"

"Uh-uh."

Steph nodded; she should've known. "That's all men are, you know—life support for a cock. All they care about is getting off themselves. A couple of quick humps and they're out the door, back to the track meet or fucking football practice." Actually, this was about all either of them had left, their desires—and their lives—shortchanged by faulty brakes. They had nothing left to do now but constantly recycle their contemplations of the perfidy of the male species. At least he could kiss good, Stephanie reckoned. At least he was cute.

Her fists clenched in the cloistered box, her dead fingers opening and closing with her ire. "I hate that prick so much I could bust right out of this goddamn coffin and wring his neck."

"Good luck," Melanie countered. "We're *underground,* remember? We're under six feet of dirt."

"Yeah, but still . . ."

It was just so enraging, being this helpless. And what would become of them? Would they eventually rot to dust? Or would they jabber away down here for eternity, writhing in their hatred, turning over one regret after another?

"Stephanie, I . . ."

Steph sighed. "What is it *now?*"

"I . . . *feel* something. Don't you?"

"I don't know what you're talk—" But the sensation put a blade to the sentence. What *was* it? All at once, Stephanie's dead heart began to tingle. . . .

"I *do,*" she whispered back, enthralled. And what a bizarre feeling it was, electric, her soul crackling. Soon the tingle felt like beautiful white fire. Then:

"Stephanie!"

"What?"

"It's—It's *him!*" Melanie exclaimed.

My God, Steph realized, she's right. . . .

It *was* him, Willy Motherfuckin' Parks. That strange graveyard alchemy kicked up; she could hear him up there, she could hear his heart, his blood, his thoughts. She was *certain* of it!

Willy Parks was in the cemetery. . . .

"Someone's with him," Melanie cited.

"Yeah, a girl," Steph agreed. She could feel her too, sense her spirit and her aura. The footsteps encroached; the nameless girl laughed in a high-pitched giggle. "I've always wanted to make it in a cemetery, Willy!"

"Yeah, well," Willy Parks replied. "Me too. And *this* cemetery . . . is special."

"Special? Why?"

"Aw, never mind."

Steph simmered. "That despicable piece of *shit!* He's bringing his new girlfriend here. To fuck her on *our graves!*"

Once again Melanie was blubbering. "How awful! How can people be so awful!"

Six feet above them, beer tabs popped. More laughter fluttered up into the night. "This is great, isn't it?" Willy asked of his consort.

"Yeah," the girl replied. "But I still wanna know what you meant, about this graveyard being special."

Steph's face turned rigid; her hatred now, her complete and total outrage, made her burn even hotter. She could hear the very thoughts in his head. . . .

Yeah, Willy Parks thought. *This place is special, all right. I'm about to fuck this chuckhead right on top of Steph and Melanie's graves!*

Melanie's sobs went rampant. Steph's hatred pounded on.

And so did Willy's thoughts above them:

And what a couple of putzes they were, jeeze! That stuck-up whining snoot Melanie, and then Steph—what a redneck slut! Boy, did I love fucking those two bitches, and, shit, they thought I loved them! What suckers. Christ, girls must've gotten wads of shit when they were passing out brains.

"Steph!" Melanie blubbered. "Did you hear that! He said I was a stuck-up whining *snoot!*"

"I heard the son of a bitch," Steph replied more calmly. *A redneck, huh, Willy?* Her dead skin burned. *A redneck slut?*

Willy laughed, sipping his beer. *And what a job I did on the two of them! Am I brilliant or what? Cutting that brake line, what a trip! I should get a medal for offing those two bimbos!*

Now Melanie was screeching. "Did you—did you—hear *that?*"

"I sure as shit did," Steph croaked, clenching her fists so hard she could've crushed rocks. "That motherfucker *killed* us!"

But now Willy was talking again. "Oh, honey, you make me so hot, Christ." Wet kissing sounds could be heard intermittently. His voice descended to a seductive whisper. "You're the most beautiful girl I've ever been with. . . ."

That did it. Steph snapped. At once, all those feelings converged, all that lost love replaced by the truth of real hatred. Suddenly she was bulling forward in the coffin, not really even thinking. She pushed against the lid, screamed, pushed again, and—

crack!

—the coffin lid split.

"Come on, Melanie!" she shouted. "We can do it! I know we can! Dig!"

And dig they did. Steph's hands eventually pushed the coffin lid completely apart, and then the concrete grave liner. Paydirt! she thought, pun intended. Her hands were tillers before her face, cutting the hard-packed soil. She chewed her dead lip, maniacal now in her determination. Cool earth crumbled and fell away as her slim body burrowed ever upward.

Then the earth broke. . . .

Moonlight glared in her eyes, moonlight in a black sky and a sea of stars. That first breath of air—the first in months—burst into her lungs. Her strength surged. It was so good to be above ground again.

And it was even better to see Willy . . .

Her dead eyes beamed; she drooled, it was so exciting. Then the rest of her body erupted from the earth.

Willy, ever the gentleman, had already pulled open his new girlfriend's black blouse, and had her black-leather skirt hiked up, and he—he was going down on her. . . .

Christ, he sounds likes a dog eating a pile of Alpo, Steph thought. Then she said, "How come you never went down on me, you selfish asshole?"

Willy looked up and, quite reasonably, screamed. The girl screamed too, once she took note of the dirt-caked corpse crawling forward through the night air. And—What a floozy! Steph concluded. A post-punk little tramp with black lipstick, Nine Inch Nails buttons, and Kool Aid–colored hair. "You gotta be shitting me, Willy! You dumped me and Melanie for this little dance-club bitch?"

Willy screamed again, while his inanely dressed paramour scurried away, her own screams flying into the night like screeching tires.

Steph was all over him at once, her smudged, white sequins sparkling. "Bimbos, huh?" she inquired of his past remark. "A redneck slut, huh?" She hauled his pants off as he kicked and flailed and screamed. "Cut the brake line, huh?"

Her dead fingers roamed his crotch, and she noted with some

satisfaction that his penis seemed intent on withdrawing back into his body. "Yeah, big man, the big football star. Well, look how big you are now, you worthless piece of garbage."

Melanie, thus far, had only managed to get her head out of her grave. "Hi, Willy," the head said.

Willy screamed again—he'd taken to screaming a lot tonight—when he saw the pulped, desiccated face speaking to him below pretty blond bangs. He screamed so hard, in fact, that the whites of his eyes began to hemorrhage.

"Come on, will you," Steph urged. "We've got work to do."

Eventually, Melanie managed to unearth herself. "You're the last guy who's ever gonna call me a stuck-up snoot." Steph laughed, fondling Willy's shrunken balls, while Melanie hoisted her dress. Willy screamed high and hard, loud as a truck horn. But then the scream cessated, when Melanie sat on his face.

"Lick, Willy." Steph chuckled. "All those times you used us to get your rocks off, well . . . now you're gonna get *us* off."

At first he fought and fought, but soon discerned that even his own jock strength was no match for scorned corpses. So Willy proceeded as ordered. He was a trooper, they had to give him that. Not many guys could so unhesitantly perform the act of cunnilingus on an eighteen-year-old girl two months dead and fresh out of her grave. Then the peeled eyes in Melanie's rawmeat face widened. She began to squirm. "I—oh! Steph! I think I just came!"

"Good for you," her sister commented. "Now it's my turn." Steph hoisted her own grave-sullied dress and assumed the position, noticing in the interim that Willy's face had turned a delightful shade of green. She plopped her putrescent pubis right on his mouth. "Lick, shithead," she commanded. The sensation was delicious, Willy's lying tongue roving the ragged vulva and distended clitoris. "That's not bad." Her eyes closed and she smiled up into the night. The sensations rose, wavelike, then crested, and Steph came in a series of shuddering throbs. But then—

"Oops!" she blurted, giggling.

Upon the final spasms of her orgasm came a sudden and unbidden release of embalming fluid, leftover urine, and other nameless putrefactive slop, which, to Willy's regret, emptied directly into his mouth. She climbed off and immediately palmed his jaw shut, whereupon he was forced to swallow the noxious flood of ichor.

"I'm so sorry, Willy," came Steph's mock apology. "What a rude thing for me to do, but then—what do you expect from a redneck?"

Willy's belly convulsed, and when he inadvertently glanced up at Melanie's car-wreck face, he threw up in grand style, the gush of vomit flying feet into the air.

"And—how do you like that?" Steph then remarked of the slew of gastric bilge. Chunks of sausage and pepperoni floated in the acrid puddle. "He bought her *pizza,* for God's sake! What a cheapskate!"

Only then, though, did Steph become aware of her sister's quietude. During the vomit fiasco, Melanie remained preoccupied, twisting Willy's scrotum around and around and around—

"Melanie!" Steph laughed. "You little dickens!"

—and then—*pop!*—gave it one good hard yank. The scrotum popped out of his groin like a tomato plucked off a vine.

Yet again Willy Parks screamed, and as his mouth went agape to do so, Melanie greedily stuffed the severed testicles into his maw.

"Be a good boy and eat them," Steph cooed, again forcing his mouth closed. Eyes squeezed shut in disgust, his jaw began to work, begetting a sound like someone eating persimmons.

Gulp.

"Good boy!"

By now Willy didn't have a whole lot of kick left in him, and the girls, having had their fill, were growing bored. After all, what more could they do to the creep?

They decided not to kill him themselves; instead, they'd let the earth assume the task. And in the seeping moonlight, then, in the teeming, gorgeous night, they buried Willy Parks alive in Steph's grave, tamping the earth down nice and hard beneath their feet. It would probably only take minutes for death to claim him, but it did give them some amusement to hear a few last muffled screams.

"God, what a *mess* I am!" Melanie exclaimed. She stood up, brushing grave dirt from her glittering white dress. "I can't be seen like this!"

Jesus, Steph pondered. She's a walking corpse, and she's worrying about her dress!

Steph shrugged. She sat down, pulled a beer off the six-pack. A moment later Melanie, shredded face and all, sat down beside her.

Steph began reflectively, "It's funny. We just had our day, and I still feel—"

"I know," Melanie agreed. "Incomplete?"

Steph swigged some beer. "I mean, Christ, we even had orgasms, but—"

"They weren't very good, were they?"

"No."

The night continued to teem. They were two sister cadavers contemplating their new place in the universe.

Something was wrong. They'd just had a wonderful revenge, yet they still felt shortchanged, unrepayed. Something was missing. What was it?

Back to the power, to their emotions, which had churned them out of the hard-packed earth. Was that it? Jesus. They were *sisters!*

It was love, wasn't it? It was still love.

Burying Willy, and subjecting him to the smorgasbord of disgust that followed, had been gratifying, but it still hadn't made them whole. Dead or not, they were still young, vivacious girls, and, no, even in the vengeance, they had not attained the one thing they'd always wanted, always needed, to be as complete as any other young woman.

They still didn't have love, did they?

What the fuck was wrong with wanting that!

Jesus Christ! Steph thought. We're two goddamn corpses! What the hell are we gonna do now? Willy was dead, or would be shortly. Their vengeance was attained. How the hell were they gonna get what they really wanted now?

But then she thought of something . . .

Sure, Melanie was a ditz, and, yes, maybe she even was a stuck-up snoot. But she's my sister, she realized. And she's real, and I love her . . .

"Hey," Steph said.

Melanie's rot-vermiculated face turned.

"I love you," Steph said. And with that profession, she put her arm around her dead sister's shoulder, turned her head, and kissed her on her corpse-swollen lips.

"We're all we've got now, sister," Steph said.

"I know," Melanie breathed.

Then, with happy tears in her dead eyes, Melanie smiled as best she could, and she returned the kiss.

GETTING WET

Alexa deMonterice

*O*h God! The end was coming. But then coming *was* the end. She laughed as she came, laughed at the ironic duality of it. To have it all be over, and the disappointment in that inevitability, and yet the sheer thrill of anticipation that went with it. Wasn't that almost as great as this moment of nerve explosion—every tactile sense from the roots of her hair to the tips of her toenails died for these exquisite seconds, only to experience glorious rebirth in her clitoris, spreading outward and rushing along her trembling thighs as they clenched and unclenched around the curves of her lover's head. His nose, lips, eyelashes, and cheekbones becoming one with her as she pulled at his head, trying to suck him inside her.

Then it was over. And just like all those times before, she ended up alone, having to clean up the mess while telling herself that this one had been the best and that he would be the last. But she had never really believed that, no matter how many times she had told it to herself. Because didn't she always have to try again just in case her last lover hadn't been the best? She knew she'd end up out there again after a while, trolling the endless sea of bars for her next fish. And when she hooked one, she always let them think *they* were the ones in control. But, of course, *she* held the rod. Again, more delicious duality.

One lover had compared her to Diane Keaton's character in *Looking for Mr. Goodbar*. Oh God! Too funny. She wasn't some sad, pathetic woman just out for a fuck to lessen her loneliness for a few hours. It was the *moment* she lived for. The moment when once again they thought *they* had the power, the magical ability to make her come; when, in fact, it was she who controlled it. It was her grinding and pushing and squeezing against their faces till she

had them right where she wanted them. I mean, who was going
down on who, huh? Whose head was captive between whose legs?
Who was not going anywhere until she decided? Me! Pretend
you're trying to get back to the womb, she'd tell them. This is
where life started for you and this is where you'll end with me
tonight. And you *will* love it. Being in control like that was almost
as thrilling as the orgasm.

Her excitement, her pleasure, was the only thing that mattered.
The pursuit of which should be a turn-on for her lover of the
moment as well. And if it wasn't, then they could get the hell out.
Actually, she'd only had to throw out one guy so far. She never
came out and told them she was only interested in getting *her* rocks
off. But she did make it pretty clear that she was particularly
interested in their oral skills. She screened them fairly well while
playing the coquette looking for a big, strong manly type. "Just
how much of a man are you, honey?" she'd purr. "Are you willing
to take the time to make me crazy, to make me beg for it?" She'd
usually punctuate the last with a squeeze of their thigh and a flick
of a long, lacquered nail along their fly. The prospect of a woman
begging for him to do it to her hit a man's ego right where it would
swell the most, so to speak. But, fortunately, she'd never had to
mess with *that* aspect of their anatomy. Uhh-uhhh. No way, honey.
She was directing the action, and after a face first visit between her
waxed thighs, neither she nor the man had any more need for
further activity.

She finished cleaning up the mess, changed the sheets and then
took a shower to wash away the sheen of sweat covering her body.
Afterward, she paused to stand nude in front of her full-length
mirror and admire herself as beads of water rolled off her hair and
down her breasts and stomach to mingle in the tightly curled nest
of hair below. Much better. Clean again. The only time she savored
sweat anywhere on her body was during her daily workout; muscles
straining against the weights, great gushes of breath powering her
on to the next rep, forcing her body to mold to her will. A body that
had graced the cover of a book on weight lifting. A physique that
had been featured in the movie *Pumping Iron Two—the Women.*
Her daily exertions had resulted in breasts that stood out and up
proudly, strong arms that could hold a man till she was good and
ready to let go, and thighs to die for.

She ran her hands over the white and pink scratches and scars on
her inner thighs, lingering over the newest ones. She liked them.

They were tribal marks of passage symbolizing the power of her womanhood. She continued to touch herself absently. She knew she couldn't possibly achieve the results she'd experienced earlier with her lover. Not even close. It frustrated her and offended her feminist sensibilities to be that dependent on a man. She had lonely female friends who told her they found pleasure in their own hands and fingers or with various electrical apparatuses. But that wasn't for her. She needed the feel of a warm, living man nuzzling her crotch, not a length of cold plastic or rubber.

She slipped into a silky nightgown, the soft material clinging to her damp form. It was as close to a lover's caress as she could hope for since her latest conquest was no more. Perhaps one night she should try just cuddling with one of them. After the sex, they were always gone. She sighed and slid beneath the crisp, clean sheets. It took her a long while to fall asleep, and then her dreams were troubled.

In only six shorts days her body spoke to her again. The urges were coming closer together, she realized with both nervousness and anticipation. But her body was insistent. It's time, it told her. It spoke softly: a gentle, feathery, moist tickle within her vagina. She knew that light, tingling kiss would turn into a pulsating ache of desire that could only be satisfied by a real kiss: a deep, wet, French kiss.

So, she gave into the feeling. She put on her tightest, shortest skirt—the crimson leather one. Red, the color of hot lust. A see-through black lace top, sans bra, and spike heels over shimmering stockings, completed her "fishing gear." Her hose glistened as she moved, like liquid poured into the form of shapely legs. After all, she thought, smoothing the clingy material over her thighs, fish needed water to swim their way toward her port. Time to get wet.

"My name is Cat," she lied to the second man who offered to buy her a drink. The first had had a jagged, chipped front tooth. It looked like it would hurt. This one's teeth were nice and even, if slightly stained by tobacco. That was okay, she wasn't planning to kiss him with her mouth.

"I'll have sex-on-the-beach," she purred at him. "I'm referring to the drink, of course. At least for now." Men loved it when she talked like that.

His opening line hadn't been the least bit clever. "What's a nice girl doing—"

She cut him off. "I'm not a nice girl," she said, and flipped her long, raven hair over her shoulders for emphasis, revealing the uninhibited state of her breasts beneath the peekaboo fabric. "But I am a little bit lonely." Two more lines they loved to hear. Naturally they all were sure they held the cure.

This guy was no different; he nipped at her hook. "I'm your man, honey."

Not so fast, she thought. She hadn't decided if she wanted to keep him or throw him back yet. She needed to check him out a bit more, look for the right signs.

The bartender set down her drink, sloshing some over the brim. "Ohhh, look. Lick it. Don't let it go to waste," she urged, offering her drink to Nice Teeth as she licked one side of the long length of glass.

He chuckled with delight at her suggestion and suggestiveness and lapped at the other side of her drink.

His tongue was longer than average and a bright pink from eating the maraschino cherries in his manhattans. How lovely, she thought.

To continue with her lure, she plucked the cherry out of his glass and broke off its stem. "Can you do this trick?" She demonstrated by popping it in her mouth and then after a few moments placed the resulting knotted stem in his drink.

He laughed again, his eyes sparkling with lust. He asked the bartender for another cherry. But, alas, he couldn't do anything to the stem with his long tongue except make it soggy.

By now the bartender, three other men, and a very drunk blond woman were all tonguing stems. Only one of the men and the woman produced a knot. She wasn't into her own sex; she preferred to wield her power over men. So, she tossed Nice Teeth away and glided over to Slick Tongue.

He needed no opening line with a tongue-twisting ability like that, but he was witty nonetheless. "Need I say more?" He laughed and held his entwined cherry stem out to her.

"Well, I don't know," she pouted, taking the stem from him and twirling it between her fingers. "I'm feeling kind of lonely. Can you help?"

"If you'll let me."

"Well, here I am," she said, and popped the stem, still moist with his saliva, into her mouth.

He moved his bar stool closer, bumping legs with her. "And here I come," he said with wink.

"Not right away, I hope." She winked back.

"Never, ever. I like to make it last a good long time. Through the night."

"That's good to hear. My last lover hardly lasted ten minutes."

"The pig! I promise I can make you happy."

"Maybe. But in the morning I'll be all alone, as always."

"Hey, wait a minute. We might be meeting in a bar and all, but who says I won't be around for breakfast? I make a mean omelette. And I could even come back after work and cook you dinner. You never know. So don't blow me off without giving yourself a chance to get to know me." He took her hand and pulled her to her feet. "Why don't we get out of this place and take a long walk by the beach and talk?"

She gaped at him. "You gotta be kidding."

"Okay, so you make me horny. But that doesn't mean I don't like to get a bit better acquainted with someone before I sleep with them."

She went with him, too stunned to resist. A guy who wanted to waste time talking?

"I've never done anything like this," she found herself telling him before she could stop herself. God! She was losing control of the situation.

"I take it you're referring to strolling on the beach hand in hand? You strike me as someone who's picked up her share of guys in bars."

"The answer to both would be yes."

"It's kind of a nice feeling—this hand-holding thing—isn't it?" He gave her hand a squeeze and tugged her closer to the lapping waves.

"I guess. I—I'm not sure." She dug her bare toes into the sand, letting the water swirl over them. "I've felt loneliness before . . . and certainly desire . . . and sometimes rage as well. But this . . ."

"You're a sad, strange woman, Cat," he said, gazing into her eyes under the moonlight as the ocean foam kissed their ankles.

"I . . ." She trailed off again, breaking eye contact. She was lost in her own tide of alien emotions. Here she was with a man who had gone along with her sexual banter; who wanted to fuck her;

who looked at her breasts, legs, and ass just like all the others. And yet he had taken the time to look her in the eyes as well, and maybe even gotten a glimpse of her soul. She felt something strange. Strange because it wasn't in her loins, but closer to her heart. No one had ever touched her there, and it scared the hell out of her. She could deal with scars on her thighs, but not on her insides. I've lost control, she thought in a panic. She gazed out at the ocean, thinking, that's me: soft and fluid one moment, powerful and crushing the next. She preferred the latter, more comfortable with the role of a dominatrix than an equal partner, or—God forbid— a submissive one. Give me back the dualities I know best, she thought. Love/hate, good/evil, beginnings/endings, life/death . . . fucking versus making love . . . No! She couldn't let *that* happen.

By the time they got back to her place, his hand a now familiar presence in hers, she was positively shell-shocked. She had lied to this guy about almost everything, including her name, and he'd practically fallen in love. What did it mean if he cared for this pretend person, the fictitious Cat? What would he say if he knew the real woman, not the one beneath the leather and lace, but deeper still? Whatever he might say at her truth, it would probably begin with a scream. He could never understand.

"Are you all right? You've gotten so quiet." He caressed her silky hair with his fingers.

"Yes," she lied some more, and then offered him some truth. "This is all so new to me."

"A relationship? A romance? This is foreign to you?"

"Yes!" The word ripped from her in anguish, and she pulled away from him. "You're not just offering to scratch my itch. You want to make me breakfast and sit around and read the paper with me!"

"Cat . . . look, if you'd rather, I'll just leave."

"Yes. No. I . . ."

He stopped her with a kiss on her mouth, and her senses reeled with combined passion and fear. His lips, tongue, and arms were firm, yet gentle. He began to undress her as if he were unwrapping fine china from a box it had been enclosed in for too long.

He whispered soft endearments over the taut muscles of her flesh. His tenderness was almost too painful to bear. And when his kisses crept toward her belly and below, she began to silently cry. He was so unlike all the others; it was like having sex with an alien creature. He'd told her his name, but she still thought of him as Slick Tongue. And it was an apt nickname: his tongue was moist and broad and he was able to make it temporarily rigid as he penetrated her with it and then sucked it back, along with her clit, into his mouth, making her gasp and clench his hair in her fists. She very nearly got off on that alone, but he made sure to leave her just on the brink, and she was horrified to realize she was ready to beg for it. No man had ever driven her so crazy with desire.

And then, the unthinkable happened: for the first time in two and a half years, she felt a man's long, throbbing rod of flesh enter her. And instead of pain and violation, she felt pleasure and something else: Joy? Love? It was indefinable. She was awash in a sea of liquid sensation, flowing with the fluid feel of him inside her—drowning.

Never before had she enjoyed the traditional coupling of naked flesh rubbing and chafing and straining. She had always thought it was so animal, so base. Always it had left her feeling impaled and bludgeoned by a punishing, bruising tool—stabbed; sacrificed on the altar of her bed. She wanted to feel as if she were being worshiped. The man's tongue, nose, lips, and breath the offerings, her vulva and clitoris the temple. His gifts given in the hopes she would please him in turn. But like many an ancient goddess, her wrath could surge to life without warning like a flash flood swallowing all in its path. She reserved the right to punish the worshiper on a whim. But not now. Not with this man tonight.

He bestowed pleasure upon pleasure to her. Just as she felt she would surely drown in this ecstasy, he came, shuddering and crying out the name he knew her by. What would it be like to hear his lips form her real name? He slumped on top of her, raining kisses on her face and breasts. Wouldn't his affections ever end?

She stroked his head absently. Her thighs were experiencing their usual postcoital tremor, along with something else deep within her soul that pulsated with joy. That something else frightened her. She tried to pull away from his embrace as he rolled over, entwined his limbs with hers and drifted off to sleep. But he was too strong and too heavy, and she lay there trapped. She finally slipped into a torturous sleep where she dreamed she was being suffocated, her face between a man's thighs.

The next morning, just as he was getting ready to make breakfast, she got rid of him. She needed to think. She went for a walk on the beach. The crashing waves and cries of the seagulls reminding her of every romantic movie scene. It was last night all over again. She kicked angrily at the sand and chased a sandpiper out of her way.

What had he done to her? What the hell was this she was feeling? She was unable to come up with any definite answers.

On the way back to her apartment she was still in such a dazed state that she walked in front of a moving car that honked and swerved, leaving her in the wake of its exhaust. She stood shaking in the middle of the street. It had been a sign, she decided; she must do something to break this disembodied feeling.

So, she did what she did best: she went to another bar that night, reeled in a fish, did the deed, cleaned up the messy sheets and her sticky thighs, and woke up alone the next morning.

Well, Ali? she asked herself, using her real name. Is this better?

"Yes!" she cried out loud. Self-assurance, independence, control! All these were better than feeling adrift in a stormy sea in a rudderless boat. So she called Slick Tongue back. Better to think of him like that than to allow his name to make him seem more real to her. He was no more than a wisp of a dream that had become a tangible nightmare.

"I'm sorry I didn't call back right away," she began by lying to him again. "I got your message from the other night." And then she found herself slipping on the truth as she said, "I was afraid. . . ."

"I know," he replied.

She wanted to scream. How dare he know her so well! But she said, "I'd like to see you tonight."

"I'm glad," he said.

And she knew he was.

He showed up with flowers and champagne and a warm, inviting smile on his magical mouth.

That alien otherness inside her moved even as her crotch grew wet. But she couldn't allow horniness to get mixed up with this other feeling—the one that led to loss of control. She knew she mustn't go on like this.

"I want you to tell me what will make you happy," he said in between kissing her breasts and throat.

Tell him! she screamed at herself before she could begin to drown again. So she did, but she didn't tell him everything.

When she felt his tongue tickling her curliest hairs, she knew it would be all right. She began to gasp with desire at his very first lick, but she felt the force of her control intermingling as well.

She squeezed her thighs around his head as she had with so many others, and her passion crested with the first crack. He struggled beneath her, increasing her excitement. And with the second crack and his smothered gasp of pain, his tongue still inside her, she shrieked. His fluids mixed with hers and his flailing became weaker as the pressure of her thighs grew stronger. She clenched her muscular legs again and crushed his skull with enough force to drive bone fragments into his eye sockets. His mouth opened wider in a final, silent scream, and in so doing he sucked in most of her vulva and then his teeth came together on her clitoris. She screamed and climaxed like with none of the others; rolling and thrashing in the riptide of her bursting desire. She laughed in between shuddering breaths. Her little death was his big death. Delicious duality was back.

As her breathing became less ragged, she gently caressed the gore of blood, bone splinters, and brain tissue between her thighs, loving the viscous, grainy feel. She shoved his lifeless body from her, whispering, "You really were the best."

Oh yes! This was the only way to share her bed with a man. She continued to take halting gasps, still feeling fluttering eddies of lingering orgasm. She would wait, savoring the sweet smell of sex and blood and death, till she got her breath back. Then she would fetch the axe and the garbage bags needed to clean up yet another lover's mess.

She smiled; she was in control again.

BACK ROW

Brian Lumley

I'll tell it exactly the way it happened.

They were showing a love story at the Odeon, a classic film from way back when, out of a different time and almost a different world. The first time I saw this picture was with my wife . . . would you believe, forty-five or more years ago? Well, the picture had outlasted her, if not our love. And who knows, maybe that's why I wanted to see it again.

I picked a rainy Wednesday afternoon when there'd be no rowdies hooting and gibbering in the back rows, just a pair or two of lovers in the double seats back there, all snuggled up and blissfully, deliciously secure and secretive in the dark. I had been a young lover myself once. . . .

But what with this ancient film—and it being a Wednesday, *and* the miserable weather and all—the old Odeon should be just about empty; maybe a few dodderers down at the front, where their eyes wouldn't feel the strain too much. But not me. I'd be up in the gods, in the next but back row. Along with my memories, my eyes seem to be the only bits that haven't faded away on me.

I was there waiting for the doors to open, my collar turned up, a fifty-pence piece ready in my hand. That's one small mercy: we oldies can get in cheap. Cheap? *Hah!* I remember when it was thruppence! As for these two kids in front of me, why, they'd be paying maybe two pounds *each!* For a bit of privacy—if you can call it that—in a moldy old flea trap like the Odeon.

Behind me a small handful of people had gathered: Darby and Joans, most of them, but a few singles too. Pensioners, mainly, like myself, I supposed they'd all come together here to chase memo-

ries of their own. And we all stood there, waiting for the doors to
open.

I had to look somewhere, and so I looked ahead of me, at these
two kids. Well, I didn't actually look *at* them—I mean, you don't,
do you? I looked around them, over them, and through them, the
way you do. But something of them stuck in my mind—not very
much, I'm afraid.

The lad would be eighteen, maybe nineteen, and the girl a year
or eighteen months younger. I didn't fix her face clearly, mind you,
but she was definitely what they call "a looker": all pink and
glowing, and a bit giggly, with a mass of shiny black hair under the
hood of her bright red plastic rain mac. White teeth and a stub of a
nose, and eyes that sparkled when she smiled. A right Little Red
Riding Hood! And all of it packed into no more than sixty-two or
-three inches; but then again, they say nice things come in small
packages. Damned if I knew what she saw in *him!* But she clung to
him so close it was like he'd hypnotized her. And you know, I had
to have a smile to myself. What, jealousy, at my age?

About the lad:

He was pale, gangly (or "gawky" as we'd say in my neck of the
woods), and hollow-cheeked. He looked more than a bit neglected,
you know?—like a good feed would fix him up no end. But it
probably wouldn't fix the fishy, unblinking stare that came through
those thick-lensed spectacles of his. He wore a black mac a bit
small for him, which made his wrists stick out like pipe stems, and
out-of-date brothel-creeper shoes like the Teds used to rock 'n' roll
in. A matched couple? Not likely! But they do say that opposites
attract. . . .

Anyway, before I could look at them more closely, if I'd wanted
to, we went in.

The Odeon has been dowdy for longer than I can remember.
Thirty years ago it was dowdy; since then it's gone well past the
point of no return. What glitter there ever was has faded, I'm
afraid, and there's no putting it back. But one thing I'll say for it:
they've never once called bingo there. When telly came in and the
cinemas slumped, the old Odeon kept right on showing films.
Somehow it came through, but not without its share of scars.

These days . . . you could plaster and paint all you like, but you
could never cover up all the wrinkles. Like some old woman
putting on her war paint, she would still turn out mutton dressed
as lamb. But that's the old Odeon. Even with the lights up full, still

the place seems so dim as to be almost misty. Misty, yes, with that clinging miasma of old places. Not haunted, no, but old and creaking and about ready to be pulled down. Or maybe my eyes weren't so good after all, or perhaps there are too many layers of dust on the chandeliers in the high ceiling. . . .

I went upstairs (taking it easy, you know, and leaning on my stick a bit) and headed for my usual seat near the back. And sure enough those young'uns were right there ahead of me, not in my row but the one behind, at the very back. Very quiet and coy, they were, as they chose one of the double seats. But I hadn't noticed them buying sweets or popcorn at the kiosk in the shabby foyer, so maybe they'd stay that way right through the show: nice and quiet.

Other patrons came upstairs, all heading for the front where there was a little more leg room and they could lean on the mahogany balcony and look down on the screen. But even so, by the time the lights started to go down in that slow way of theirs, there still couldn't have been more than a couple of dozen people in all up there in the gods, and most of them in the front two rows. Me and the kids, we had the back entirely to ourselves. It was a poor showing even for a Wednesday; maybe there'd be more people in the cheap seats downstairs.

In the old days this was the part I'd always liked best. The lights dimming, organ music (but only recorded, even in my time), and the curtains on stage slowly swishing open to reveal a dull, pearly, vacant screen. Then there would be the Queen, and the curtains would close again while the lights died completely. Followed by the show: the Pathé News, a short supporting film, a cartoon, the trailers—God only knows why they'd called them that, since they didn't trail but came before!—and finally the feature film. Oh, yes, and between the cartoon and the main show there would be an intermission, when the ice cream ladies came down the aisles with their trays. And at the end, the Queen again.

Funny thing, but I can't go back as far as the King. I mean, *I* can, but my memory can't or won't! And even remembering what I can, I'm not sure I have it exactly right. That's what getting old does to you. Anyway, the whole thing from going in to coming out would last as long as two and a half to three whole hours. *That* was value! Nowadays, you get the previews, local advertisements, the feature film . . . and that's it. Or if you're lucky there *might* be a short supporting picture. And here's me saying I was surprised at the poor turnout!

Well, the trailers weren't much, and the local ads were noisy,
totally colorless, and not even up-to-date—Paul's Unisex Hair-
dressing Salon had shut down months ago! Then the briefest of
brief intervals when the lights came halfway up; and suddenly it
dawned on me that I hadn't heard a single peep out of the young
couple behind me in the back row. Well, maybe the very faintest
whisper or giggle or two. Certainly nothing to complain about.

The seats were stepped down in tiers, so that my row was maybe
six inches lower than theirs. I turned just a little in my seat
(pretending to make myself comfortable), and sneaked a quick
backward glance. My eyes trapped a snapshot of the pair sitting
very close and wasting half their seat; the girl was crammed in one
corner, and the pale lad had a black-clad arm thrown lightly
around her red-clad shoulders. And his fish eyes behind their thick
lenses swiveled to meet mine, expressionless but probably wishing
I'd go away.

Then it was dark again and the titles rolling, and there was I,
settling down to enjoy this old picture, along with one or two old-
fashioned memories. . . .

That was when it started: the carrying-on in the back row. Of
course, I'd seen it coming when I glanced back at them. Two kids
like that sitting there in their rain macs! You don't have to be some
kind of dirty old man to see through that old ploy. It's amazing
what can go on—or come off—under a rain mac.

Very soon buttons would slowly be giving way, one by one, to
trembly, groping fingers under the shiny plastic; garments would
be loosened, warm, naked flesh cautiously exposed—but not to
view. No usherette's flashlight beam would find them out, and
certainly not the prying eyes of some old duffer in the row in front.
Indeed, the fact that I was there was probably adding to their
excitement. It amused me to think of myself as a prop in their
loveplay—or as a wrench in their wet works, whom they must
somehow deceive, even knowing that I wasn't deceived?

And all the time this sick-looking excuse for a youth pretending
the exploratory hand had nothing to do with him, while the girl
feigned total ignorance of its creeping advance upon her nipples—
and they would only be its first objective. All of this assuming, of
course, that they were just beginners. Oh, yes, it's a funny business,
love in the back row of a cinema.

First there was the heavy breathing. Ah, but there's heavy and
there's heavy! And the moaning, very low at first but gradually

becoming clearly audible. I quickly changed my mind, restructuring the scenario I'd devised for them. They weren't new to it, these two; by now *all* of the buttons would be loose, and just about everything else, for that matter! No exploratory work here. This was old ground, gone over many, many times before, together or with others. No prelude, but a full-blown orchestration, which would gradually build to a crescendo.

Would they actually do it, I wondered? Right there in the back row? Fifteen minutes ago I'd seen myself as some sort of obstacle they would have to overcome; now I was thinking they didn't give a damn about me, didn't care that I was there at all. I might as well not exist for these two, not tonight. They had the darkness and each other—what the hell difference did the presence of one old man make? An old man who was probably deaf anyway?

A knee had found its way up onto the collar of my seat back; I felt its gentle pressure, then its vibration starting up like a mild electric current, building to a throb that came right through the wood and the padding to my shoulders. A good old knee-trembler, as we'd called it in my day, when the body's passion proves too great to be contained. And all the time the moaning increasing in pitch, until it rose just a little above the whirring of the projector where it aimed its white, flickering curtain of beams at the screen to form the moving pictures.

It dawned on me then that I was a voyeur. Without even looking at them I'd become a party to their every action. But an unwilling party . . . wasn't I? I had come here to see a film, not to get caught up in the animal excitement of lusting young lovers. And yet I *was* caught up in it!

They had aroused me—*me*, an old man! With their panting, moaning, and slobbering. I was sweating with their sweat, shaking with their vibrations. And all I could do was sit there, stricken and trembling like a man immobilized as by the touch of some strange female's hand in his most private place; yes, actually *feeling* as if some unknown woman had taken the seat next to mine and started to fondle me! That's how engrossed I had become with what was happening behind me, there in the back row.

Suddenly I was startled to realize that we were into the last reel. My God!—but what had happened here? Where had my film and my memories gone? A little bit of nostalgia was all I had wanted. And I'd missed it all, everything, because of them.

Them . . .

Why, I could even smell them now! Musty, sweet, sexual . . . biological! I could smell their sex! And a mouth gobbling away at flesh only inches from my ears! And a frantic gasping coming faster and faster, bringing pictures of some half-exhausted dog steaming away on a bitch!

Lovers? Animal excitement? They *were* animals! Young animals; and right now they were feasting on each other like . . . like vampires! Oh, I suppose you could call it petting, kissing, "canoodling"—but not my kind of canoodling. Not the kind me and my lass had indulged in all those years ago. Kissing? I could hear them *sucking* at each other, foaming away like hard acid eating into soft wood. And suddenly I was angry.

Angry with myself, with them, with everything. The film had only fifteen minutes to run and everything felt . . . ruined. Well, and now I'd ruin it for them too. For him, anyway. You won't come, you young bugger! I thought. You've denied me my pleasure, and now I'll deny you yours.

Abruptly I turned the top half of my body, my head, and spat out: "Now listen, you two—"

They were like one person, fused together, almost prone on their long seat. The hoods of their macs were up and crushed together, and I swear I saw steam—the smoke of their sex—escaping from the darkness where their faces were locked like tightly clasped hands. The slobbering stopped on the instant, and a moment later . . . I heard a growl!

No, it was a snarl. A harshly hissed warning not to interfere. And I didn't.

Oh, pale and sickly he might seem, but he was young and I was old. His bones would bend where mine would snap like twigs. I could feel his contempt like a physical thing—even as I *had been* feeling it for the last ninety minutes! Of course, for who else but a contemptuous lout would have dared all of this with me sitting there right in front of him? And the girl was just as bad if not worse.

"I . . . I . . . I'm disgusted!" I mumbled. And then I quickly turned my face back to the screen, and watched the rest of the film through a wash of hot, shameful tears. Doddering old fool that I was . . .

Just before the lights went up, I sensed movement behind me and thought I heard them leave. At least I heard light footsteps treading the carpet along the back row, quietly receding. Of course it could be the girl, on her way to "tidy herself up" in the ladies. But because *he* might still be there, behind me in the back row, sneering at me, I didn't look to see.

Then the film was over and as the people down front began filing out, still I sat there. Because I could still feel someone behind me, hot and salty. Because it might be him, and he'd look at me, fishy-eyed and threatening, through those steamed-up glasses of his.

Eventually I had to make a move. Maybe they had both gone after all and I was just being an old coward. I stood up, glanced into the back row, and saw—

God! What had he done to her?

The rain mac was open from top to bottom. She—what was left of her—was slumped down inside it. There was little of flesh on her face, just raw red. Breasts were gone, right down to steaming ribs. The belly was open, eviscerated, a laid-back gash that opened down to the spread thighs. And down there, no innards or sexual parts at all. If I hadn't seen her before, I couldn't even have said it was a girl at all.

These were my thoughts before I noticed the true color of the mac. I had only thought it was red at first glance because my mind had refused to accept so much red that wasn't plastic. But then I saw his specs, crushed and broken on the blackened, blood-soaked baize of the double seat. . . .

That's my statement, Sergeant, and there's nothing else I can tell you—except there's something terrible loose in this town that eats living guts and looks like a pretty girl.

GODFLESH

Brian Hodge

*B*eing as she was a woman who prided herself on walking her own deliberate path, imagine, then, the irony that her horizons were forever broadened by the ecstatic man with no legs.

She was Ellen by day, and knew the aisles of the bookstore as well as the creases in her palm, the smoky gray of her eyes, the finely wrought lines that inscribed the corners of her mouth and lent it warmth and wisdom, as if etched by a loving sculptor. She walked the aisles with her modest skirt brushing against her knees, and could smell every page along the gauntlets of spines. For the patient customer, it was a trip well rewarded. Every book should be so matched to a loving home.

There had been nothing different about that day, right up to the very moment they left the bookstore, she and Jude letting the evening clerks take over. With that taut face-lift, Jude could have been an older sister, or so she thought. Thought she knew what made Ellen tick. A common mistake, but then Jude's idea of a deep read was Danielle Steel over Jackie Collins. Jude already had the endings worked out for most anyone she could ever meet.

They left together for the parking lot down the street. The bookstore's neighborhood was like much of the city itself: old and charmingly crumbled by day, though not a place most would want to walk alone at night. The peeling doorways, the odd bricks set just out of step with the others, the derelict and sagging smoke-stacks and chimneys . . . they hooked strange shadows that worsened as day dwindled into evening, and the shadows gave birth to night people.

They joined the flow, Jude's brisk footsteps clicking at her side. Urban minnows, that's what they all were, and God forbid anyone should fall out of step. Were it not for nights, Ellen knew she would one day tear out her hair, an allergic reaction to this sunlight world and the prefab molds it demanded.

". . . and then do you know what that little doofus asked me?" Jude was saying. "He asked, 'Do you have *The Old Man and the Sea* in Cliff's Notes?' I told him the original was barely a hundred pages, so why didn't he read that, and he just looked at me—"

They approached a break in the buildings, the mouth of an alley that gaped back like a dirty, leprous throat. Yet inviting, all the same, with mysteries lying just behind those crusty locked doors. Back rooms often tweaked her curiosity.

"—just *looked* at me, like I'd suggested, 'Here, why don't you bite this brick in half.' So I said, 'Listen, I can summarize it for you in fifteen words or less: Man catches fish, man battles fish, man loses dead fish to hungry shar—'" Jude froze, except for her arm, as she began to point along the alley. "Oh my *God.*" Her arm recoiled back to her side. "Don't look, Ellen, just don't look."

It was the wrong thing to say, and too late anyway. Ellen wouldn't have missed anything that got Jude to interrupt herself.

The man looked to be in his early forties, and she'd never have mistaken him for one of the street people, one of those who cruised around in their wheelchairs with sad stories of cause and effect: car wreck and loss of livelihood; war wounds and loss of stability. From this distance—say, twenty feet along that wall?—his clothing looked neat and new, his hair well-barbered. He might have been any reasonably attractive man who'd made the best of his life after losing both legs at the hip.

Then again, he *was* masturbating. In his wheelchair. It did *not* look as if he were merely adjusting his crotch. He was wholly absorbed in the act—heart, soul, and both hands.

"He's—He's right out in the open!" Jude said, adding her disgust to that of the less self-absorbed passersby. "I . . . I don't think he's even aware anybody's watching!"

No. No, he wasn't, was he? His exultant abandon—Ellen found this the most fascinating aspect of the display. His choice of locale and timing may have been awry, but she saw on his face more passion and ecstasy than she'd noticed on the faces of last week's eight or ten lovers combined.

A Mona Lisa smile brushed her lips, unnoticed as Jude yanked at her arm.

"Come on, come *on,*" said Jude. "A nice proper thing like you, a sight like that can scar you for years. I had a neighbor? Liked to show himself to other neighbors? To this very day Sylvia Miller gets nauseated by the sight of knockwurst." Jude shuddered. "Oh, if only I had a bucket of water, I'd douse that pervert's fire. You shouldn't have to see things like that."

If you only knew, Ellen thought, and let Jude believe she was saving her from something she'd in fact watched maybe two thousand times before.

Ellen could be kind that way.

And the days took care of themselves.

By night, Elle; just Elle. "What's in a name?" it had been asked, and she'd decided plenty. With the lopping off of a single letter, she had created an entirely different life.

She even felt different when that was what others called her, what she called herself. "Ellen" was safe and respectable, a fine name to endorse on the back of paychecks. But "Elle" rang with mystery and resonance, conjured a slick wet alchemy of surrender and seduction.

For years now that name had been eagerly welcomed by the sort of clubs that are frequented only by those who know where to find them, whose new members arrive by word of mouth, where no one is ejected back to the streets for improper conduct, because everyone there knows precisely what everyone else has come for.

Her beauty and willingness to experiment were prized. She was almost tall, not quite. Her raven hair, when unbound, contrasted with her pale luminous skin and ripe lips in delicious nocturnal severity. She had a twenty-three-inch waist but could corset it down to eighteen; men and women alike loved to place their hands around it, or nuzzle over the smooth tight curves on their way to the drenched heat between her thighs.

Tonight's lovers were no exception, at times all six hands caressing her tiny middle, some lightly tender, others rough and groping with urgency. The club's name was the Inner Circle, and variety was everybody's spice.

She'd spent the past couple of hours as part of a foursome, one of her preferred configurations. Two men and two women—she found a perfect symmetry there, something intended by nature, along with the four winds and seasons, the cardinal points of a compass. The Inner Circle offered an orgiastic central room aglow with gauzy mood lighting, or more private quarters with plenty of cushions and sprawl, and they'd opted for the latter.

She filled her mouth with Daniel while Mitch filled her from behind; she cradled Jill, kissing her deeply, as the men traded off between the girl's legs; she and Jill tongued one another's feverish clits while Daniel and Mitch were yet locked inside them; Jill straddled her mouth while holding her ankles wide . . . and in Elle's broad experience you usually needed more men, because their glands betrayed them and they wore out so much sooner. Still, they gave their all, and she drank it with her mouth, cunt, anus. She cried out loudly, in cycles, pulled the others into her singly, as pairs, all three. She made a dinner of semen, a dessert of the musky dew on Jill's swollen and petaled cleft.

And there was always so much silence when bodies fell still, unable to give or take any more. It always felt as if the world had just ended and they all lay naked and wet in the ashes.

"You're ravenous," Daniel told her. Blond, well-toned, he lay in a sweaty half curl near her side, reaching over with one finger to probe beneath the edge of the black corset. Jill and Mitch lay in their own raw exhausted tangle a few feet over. "I'd like to see you again."

"You might," she said. "I'm no stranger here."

"So I understand." Grinning, he elbowed closer, crawling like a soldier. "How long've you been coming here? Double entendre not intended."

"Look, you don't have to engage me in conversation, all right? I fucked you tonight, and I'll probably fuck you again."

He rolled onto his back, relaxed, unfazed. "I wish I was nineteen again," he sighed. "I could come five times a night when I was nineteen. But the sad thing was, I was alone for most of it." He peeked at her, hopeful. "Are you feeling pity for me yet?"

He was so obvious, and knew it, that Elle had to laugh in spite of herself. "You late bloomers, you're so maudlin when you start dwelling on what you've missed."

Daniel said he was valiantly fighting the pull of gravity, here on the downhill side of the sexual bell curve. Confessed he was thirty-five—coincidence, or karma? She was closing fast on thirty-five herself, but then weren't they all, for the first or second or tenth time.

She let him talk, and he was pleasant enough without seeming possessive. A few of the guys in these places, in spite of their laissez-faire posturing, they nailed you once and it was as though they'd staked a claim. So she let Daniel talk, but already her thoughts were drifting ahead. Tomorrow night, or the night after . . . future nights at other clubs, wondering where she'd be, what she'd be doing, who she'd be doing it with.

Maybe at the Purgatorium, with the rings through her hardened nipples and chained to a leather belt while some hooded dominatrix violated her with a strap-on phallus.

Or maybe with the Jezebel Society, where gang-bangs were a specialty, and where, on knees and elbows, she could be triply penetrated while massaging a cock in each hand.

Or elsewhere, with company even more exotic, but always sure to wring more from the experience than her partners. It was a kind of challenge, something bone-deep and primal.

And she wondered if, wherever she'd be, after she was sated and lay breathing heavily, she'd once more start dreaming of the next time before the sticky fluids of that night had even dried.

Could you even completely look forward to that next time when you could so easily forecast your pose by its end? Even in private clubs like the Inner Circle, the Purgatorium, et al., sex could get as routine and predictable as some fat suburban couple's half-hearted hump scheduled for the second Tuesday of each month. It was only a matter of degree.

And she wondered if considering these things, in a room with three other nude people whose potent sexuality had just soaked the walls, meant that she was bored.

Figuring that, in the asking, she already had her answer.

A few days later, Ellen came back from lunch, took one look behind the counter, and wondered if one of Jude's facial nips and tucks had begun to unravel. The woman's forehead appeared ready to burst veins.

"He's . . . *upstairs,*" she said through clenched teeth.

Ellen frowned. "Who? Who is?"

"That . . . that *creature.*" Jude seemed to need the counter to remain vertical. "From the alley."

"*Ohhh,*" she said, and frowned again, more thoughtfully. "Was everything in place when he came in?"

Jude's eyes widened, quite horrified at the very notion she'd have glanced down to check. "You see, you *see*—it's types like his

that make me think Affirmative Action is a terrible imposition on
the rest of us. No telling what he's doing up there."

Ellen started for the stairs. "Maybe he needs help reaching a
book. We don't have elevators for each shelf, did you ever think of
that?"

"You're going up?" Jude clutched the counter, all bony white
knuckles and maroon nails. "What if he has his willy out again?"

Over her shoulder, Ellen smiled with reassurance. "Then I'll
suggest he find a more appropriate bookmark."

This befuddled poor Jude. Upstairs, Ellen began to check the
aisles, the shelves older and taller and dustier up here, home to the
store's used and vintage and rare books. She'd always accorded a
greater respect to the browsers who spent their time here.

She found him in fiction, as sturdy and vital in his chair as if it
were an outgrowth of him. He sat engrossed in a book, not so
deeply that he didn't notice her approach. His face lit with a self-
effacing smile, and she tried not to recall how it had looked the
other day, self-pleasured and unashamed. And so powerfully
attuned to his body. Not one in a thousand could get past his lack
of discretion, and she supposed that finding this a simple matter
made *her* the odd one as well.

"Can I help you?" she asked.

He pointed at the second shelf from the top. "Even chimps use
tools to get what they can't reach, but . . ." He spread his empty
hands. "Eleventh from the left, if you wouldn't mind."

She stretched, pulled it down, looked over the cover before
handing it to him. "De Sade, *Justine*. Not too much call for that."

His grin was apologetic, wholly engaging, set in a weathered
ruddy face. A shock of hair tumbled over his forehead. "Loaned
mine out and never got it back. Home feels incomplete without it."

Ellen smiled back, or maybe it was Elle this time. Elle in
daylight, rattling at her nighttime prison. "Myself, I'm partial to
The 120 Days of Sodom."

He seemed merely delighted, not surprised. "I'm sure we each
have our reasons." Vigorously, he patted *Justine*'s cover as if it
were the shoulder of an old friend. "I appreciate his philosophy
here. The utter lack of reward for living a virtuous life. And every
one of these sick sons of bitches in here states his reasons for acting
like a depraved monster with such eloquence it makes you want to
cry." He shrugged. "But obviously you know that."

Her grin turned mildly wicked, and she checked to make sure

they were alone. "You want to know what *I* found most eloquent? When Justine's captured by the bandit, and de Sade gets across the idea of a blowjob without using one concrete anatomical reference. I loved that."

And thus it went on, impromptu critiques and appreciation of the works of a man who'd scandalized a continent, whose debauches were legend, whose name itself had enriched the vocabulary of the erotic. Time got away from them, and once she started to laugh as she imagined what by now must have been going through Jude's mind downstairs. The poor woman frantic, calling paramedics, priests, a SWAT team. She *should* go quell Jude's fears.

"I'm enjoying this," he said at last. "I really am. You know the way you can just tell, sometimes, that you can talk to someone and let a half hour go by and you won't even know it? I knew you'd be someone I could talk to."

"And how's that?" She had to know. He was either far more intuitive than Jude, and most of the day-herd who muddled through downstairs, or she'd let something of night inside shine free.

"You didn't look away on the street the other afternoon. You held your ground . . . and watched." His eye contact was bold, candid.

She stood there, tongue tip wedged between her front teeth, clothed, yet her garments may as well have been sheer. Caught. She was caught. Knowing it had to come someday, but always taking for granted the person would at least have legs. *Caught.*

"It was the look on your face," she whispered. "I—I didn't even think you noticed me then. . . ."

As he laughed and rolled his eyes, she found his easy candor extraordinary. And while she'd known plenty of exhibitionists, she got no sense that his pleasure had derived from being watched. It had been grounded in the physical, she was sure of it.

"I get carried away sometimes. I really shouldn't, but when it feels that good, and the mood strikes . . ." He shrugged, palms up. "You know, you may think it doesn't, but your face gives you away too. Like *does* know like, when it knows what to look for; I don't think I'm completely off base here, am I?"

A blush threatened to warm her cheeks. Embarrassment? She'd not even thought it possible anymore. The challenge in her tone of voice was merely affectation: "What is it you think you see?"

He appraised. "In your eyes. It's always in the eyes. This look when your guard slips. Something unsatisfied, maybe a little angry. Okay. I know—it's like someone just stole the last sliver of chocolate torte right out from under your fork."

Ellen's laugh was soft, low, throaty, half pleasure and half challenge. Chocolate and sex. This man may have had no legs, but he most definitely had her number.

"Look," she said, "I have to be getting back to work. But I think I'm going to need your name . . . and some way of getting hold of you later."

His name was Adam, and the address he gave took her to a dim neighborhood where her footsteps were solitary echoes against walls of brick and stone, where the pale faces of residents peeped out from behind barred windows. Everything malingered beneath a stubborn dusting of industrial fallout, and the last of the year's greenery twined dead and brown around sagging wrought-iron fences. Privacy would be valued here, and respected.

Adam played the proper host, skimming through his apartment and around corners as quickly as if he were on a basketball court. He mixed fine drinks, served hors d'oeuvres that probably hadn't come from a deli. He showed her his books, including the freshly reinstated *Justine*. He let her notice for herself his collection of fetish videos, and be the one to suggest slipping a tape into the VCR. There was a lot in the way of nipple clamps and whimpering, later the obligatory golden shower, and they were really just marking time here, weren't they? She might've yawned once. Adam shut it off before the end.

"It's been a while since I've watched this," he said. "Been a while since it even did anything for me."

"So why sit through this much if it's that passé to you now?"

He shrugged easily. "Humoring you?"

"Oh, that's a laugh," she said, and she was Elle again, had become Elle without one bit of effort. Adam recognized this. Like knows like, and from here it was a very short trip to the bedroom.

Unclothed, his body was a peculiar marvel. Incomplete, but hard and sculpted, like a magnificent Greek statue that vandals had smashed in two. His genitals seemed all the more for it, large and immodest; his lower trunk flexed with new rhythms she'd never felt without the normal counterbalance of legs. As he meshed with her, braced upon two powerful arms, she could run her hands along the tapering curve of his back, cup the clenching muscles of his ass. Could run her hands farther down and cup the smooth rounded stumps where his legs just *ended.* She couldn't think of him as an amputee. It felt as if Adam were complete, whole, and his hips met some other plane, where his legs existed in another dimension.

For hours they rolled, locking themselves into twisted new arrangements. Positions once denied her because of one set of legs or the other getting in the way were now accessible. And Adam was tireless, his commitment to ecstasy for a long time bordering on possession, then tipping far beyond. He had a whole body's worth of passion compressed into half the mass. Each time he came it was with a straining convulsion of ardor, racked with groans and shudders that might've been endearing were they not so intensely animal. For any less experienced a woman, Elle decided, his plunge into the heart of his own pleasure would've been frightening.

But for herself? It was maddening, feeling for the first time ever that she had been left behind, that there was no way she could draw more from the most ravaging of fucks than her partner. He had eclipsed her, and if at the bookstore he'd nearly prompted in her a flush of embarrassment, he had now done the unthinkable: He had inspired envy.

I want whatever it is you have inside, she thought, and lay as stunned as if a new galaxy had opened before her. Lay with him in the sweat-soaked afterglow, her cunt lips puffy and throbbing. It lasted long moments, even as Adam stirred, even as he traced a hand along her face.

Even as he said, "If you stay with me, you . . . you may not be seeing me this whole for much longer," and she found it a peculiar thing to say. But consider her life.

It certainly was no stranger than hearing someone confess his love.

Their relationship grew from that night, a happy coexistence of need and availability, willingness and daring. She didn't know how long it would last, but this was the way things were done on their level. Emotions and attachment rarely figured in; it was more the delight of connecting with someone who didn't judge, who understood that not everyone craved a permanent partner at his or her side through life. Who trusted the physical body's immediacy more than a bamboozled heart.

It saved time. It saved money. It saved pretense.

Adam happily listened to her recount various liaisons at her nocturnal haunts, his erection like a club curving out from the base of his body. He would close his eyes, smiling as she conjured for him images that would drive the average man to frenzied fits of jealousy and despair: Elle, flogging the back of a submissive man until he rimmed her with a quivering tongue; coaxing an orgasm from the sluggish genitals of an uncut transsexual; bending a girlfriend over her lap and paddling her bottom cherry red while a nervous old couple watched from chairs.

Adam listened, and Adam trembled. She had read, one memorable lunch break, that Salvador Dali could think himself to orgasm; she wondered if Adam wasn't far away from it himself.

"Your turn," she demanded once, in an uncharacteristic sense of quid pro quo. "You've hardly told me a thing about yourself. I want to know all the dirty stuff you did before you met me." Then, with a grin, "Besides pulling over for quickies with yourself in the alley."

He pretended to consider sharing. "I know some people, you're not the only one with a members-only pass. . . ."

He teased her with silence then. Adam's smile was annoyingly aloof, smug, even. He could be *so* superior when he wanted, all in fun, but he knew damn well how curious she was, that she wondered if he'd not had some esoteric training to channel sexual energy, let it feed upon itself like nuclear fusion. Something to do with Indian chakras, perhaps; tantric sex magick. *Teach me too,* was the unspoken gist of her hunger. *Teach me or I'll strangle you.*

"So what does it take to meet these people," she asked, "or am I not good enough?" Guilt—that was a fair tactic. "You're ashamed of me, is that it? Not worth fucking in front of your friends?"

His weather-worn face creased with a heartfelt smile. "You may be ready after all." He ran a hand along her body, lingering here, there, anyplace where bones joined. "But then, Elle"—and it sounded anything but rhetorical the way he said it—"what have you got to lose?"

Adam took her to another unfamiliar neighborhood; this newest stop on the search for the bigger and better orgasm was a no-man's-land where residential met industrial and both had died of blight. The building of intent was a church whose congregation had long since moved away, broken up, lost faith . . . something. They'd left behind an orphaned edifice surrounded by trees stripped bare by smokestacks that had themselves died, all of them now in a stark eternal autumn. The church sat Gothically stolid, sooty and gray.

"Privately owned now," he said, and she wheeled him up a ramp at one side of the steps. It looked to be the only thing kept in good repair.

He unlocked the door, then stopped inside the nave, and before her eyes could adjust to the dimness, dangled a black strip of blindfold. "I'm afraid I have to insist."

Elle stiffened. His demand reeked of threat—how well *did* she really know him? Curious women died all the time, led to hellish ends by their hungers and strangers who betrayed misplaced trust. But back out now and she was a coward, a poseur. Adam knew that, of course, could easily exploit her sense of self.

She bent at the waist, let him fasten it around her head, and a cool cathedral night descended upon her. "If you cannibalize me," she said, "I'll haunt you till you die," then she bit firmly on his ear. He just laughed.

Elle rested her hand on one of the grips of his chair as he wheeled forward, let him lead her along as if blind. They passed through swinging wood doors; she shuffled her feet, seeking clues. Farther still, and in this dark nucleus of intuition the room felt vast—the sanctuary, but a sanctuary redefined. It smelled of sex and sweat and ecstasies.

Her senses expanded, took in the others that surrounded them. Whispers on the periphery, a crawling sensation of being watched, appraised, admired. The menace of the unknown. Movement— were these others drawing closer?

Adam stopped, had her lower herself to the floor while he swung from his chair and joined her. His mouth pressed roughly to hers, and his hands rose to strip her clothes away. Moments later his hands were joined by others. Naked, blind, she was laid back on cushions that shielded her from a floor that felt old, nobody's priority.

"Beautiful," came someone's voice, "even if she *is* whole."

She submitted to the hands that stroked, caressed, and in their numbers lost track of Adam. He was subsumed to the mass around her. Her back arched, her mouth parted to suck a finger that slipped past her lips. Her nipples stiffened beneath circling palms. Their hands gave a hundred delights, promised a thousand more.

They opened her legs then, swung her ankles wide, and as one checked her wetness, then murmured approval; she heard the rustle of someone else moving into position. She was entered then, and gasped. It was *huge,* pushing deep, deeper still. What began as a groan became a wailing cry, treading that delicious threshold separating rapture from agony. She was filled near to being split, yet still wasn't aware of a male body hovering over her. There was no press of hips against hers.

Elle reached down with her hand, felt herself caught by Adam. "One finger," he whispered in her ear, and she'd found him again. "One finger's all you get."

Trembling, slowly rolling her hips with the rhythm set up by the massive phallus, she extended one finger. Her hand was guided by his . . . and she touched, glided a few inches. Flesh. It was flesh, firm and hard.

"Satisfied?" he asked, and she was and she wasn't. *Nobody* could be that big . . . could they?

It wasn't for the mind to ponder—she let go of the thought, surrendered to the here and now, the reality of sensation. She drew a deep breath and braced herself, elbows on the floor. Took it. Took it all in. Thrust back with muscled hips and grunts through feral clenched teeth, feeling as if she were at war with this monstrous thing inside her. Riding it until it brought her low and sent her soaring, and her voice pealed from rafters gone dead with dust.

Drenched in sweat, she fell back into someone's arms, felt her lover withdraw, receding into a blackness that was total, her sole world. They waited until she got her breath, then a hand was on her chin, urging her lips to part. She obliged, eager to surmount exhaustion, prove herself worthy. Whoever these people were, she wanted to be one of them, take what they offered, give what she had. Her lips parted and her tongue serpentined out to explore what her eyes were denied. She touched warmth—

It was at her mouth.

She smelled herself on the gigantic phallus, tasted herself a moment later. Opened wide, wider, could scarcely accommodate a few inches without her jaw cracking. *What* was *it?* And she raised one hand, wrapped her fingers around it, felt firm flesh, muscle—

And it slowly withdrew, teasingly, before she could identify what
seemed so familiar, so alien, so tantalizing. Around her, far and
near, came soft murmurs of approval, appreciation, acceptance.

Adam's hands were at the back of her head, gently undoing the
knot, and when the blindfold was drawn away, she blinked into the
light, forgot to breathe. Whatever she'd expected, it wasn't *this*.

She found herself in the center of the old sanctuary, beneath
soaring ceilings and the watchful eyes of suffering figures in the
stained-glass windows, some pocked with vandals' holes. Pews and
pulpit were gone, in their place a cushioned playground for these
thirty-plus members who had welcomed her, even though she
wasn't at all like them.

Elle looked straight into the eyes of the young woman sitting in
the V of her outstretched legs. So this was her lover? There was a
thin, wanton quality to her as she reclined on her haunches,
meeting Elle's gaze with a hunger almost masculine. It was a role
she played well. Elle followed the contours of her body, from the
small breasts to the slim hips, to the tapering length of her left leg.
There was no foot, just the smooth bony head formed by her ankle.
Very phallic.

At the moment, quite wet.

And she had no right leg at all.

Elle whirled, met Adam's smile. His pride. And let herself be
taken into his arms. At least he had them.

Not so, many of those around her. They were all missing bits and
pieces, some more than others. Feet, lower legs, or the entire limb.
A few, like Adam, had neither. Others had sacrificed arms along
the way. A couple, she saw, were but heads and a single arm
attached to naked trunks. They were smooth and they were
sculpted, every one of them, and if they looked upon her with
anything, it was with longing. Not to be like her again . . . but to
make her one of them.

"You do it to yourselves, don't you?" she whispered to Adam.
"These weren't accidents."

He grinned, got Freudian on her. "There *are* no accidents."

"I don't understand." But then, in looking around at them, an
entire roomful of broken statuary, she couldn't say she didn't like
it. Whatever their reasons, *this* was commitment, so far beyond the
Inner Circle that she could never go back there.

"You will," Adam told her, then scooted off to new partners, as
did the others. Recombinant pairs, trios, groups.

And she watched, a privileged witness.

They could do the most astonishing things.

Adam explained later, after the two of them had returned to his apartment. She was very quiet, cataloguing everything she'd experienced but finding that even in her vast erotic repertoire there was no place for this.

She drew herself together on the sofa, hands around a mug of coffee. Feeling loose inside, liquid, where muscles had stretched.

"How did it start?" she asked.

"How does anything start?" Adam said, then laughed softly to himself. "Transcendence. That's what anyone wants out of life, isn't it? Some way of getting past it. Or getting more out of it." He paused, changed gears. "Ever hear of the Gnostics?"

She seesawed her hand.

"They were several splinter groups from the early Church, a couple thousand years ago. Didn't last long, by comparison. The party line condemned them as heretics. Progressive in their day, in a lot of ways. But then they had this self-loathing kick they were on. Since the material world fell short of the spirit, it was bad, themselves included. So, automatically, anything that created them had to be bad too, so their lives were mainly spent showing contempt for it all, until they could return to the spirit. Each branch had its ways. The ascetics denied themselves everything. The libertines, they pleasured themselves and fucked each other left and right. Overindulgence as the way to paradise . . . people after my own heart." Adam winked. "And yours too, *ma chérie?*"

Elle smiled weakly; she felt rubbery inside and out. "I don't think my goals were that lofty."

"Oh, mine neither, hell no," he said, laughing. "Anyway. Even among the Gnostics there was a lunatic fringe. Most all of them had the idea that the body was a prison that kept the spirit shackled, but this fringe, now they did something about it. Had a habit of cutting parts of themselves away to reduce the size of the prison."

She began to piece it together then, amputation in an erotic context; the less body one has to dilute pleasure, the greater must be its concentration in the flesh that remains.

"And so the two of those approaches got combined, over time?"

"I don't know. Probably." Adam looked dumbfounded. "Who knows how anything really happens? It's not like we trace ourselves back for centuries, nothing like that. It's just something that someone stumbled onto a while back, and found out . . . works."

Languidly, Elle slipped from the sofa, wandered to a window, stared into the night. A sickly glow of sodium lights cast pools amid the blackened hulks of brick and steel, dessicated hives of isolation. How she hated it out there, its cold hard rot.

"Everything revives," she said, "if you give it time."

Their procedures were strictly of a back-room variety, the amputations performed by a surgeon no longer allowed by law to practice his craft, who still liked to keep his hands active. It was an ideal arrangement, and the discarded parts were safely burned in an industrial incinerator.

Elle had him begin with her foot.

She found that phantom pains were scarcely a problem when you had done away with something voluntarily. She grew new skin, and beneath it, it seemed, new nerves. It was an awakening, and while the world slept beneath snow, she was healed enough to give this new sexual organ its first workout. Found she could come without a single touch between her legs.

At the bookstore, sympathy flowed freely, especially from Jude, and they all remarked what a wonderful attitude Ellen had in spite of her accident. She was deliberately vague on particulars, felt touched by Jude's concern that it might now be more difficult for her to find a man, one who would overlook her handicap.

"If you have one tiny flaw," Jude said, "they can turn around and be such coldhearted bastards," and then she smiled nervously and checked herself in a compact mirror. Ellen assumed it was time for another face-lift.

And Ellen, with her mind already made up to proceed, wondered how she would ever be able to explain away the rest of her leg.

She was up and around again by spring, the itch of healing and new growth mostly behind her. Spending most of her free hours at the former church, crutching her way about as she explored both edifice and companions. They were a very insular group, came to be with each other even when they left their clothes on. Of course—who else could they talk to? They'd cut themselves apart in more ways than one.

She often lay with Adam in the dying light of afternoon, both of them washed in colors the sun picked up as it streamed through stained glass. Overhead, the Virgin Mary held a little lamb; its fleece was dark with soot.

"You bastard," she said, "you didn't wait for me." But there was no anger in it, and it made Adam smile, made him laugh.

He touched her face with his sole remaining hand, an act she would relish for however long it might last. Not forever. Elle curled in closer, pressed her mouth over the smooth pink stub that jutted from his left shoulder, flushing in pleasure as he gasped.

"Has anybody ever gone all the way?" she wondered. "Cut off everything?"

Adam nodded. "There've been a few."

She groaned, murmuring wordlessly with fantasies of narrowing herself to a focused bundle of overloaded nerves, a single vast erogenous zone. "I wonder what it's like."

"I don't know. But I get the idea that . . . that it's like being a god." Adam stirred, flexed; seemed to ripple with each caress of hand and mouth, breeze and dust mote. "By that time, you know, it's up to everybody else to care for you. Take care of your needs. You're mostly a receptacle by then."

"What did the others say about it? And where are they now?"

"They quit talking," he said. "And pretty soon . . . they quit eating. But they still smiled."

They knew something, she thought. *Or felt something the rest of us aren't even close to yet. . . .*

Yet.

She forced his hand down to her hip, the exposed stump hot, tingling. Raw and alive with promise. "I'll be better at it than you will. When I get that far. I'll feel more than you."

Said this with a tremor and a smile.

Could she cut herself down an inch at a time, feel gradations of pleasure with each successive chopping? If she lopped off a finger herself, would it be a new form of masturbation? Such paths to explore, down this avenue of the blade.

"We'll just have to see about that," he said, "won't we?"

And Elle wondered if she could convince him to hang onto that

one last arm at least until she went in for her other leg, so that
Adam might be the one to hold the scalpel for that first symbolic
incision.

    That would be divine.

    It would almost be something like love.

THE CONTRIBUTORS

Gary Bowen

Bowen is the author of *Diary of a Vampire* and a collection of erotic science fiction, *Queer Destinies*. In the works are a second novel and collection. In addition, Maryland's Bowen has published more than a hundred pieces of short fiction in venues ranging from *Drummer* to *Dead of Night* magazines. Bowen is the consulting editor for Obelisk Books.

Ramsey Campbell

England's Campbell has been writing ghost and horror stories for more than thirty years. A selection from his first three decades, *Alone with the Horrors,* received the 1994 World Fantasy Award and the Stoker Award of the Horror Writers Association. His novel *The Long Lost* was given the British Fantasy Award, and both books gained him the *Liverpool Daily Post & Echo* Award for Literature. His most recent novel is *The One Safe Place.*

Alexa deMonterice

New Yorker deMonterice has upcoming stories in *Cyber-Psychos A.O.D., Scifant,* and *Bohemian Chronicle.* As associate editor at *Space & Time* magazine, she is also finishing work on her first novel, which blends horror, mystery, and science fiction.

Christa Faust

Faust is a former professional dominatrix who has recently given up that profession to become a writer. She has had short fiction published in such anthologies as *Young Blood, Millennium,* and *Love in Vein.* The Californian, who occasionally collaborates with Poppy Z. Brite, is currently working on her first novel.

Michael Garrett

Garrett sold numerous erotic thrillers to men's magazines before joining forces with Jeff Gelb to create the Hot Blood series. His work has recently appeared in the Shock Rock series and the *Fear Itself* anthology. He is an instructor for the Writer's Digest School and teaches weekend writing seminars. Garrett lives in Alabama.

Jeff Gelb

Gelb and Garrett came up with the idea for the Hot Blood series in a pool in New Orleans in 1987, and the rest is history. Gelb is the editor of the *Shock Rock* and *Fear Itself* series, and is developing *Danger!,* a suspense anthology, with Garrett. Gelb is also a comics historian and novice comics scripter for *Bettie Page* comics. He lives in California.

Brian Hodge

Hodge has written for film, comics, and books, including his most recent, *Prototype.* He has also published fifty-some short stories and novelettes in a variety of anthologies, and has recently turned his attention to crime fiction. The Illinois resident says he is, by nature, very curious and experimental, but so far still has all his original limbs.

Bruce Jones

California's Jones is an illustrator and writer with extensive TV credits, including many episodes during the first season of HBO's

Hitchhiker series, and the TV movie "My Boyfriend's Back." His novels include *Stalker's Moon, In Deep, Game Running,* and the upcoming *Maximum Velocity.*

Edward Lee

Maryland's Lee has sold nine horror novels, most recently *Sacrifice.* With t-Winter Damon, Lee has cowritten the screenplay to Rex Miller's *Slob,* as well as the books *The Epicycle* and *Shifters.* Lee is also marketing collaborative novels with Elizabeth Staffen and fellow Hot Blood contributor Alexa deMonterice.

Brian Lumley

England's Lumley is the author of more than twenty horror novels, including the highly successful Psychomech and Necroscope series. Since publication of *Bloodwars,* the final volume of his massive Vampire World Trilogy, he has been arranging more collections of short stories, and is currently working on the new two-volume *Necroscope: The Lost Years.*

Graham Masterton

Nowadays a frequent traveler to Eastern Europe, where his horror novels have achieved extraordinary success, Masterton has recently completed two collections of short stories and two ghost novels, *Spirit* and *The House that Jack Built.* He lives in England.

Yvonne Navarro

Navarro's fiction and illustrations have appeared in more than forty publications. Her first novel, *Afterage,* was nominated for a Bram Stoker award, and her second, *Deadrush,* was recently published. Illinois resident Navarro is also the author of the novelization of the MGM movie *Species.*

Michael Newton

Indiana's Newton has published 114 books since 1977, with ten others pending release and three more under contract. In addition to fifty-odd installments of the Mack Bolan Executioner series, his recent works include *Raising Hell, Silent Rage,* and *Cat and Mouse* (from Pocket Books).

Tom Piccirilli

New York's Piccirilli reasons that all the vowels in his name helped propel his Pocket Books horror novel *Dark Father* to best-sellerdom in Italy. Co-editor of *Pirate Writings* and *Space & Time* magazines, his collection of witchcraft tales, *Pentacle,* was recently published.

Wendy Rathbone

California's Rathbone has written stories for *Writers of the Future Vol. 8, Air Fish, TechnoSex, Prisoners of the Night,* and others, and such magazines as *Midnight Graffiti* and *Figment.* Her poetry appears regularly in *Asmiov's SF, Aboriginal SF,* and others, and has been published in two chapbooks, *Anything to Do with Dreams,* and *Moon Canoes.* She is working on her third novel.

John B. Rosenman

Rosenman's first novel, *The Best Laugh Last,* went through two printings in 1981–82. Since then he has sold fiction to eighty magazines and anthologies, including *The Horror Show, Cemetery Dance, New Blood, Iniquities, Terminal Fright, Dead of Night Magazine, Galaxy, Offworld,* and *Starshore.* An editor of *Dark Regions,* Rosenman is also an English professor at Norfolk State University.

Brinke Stevens

California's Stevens is a world-renowned "Scream Queen" with over two dozen film credits. Among her most recent film roles is

Mommy, directed by Max Allan Collins from his short story in *Fear Itself.* Stevens is the heroine of comic books, trading cards, and model kits. When not acting, she's at work on movie scripts, short fiction, and a children's book.

Lucy Taylor

Taylor's horror fiction has appeared in *Hotter Blood, The Hot Blood Series: Deadly After Dark, Northern Frights, The Mammoth Book of Erotic Horror,* and many others. Her work has also appeared in such publications as *Pulphouse* and *Cemetery Dance.* Her collections include *Close to the Bone, The Flesh Artist,* and *Unnatural Acts and Other Stories.* The Colorado resident's novel, *The Safety of Unknown Cities,* appeared in 1995.

Edo van Belkom

Edo van Belkom is the author of *Wyrm Wolf* and of over 80 short stories that have appeared in anthologies such as *Shock Rock 2, Fear Itself, Year's Best Horror 20,* and the *Northern Frights* series. He is a contributing editor of the *SFWA Bulletin* and *Horror* magazine and lives in Ontario.